THE SCARLET
BISHOP

THE DARK HARVEST TRILOGY

The Dark Faith
The Scarlet Bishop
The Threefold Cord

THE SCARLET
BISHOP

JEREMIAH W. MONTGOMERY

PUBLISHING
P.O. BOX 817 • PHILLIPSBURG • NEW JERSEY 08865-0817

ISBN: 978-1-59638-188-9 (pbk)
ISBN: 978-1-59638-896-3 (ePub)
ISBN: 978-1-59638-897-0 (Mobi)

Printed in the United States of America

Library of Congress Control Number: 2013940158

To Dad, Donald, and Douglas

CONTENTS

PART I

FELL WINTER

PROLOGUE

Outside, the sky was falling in small white shards.

It had been years since Mereclestour had seen snow for Adventide, and even longer since the city's Great Cathedral had hosted a royal wedding. But never in the history of the land of Mersex had the cathedral hosted a royal wedding on the holy feast day.

Until today.

"It has been a remarkable year, sire." Stonoric stood before the window with his younger companion. In contrast to the clear glass, his tone was opaque.

"Indeed it has, cousin. And it is not over yet."

"No." Stonoric lingered over the word, hoping the king would invite him to speak freely.

Wodic picked up the cue. "You wish to say more. Tell me."

Stonoric gazed through the high window as he gathered his thoughts. Great gusts of wind buffeted the snow as it fell, unseen fingers menacing the white flakes. For its own part, the snow was helpless. Overwhelmed by forces beyond its control, it could but plunge to an uncertain landing.

Stonoric sympathized with the snow. Loyalty to king and country flowed in his veins. He would no sooner contradict the former than betray the latter. But what if the *king* were in danger of betraying the country? Surely those who loved both must speak, even if they risked contradicting their sovereign?

11

He took a deep breath. It was now or never. "Sire, I am ... disquieted by the events of the last four months."

"*Disquieted* is the language of an ambassador." Wodic did not turn from the window, but his eyes glanced sideways, up to Stonoric's face. "It ill befits a duke. We are not at court, cousin. Speak your mind."

"As you wish, sire. I put it to you plainly—I do not like the way events have unfolded since the arrival of the new archbishop. His agents are everywhere, and his embassies to the Dyfanni have been numerous. He has brought these barbarians to your court, and—"

"And today he will bring one to my bed." Now Wodic did face him. "That's what this is really about, isn't it, cousin? You do not wish me to marry Caileamach."

Stonoric inclined his head. "I confess that I do not."

"Do you object to all Dyfanni, or merely to her?"

"The last time the Dyfanni crossed their mountains, it was to attack my city and your kingdom." Wodic had been Stonoric's ward and had fought alongside the duke at Hoccaster. "Surely you remember."

"I do. But that was twenty years ago."

"And in these twenty years, they have refused all parleymen. Now, suddenly, they offer their high princess in marriage? *Now* they are pleased to make a Mersian king their high chieftain? I am suspicious, sire."

"And we are just as pleased to make a Dyfanni princess our Mersian queen!" Wodic laughed. "The world is changing, cousin. The old guard of the Dyfanni are dying."

"Your bride's own father among them."

"Yes, exactly. And besides this, the Red Order is very persuasive." Wodic glanced back out the window. "All monks claim to work for God, but in this case I actually believe it. They have been a godsend to us, at least! Have you heard the reports of their miracles?"

Stonoric snorted. "Perhaps the death of Princess Caileamach's father was one such 'miracle'!"

"What do you mean?"

"Do you not find it remarkably coincidental that those who would have most opposed this union—your own father, and now hers—have died under questionable circumstances?"

"Remarkable, yes. Coincidental? Perhaps. Or perhaps supernatural." Wodic shrugged. "Either way, cousin, it has worked to our advantage. My marriage will cement a union between Mersex and Dyfann. What my father could not do with myriad swords, I have done with mere words. Think of it!" The king's eyes flashed. "Who will call me Wodic the Weak now?"

"No one, sire. But that is not the point."

"Perhaps not for you, cousin. But for me it is *the* point. A king must project strength in order to protect his people. One who is perceived as weak invites invaders. Do not think I haven't heard the whispers, Stonoric!"

"Sire—"

The king held up a hand. "To repel this perception I was prepared to invade Dyfann at great cost of blood and treasure. Now, thanks to the Red Order, almost all of Dyfann has submitted *voluntarily*—without a single drop of Mersian blood spilt. Word of their surrender will travel across land and sea. Those who hear will marvel. Those who contemplated moving against us will stay home. And you, cousin, will not even you yourself sleep easier without the constant threat of an enemy beyond our borders?"

"Not if it means an enemy within our borders."

Wodic snorted. "The Dyfanni will not attack us. After today, they would have as much to lose as we."

"It is not the Dyfanni who concern me, sire. It is the Red Order."

Irritation entered Wodic's voice. "The Red Order has given us Dyfann. Is that the stroke of an enemy, cousin?"

"Yet think of the speed with which they gave it, sire!"

"What of it?"

"It took the archbishop and his red monks but four months to bring the barbarians to capitulation. Four months! And how did they do it? Missionary labors and miracles, they say. But the truth is, we don't know."

"Do you deny the supernatural, cousin?"

"In the present case I neither affirm nor deny it." Stonoric let the urgency within him kindle his words. "Sire, here is my point—our own country is teeming with these same red monks. They are everywhere, and most of them are foreigners. We can be sure they have power, but what we cannot be sure of are their loyalties. Across the sea they serve the emperor. How do we know they do not do so here?"

"The Church has no teeth without the patronage of the throne. The Red Order's loyalties lie with the hand that feeds them. On Midgaddan that hand was the emperor's. Here it is mine."

"I worry that you are wrong, sire."

"You worry too much, cousin." Wodic turned from the window. "The Red Order intends to build new cathedrals in each of the royal cities. Does that not show good faith?"

"It depends. Who will pay?"

Before the king could answer, footsteps echoed in the corridor behind them.

"Your Majesty." The clear voice spoke Vilguran.

Stonoric and the king turned. Two men approached, and Stonoric commanded his features to remain neutral.

Speak of the devil...

"Archbishop Simnor." Wodic smiled his welcome. "We were just talking about you."

"Is that so, Your Majesty?"

"Duke Stonoric has just asked how the Red Order intends to pay for our new cathedrals. Would you care to answer for yourself?"

Apart from his splendid vestments, the Archbishop of Mereclestour was a man of average appearance. Except for his eyes. Like most people, Simnor had black pupils. But unlike anybody else, the irises of the archbishop's eyes were also solid black. These eyes now turned to Stonoric.

Gaping eyes—like looking into a pit. The thought had crossed Stonoric's mind more than once.

"You have a question, my lord?"

"I do, Your Grace. Grand edifices demand grand sums. Who will pay for these new cathedrals? More taxes would not be popular."

"Very true, my lord." Simnor smiled. "Thankfully, more taxes will not be necessary. The Dyfanni have opened both their hearts and their coffers to the message of the Saving Blood. Their contributions will build the new cathedrals."

"The last time the Dyfanni came to Mersex, they tried to burn my city—including its church."

"That was a long time ago, my lord. Long before the Saving Blood came to Dyfann."

"Quite. Now the Dyfanni are going to build *five* new cathedrals . . . in *Mersex?*"

"Yes."

"Their gifts must have been prodigious to afford so much."

"My lord underestimates both the wealth and the generosity of the Dyfanni people."

Before more could be said, there was a cough. It came from the hooded red monk standing a few paces behind the archbishop.

Stonoric had barely noticed the man before, for the archbishop seldom lacked the company of the Red Order. But as he looked at the hooded figure now, he noticed that the man's robe was of a fine and glossy material rather than the ordinary dyed wool.

Must be of some rank. I wonder who he is?

15

But the red monk neither lowered his hood nor opened his lips. He simply turned his faceless head toward the archbishop.

"Though he knows it is not his place to speak," Simnor interpreted, "my brother reminds us that we have little time before the ceremony begins. That is why we came to find Your Majesty. Are you ready, sire?"

"We are." Wodic put his arm on Stonoric's shoulder. "Come, cousin. It is time for us to make history."

The nave of Mereclestour Cathedral was a long hall of white stone. Great columns ran along both sides of its length to support the high ceiling and two long balconies that faced one another across the center aisle. Above these balconies, the windows alternated between clear and stained glass.

Similar to the windows, the hangings below the balconies alternated between two new banners. The ensign of Archbishop Simnor contained a large white cross with the roots of a tree, set amidst a field of scarlet. The new royal standard took the traditional banner of Mersex—the diagonal cross of Saint Aelbus, colored in gold on a field of red—and replaced two of the four triangular sections. The top section had changed to white, and the bottom was now green.

"*A symbol of unity between our peoples,*" Wodic had explained. If Stonoric had not been standing next to the king in front of the altar, he would have scowled. He hated the new flag.

The royal wedding rites took longer than most. This was not only because of the necessary pageantry involved with royal persons, but also because of the languages involved. As a service of the Church, the rites were in Vilguran. Yet because of the public nature of the occasion, a translator repeated each portion of the archbishop's words in Mersian. But since most of the Dyfanni guests did not speak Mersian, yet another translator repeated the ceremony in Dyfannish.

Thus echoed in two languages, the archbishop was somewhere mid-homily when Stonoric let his gaze and attention drift out over the crowd. Despite its size, Mereclestour Cathedral was full. Churchmen, nobles, and other courtiers from both Mersex and Dyfann sat on the balconies and in the front rows. Behind them, buffered by several ranks of soldiers, were the commoners. The contrast between the nobles in their finery, the soldiers in their red tunics, and the rest in their best rags was striking.

Stonoric's eyes stopped near one of the walls at the front of the commoners' section. There, just under one of the balconies, something stirred one of the hanging banners. The duke focused his eyes on the spot.

The danger was not immediately obvious. A man handed a bundle to somebody behind the hanging. The bundle was wrapped in a shawl of some sort, and the recipient looked to be wearing a bonnet.

The duke relaxed. *Just a nursing mother.*

He was about to look away when he saw the shawl fall. Immediately the bundle vanished behind the banner, but not before Stonoric caught a glint of metal in the motion.

His hackles stood on end. That was no baby!

He glanced down at the two guard captains standing at the foot of the dais and tried to convey urgency with his expression. But it was no use. Both men were looking up at the archbishop, who was nearing his conclusion.

"By the power vested in me by Almighty God, I now pronounce you man and wife. What therefore God hath yoked together, let not man put asun—"

Twin shouts resounded from the far back of the nave.

"Traitorous king!"

"Barbarous wench!"

All eyes turned to see two men, one on either side of the hall, standing beneath a hanging banner. Each man carried a lit torch, and in the next moment each had put fire to the banner above him. The flames seemed to leap onto the long cloth.

Both captains standing below Stonoric jumped into action, calling out orders as they dashed down the aisle.

"Give way!"

"Get water!"

"Seize those two men!"

Chaos erupted. The line of soldiers dividing nobles from commoners broke as every guardsman hastened to obey his superiors. At the same time, the crowd of commoners, stuck between the fire and the soldiers, surged toward the doors to escape. Men were shouting. Soldiers were cursing. Women were screaming. And babies were crying.

The sound of crying children brought Stonoric's mind back to the front of the commoners' section—to the place where he had seen the men handling the bundle.

The place was empty.

Where did they go?

A woman screamed again.

Looking up, Stonoric found the source of the noise on the balcony opposite him. There he saw a rough fellow holding a Dyfanni noblewoman from behind. The man held a gleaming knife to her throat.

"Back off!" the man growled to the Dyfanni chieftains starting to close in around him. "Back off, I say, or the barbarian wench bleeds out!"

By this time, the fire at the back of the nave had been put out, and a semblance of order had returned to the nave floor. All eyes turned to the drama unfolding on the balcony.

Beside Stonoric, the king was apoplectic. "Unhand the lady, you vermin! Whatever your game, you cannot possibly hope to win."

The man spat out over the balcony. "That's where you're wrong, king! We've won already!" As he spoke, the man's eyes darted to the balcony facing him—the balcony directly behind the duke!

Stonoric turned his head to follow the man's gaze, and his breath caught in his chest.

Above him, less than ten yards distant, stood two men with loaded crossbows.

The weapons were pointed at Wodic and Caileamach.

Curse my stupidity. It was all a ruse!

Stonoric leapt at the king and queen.

"Your Majesties, look out!"

From the balcony, the crossbows fired.

It is a rule worth remembering as long as one lives: the past may be forgiven, but it cannot be outrun. Those who face their history with honesty may obtain pardon and power. But those who refuse the truth find only fear and flight. True, they may escape consequences for a season . . . but they can never evade conscience.

Outside Urras Monastery, the waves of the northern sea battered high, solid cliffs. Where the land was lower, the cold water lapped over long, pallid sands. In the dark of the night, this steady assault beat a ceaseless, pounding cadence—the drum of general providence.

Inside the abbey, the light of many lamps fell between blazing hearths upon a long table in Saint Calum's Hall. Here the brothers and sisters would soon sit to celebrate the Midwinter Feast. Against the cold without, this seasonal observance was a steady, quiet reminder of providential preservation and provision.

Urien stood near one end of the table, gazing into the fire.

Though it had been less than a month since she had come to Urras, in most ways Urien already felt like part of the community. At first, the brothers' and sisters' natural curiosity had begotten many questions.

Her accent was Dyfanni, wasn't it? How had she come to arrive on a ship from Caeldora?

How had she met Morumus and Oethur?

Where had she learned Vilguran?

But the brothers and sisters soon learned that Urien did not wish to discuss her prior life. And from that point forward, inquisition gave way to a compassionate welcome.

Some stories are best told in silence.

Yet there was one way in which Urien still felt separated from the monks of Urras. For all her integration, she remained an outsider here in one very significant respect. She had renounced the Dark Faith while she was yet in Caeldora, but she had not embraced what the monks insisted was the True Faith.

I am not an Aesusian.

This difference created far more tension for Urien than it did for the rest of the community. For their part, the others did not treat her any differently. Though they knew of Urien's unbelief, and though they did not in any way condone it, they yet showed her the same love and respect that they demonstrated toward one another. Urien found this . . . remarkable.

Also remarkable was the fact that she was encouraged to ask hard questions. Unlike her brother, Somnadh, the inhabitants of Urras never got angry when their faith was questioned. They did not evade her challenges by changing the subject, nor did they dismiss her difficulties with pious flufferies. Instead they responded with calm, reflective answers—and if they didn't know the answer, they admitted it.

Urien found such honesty both refreshing and frustrating. Refreshing for its humility. But it was frustrating because these monks were so insistent that their god spoke in Holy Writ. How could they be so sure?

For a time Urien had been certain it must all be a pretense. For a while she had believed that if she pushed hard enough, she would find a crack. Yet try as she might, she had not managed to exhaust anybody's patience.

Except her own!

It is their confidence. That is what frustrates me. Yet Urien knew frustration was but the tip of her feelings. And the memory she couldn't escape rose unbidden.

That girl in Caeldora was confident, too . . .

Urien turned away from the flames. About halfway down the table on the opposite side, Abbess Nahenna was setting out plates for the feast. Urien hurried along the length of her own side to catch up, leaving a line of wooden dishes clattering in her wake.

Hearing the noise, the abbess looked up. "There is no need to rush, child."

"Yes, ma'am." Urien slowed her pace.

Like the hall in which they labored, Abbess Nahenna was a woman of light and warmth. She was one of those people who smile with their eyes, and hers nearly always bore the spark of some quiet delight. Though the lines on her face hinted of many seasons, the contours of those creases told a joyful tale. There was a strong motherly aura about Nahenna, though she and abbot Nerias had never had children of their own.

As Urien and the abbess reached the far end of the table, a loud crack in the near hearth sent one of the logs tumbling out of the fire.

The abbess grabbed for a poker.

"Urien, would you go and begin fetching the goblets? I will follow you as soon as I fix this fire."

"Yes, ma'am." As she moved back down the length of the table to exit the room, Urien's gaze drifted back toward the fire, where she had started—

"May Aesus forgive you!"

The murdered girl's words seemed to echo from the flames. Urien whisked out the door of the hall into the corridor beyond, trying to outrun the whispered memory . . .

And failing.

Her own reply haunted her as much as the girl's grace.

"How can you say such things to one who will soon carry your blood in a basin?"

"Because I must. Even as he has forgiven me, so I forgive you. And I pray that he might yet rescue you from this darkness."

"No! No, you cannot!"

But she had.

And then there had been that other monk, Donnach, the same day. . . . *No.* With a firm effort, she refused to relive any more of it.

For years Urien had held faith in the Mother. For years she had served the great goddess tree.

Wasted years.

The Mother had proven to be just a tree. In the end, Urien had put the fire to it herself.

Could she ever believe in anything again?

She rounded a corner in the corridor—

And nearly toppled a monk traveling in the opposite direction.

"In a hurry, sister?"

The monk, who had drawn back just in time to prevent the collision, smiled at her. Urien recognized him at once.

"Landu." Somehow, she was not surprised.

"Urien. What a coincidence." The Lothairin had black tonsured hair and clear blue eyes.

"Coincidences must be more frequent here than elsewhere."

Landu laughed. "It is a small island, is it not?"

Too small. Urien could not seem to go more than a day without a 'coincidence' bringing Landu into her company. "I have to go."

"May I sit with you tonight at the feast?"

"No. I am to sit beside the abbess."

"Oh."

Urien stepped past the disappointed monk and continued her way down the corridor. Though she did not look back, she could feel Landu's eyes watching her departure. He was not an unhandsome monk. She simply was not interested.

I won't be here long enough.

Despite the generosity of the abbot and abbess, Urien knew she had to leave the monastery. For all the kindness demonstrated toward her, she did not belong here. She was the fallen servant of a fallen goddess . . .

The Mother is just a tree, and I am just a murderer. Would they accept me so freely if they knew?

In the spring, she would ask to leave. It was the only way.

What will the abbot and abbess say then, when they realize I won't convert?

Her brother had treated her well, too—until she had denounced his faith . . .

"I hate *the Mother! I hate her, Somnadh! Do you hear me?* I hate her!"

The echo of her last words to her brother lay like a millstone on Urien's heart. Where was Somnadh now? Would she ever see him again? Would he want to see her, after what she had done?

She sighed.

Do I want to leave Urras?

For now, the question did not matter. It was midwinter, and ships did not venture to or from the mainland except at direst need. Until the weather broke, she needn't make the decision.

Urien picked up her pace.

For now, all she needed to do was find goblets for the feast.

A few hours later, life and light filled Saint Calum's Hall as Urien took her place next to Abbess Nahenna, near the center of the long table. Across from them, Abbot Nerias rose to his feet.

"My beloved brothers and sisters, it gladdens my heart to see us all gathered here this evening." The abbot swept his gaze from one end of the hall to the other as he spoke. "Though the days be cold and short without these walls, here within we have hearths and hearts warmed by the bounty of our God." He gestured to the full spread on the board before them. "'Taste and see that the Lord is good; the man is blessed who in him rests!'"

The brothers and sisters continued the quotation in reply. "'Fear the Lord, his holy sons, for those who fear him have no want!'"

Nerias intoned the concluding verse: "'Lions do suffer and are hungering, but those who seek the Lord want no good thing!'"

With these words, the Midwinter Feast began.

The Midwinter Feast was a celebration peculiar to the Church in the North. Abbess Nahenna had explained it to Urien thus:

The Church in Nornindaal and Lothair, which included the island of Urras, took its faith and practice only from Holy Writ. According to Holy Writ, the only religious holy day commanded in Writ was Aesusday—the first day of every week. The Church and her members were free to observe other occasions of thanksgiving if they chose, but they were not to elevate such celebrations to the same spiritual level as Aesusday.

For this reason, the Church in the North did not celebrate Adventide—a religious holy day observed by the Church in Mersex and on the continent of Midgaddan. Instead, they held a regular feast on the next day. At this Midwinter Feast, the monks of Urras would give especial thanks for the birth of Aesus—but they would do so without adding to Holy Writ.

It seemed a subtle distinction, but Urien thought she understood the principle. The Aesusian monks believed their god spoke to them *only* in their book. If this were true, then it made sense that they should be careful to frame their devotion *only* in accord with their book.

As the feast got underway, Urien occupied herself with the simple pleasures of eating and drinking. All along the board, brown-robed brothers on one side and grey-robed sisters facing them did the same. Full jugs and platters passed up and down the length of the table, losing a bit of their heft at each stop along the way. Conversation was free and convivial—the brothers beamed and the sisters smiled. Although life in Urras Monastery was not always easy, on this night everybody seemed happy and content.

Urien saw Morumus and Oethur sitting side by side about halfway down the table to her right. Though inseparable, in many ways the two men were opposites. Morumus was dark featured and brooding. On most days his brown eyes and brow bore a grim intensity. Oethur, in contrast, was fair featured, tall, and gregarious. Though he could be serious—Urien had seen this in Caeldora—the Norn was not normally so disposed.

At present, for example, Oethur was engaged in pilfering a slice of buttered bread from Morumus's plate. He did this with gestures of exaggerated stealth . . .

Morumus was the closest thing Urien had to a friend, and normally she made it a point to sit with him and Oethur. Yet on this occasion, as Abbess Nahenna's special guest, she sat near the center of the table.

Across from Urien, the abbot's honored guest was Feindir, a large, silent monk.

"Would you like some bread, Feindir?" She offered him a basket of small dark loaves.

Feindir nodded and smiled.

Though he always seemed cheerful, Feindir never spoke—for most of his tongue had been cut out. The abbess told Urien that Feindir would reveal nothing of how this had happened. The one time he had been asked to write an account, he simply had copied down a verse from Holy Writ:

"But having knelt, Saint Stephrin cried out with a great voice, 'Lord, set not this sin against them.'"

The moment before Feindir took the basket from her hands, the edge of Urien's sleeve caught on a sliver in the table. The wool drew back, revealing an ornate tattoo on her forearm—

Urien jerked her arm back, her breath catching in her throat. Had anybody noticed?

She looked up, and her eyes met Feindir's. He smiled again, shook his head, and looked away.

Urien sighed.

Meanwhile, back down the table, Morumus had noticed Oethur's knavery.

"False grabber!" Morumus growled in an attempted Nornish accent and deliberately poor Vilguran.

As Morumus and Oethur erupted in laughter, Urien smiled.

Of all the people on Urras, only Morumus had any knowledge of her former life. But apart from asking her to translate that horrible book—no, she would not think of *that* tonight—he had spoken of her past only once, on the day when their ship had come within sight of Urras.

"I won't denounce you, Urien. . . . No one here will learn of your past from me. Not even Oethur."

"Thank you, Morumus."

"But I cannot absolve you, either . . ."

"I know. Nobody can."

"No, that's not true. Remember Donnach's words: forgiveness is God's free gift to those who put their trust in Aesus."

"I don't—"

"*I know you don't believe this yet. Grace doesn't come to us naturally. But there are people here who are willing to help you understand, if you desire—myself included.*"

Urien didn't know yet if she could believe. Yet as she sat amidst these merry monks at their Midwinter Feast, she knew one thing for certain:

She very much *wished* all this joy might be true.

In the sky above Dericus, a bank of clouds passed over the face of the full moon.

Standing in a recessed doorway far below, the *Lunumbir* smiled.

Perfect timing.

As the moon's shadow fell upon the street before him, the Lunumbir left the concealment of his alcove. Regular, uniformed *Lumanae*—the "Hands of the Moon," the imperial bodyguards—were intended to be noticed. But the emperor insisted that his highest-ranking, deep-cover operatives incarnate their name.

Lunumbir, "Shadow of the Moon."

Habitual discretion and utmost secrecy flowed in his veins.

Across the street, bawdy laughter and bright light seeped from the door and windows of the dingy pub. From the volume, it sounded like a full house at The Lucky Jug.

The Lunumbir frowned. Tonight's operation would be a risk. *But a necessary risk. We cannot afford to lose him again.*

More than a month had passed since the cluster of grim events that had necessitated tonight's activities. First had come the murder of the bishop of Aevor. Then the slaughter at Lorudin Abbey. Last had been the two dead monks in Naud—one from Lorudin, the other a legate of the Red Order.

When word of the carnage had reached Versaden, the emperor had demanded answers. The task of finding those answers had fallen, as it always did, to the Lumanae.

Witnesses had reported two monks leaving the scene at Naud. One of them had boarded a ship bound for Aeld Gowan—the island north of the Narrow Channel, and beyond the borders of the Imperium. The other had fled inland.

Tonight, that inland monk was sitting inside The Lucky Jug.

It had not been an easy chase. The monk had managed to get a considerable distance from Naud before the Lumanae had begun tracking him. For a period of time, he had disappeared among the small villages along the River Lor. After that he had appeared in Aevor, only to evade capture and disappear again. And while this narrow escape had been doubtless due more to providence than to skill, the monk had proven circumspect thereafter. Not until he had settled in Dericus as a beggar had he again dropped his guard. While drinking himself into oblivion one night, the monk had shared his woes with a fellow beggar.

Who happened to be a paid informant of the Lumanae.

The Lunumbir never smiled. But as he reached the door of the pub, he allowed his frown to flatten into a grim line. He had finally caught up with the last man in Caeldora who could tell him what had happened had at Lorudin Abbey.

Covering his face with a wool scarf, he lifted the latch and pushed open the door.

After the darkness without, the bright interior of The Lucky Jug made the Lunumbir squint. Like many similar haunts, it was larger on the inside than he would have guessed. The bar itself was near the back, and small tables lined the outside walls—intermitted only by a pair of large hearths. Long trestle tables dominated the center of the room, their benches crowded with numerous rough customers, a scattering of genuine rogues, and more than a few immodestly clad women. The whole place had a grimy, unwashed appearance. It smelt it, too.

The Lunumbir tugged his scarf tighter—and not simply for secrecy's sake. A full house indeed.

Scanning the room, he saw a pair of his men seated near the middle of the farthest trestle bench, disguised as tradesmen. Two others, wearing the heavy cloaks preferred by highwaymen, had tucked themselves by a small table next to one of the hearths. A few paces away from the latter pair sat the long-sought fugitive monk. He sat at the end of a long table and stared bleary-eyed into the flickering flames.

The other Lumanae saw their captain enter and made the private signal.

They were ready.

The Lunumbir made his way toward the monk. He turned his head this way and that as he went—a feigned attempt to find a seat. The regular denizens of The Lucky Jug watched his search with apprehension. He could almost see the question in their faces . . .

What kind of character needs to hide his face in a place like this?

For his part, the Lunumbir encouraged their suspicion. He returned hard looks to their stares and tugged his scarf tighter—a clear warning not to look too close.

This was all it took. The crowd assumed the worst and closed ranks. Men and women slid closer together, closing off the spaces near the centers of the benches. Consequently, by the time he reached the far end, the edge of the bench opposite the monk was empty.

The Lunumbir sat down facing his quarry. The monk acknowledged his presence with a grunt but did not look away from the fire. The man had a stretched, tattered appearance. Whatever had happened at Lorudin, the days thereafter had not been kind.

"May I buy you a drink?" There was no need for the Lunumbir to feign his pity—not at this point.

This time the monk did look in his direction. "Who are you?" Bloodshot eyes narrowed. "Why are you covering your face?" Given the man's glazed look and slurred speech, the empty tankard before him had not been his first.

"This?" The Lunumbir touched his scarf, then gestured to the room at large. "This place . . . it stinks. I am amazed anyone can stand it."

The monk snorted, but the almost-laugh turned into a shrug. "You get used to it." He turned back to the fire. "I'll have that drink now, if you're offering."

The Lunumbir raised his arm for a waitress. Across the room, he saw one take notice and begin moving toward him. Before lowering his arm, he opened and closed his fist twice. It was a quick, unremarkable gesture. But his men had been watching for it.

The two disguised Lumanae seated at the middle of the far table began to argue.

"Watch your mouth, you son of a jackdaw!" One of them stood up, his face red.

"Jackdaw?" The other spit out the word and jumped up to face him. "I think you're confused, mate—you talkin' about my mother, or your wife?"

"I'm talkin' about sendin' you to Beln'ol, bloke!" The first man threw a punch.

The Lunumbir saw the second man smile as he ducked the blow and dived at his fellow.

"Hey, watch ou—!" A big fellow seated nearby leaned away from the brawlers, but to no avail. The two Lumanae went sprawling into their neighbors—including the erstwhile protestor.

As intended, the conflagration spread like flames from a shattered lamp. It did not take much to start a melee in a house full of ale—especially one as full as The Lucky Jug on the night of a full moon. In less than a minute, the benches had emptied—and the blows were flying.

The Lunumbir and the monk rose to their feet in the same moment.

"Going somewhere?"

"I must get away..." The monk's voice trembled as he tried to push past the Lunumbir.

"Not tonight." The Lunumbir stepped sideways to block his escape.

"What—?" The monk took a step back. Drink had dulled his wits, but those bits that remained must have sensed the trap, for he turned to flee.

Too late. The other two Lumanae—the ones who had sat close by at the table next to the hearth—now stood blocking his escape.

In the boiling cauldron of The Lucky Jug, nobody noticed the short struggle that ensued. One of the two Lumanae grabbed the monk and pinned his arms, while the other held a soaked cloth over his face. The monk struggled, but not for long. As he sagged into unconsciousness, the Lunumbir drew a short sword from beneath his cloak.

"Let's go. I'll clear a path."

About an hour later, Ortto awoke with a start. His head throbbed with something worse than a hangover, and he felt something cold and damp running down his face into the neck of his robe. As he became more alert, he realized why: somebody had just dumped a bucket of cold water over his head.

Opening his eyes, Ortto saw that he was in a small room. A meager lamp on a table in one corner provided the only illumination, and in its dim glow he saw the silhouettes of five men. He could not see their faces, but he recognized the voice that spoke. It was that of the man who had offered to buy him a drink at The Lucky Jug—the man who had hidden his face with a scarf.

"You're awake."

"I'm getting there."

"If you wish to live out this night, you will get there quickly."

"I'm there now."

"Good." The shadowy figure took a step toward him. "Then we shall waste no more time. You will answer my questions. If you answer completely and truthfully, you will live. If you lie but once, I will cut your throat. Is that clear?"

"Yes."

"What is your name?"

"Ortto."

"You were a monk at Lorudin Abbey. Is it so?"

The mention of Lorudin made Ortto's heart skip a beat. He tried to stand and found that he could not move. Looking down, he realized why: thick ropes bound him to a heavy chair.

One of the other figures offered a long knife to the inquisitor.

"Maybe this'll loosen his tongue, Captain."

The captain waved it away. "It needn't come to that, unless he fails to answer." He turned back to Ortto. "To fail to answer is to lie and will bear the same penalty. Is that clear?"

Ortto nodded. "I was a monk at Lorudin Abbey."

"Yet you survived the slaughter."

"Yes."

"Who killed your brothers?"

"The Red Order."

36

Though several other of the figures gave low whistles, the captain's voice remained impassive. "The Red Order, you say? Did I not warn you against lying, monk?"

Hot sweat mingled with the cold water running down Ortto's back. "It's true, sir, I promise! Most of them wore black hoods, but their leader was a legate of the Red Order—Ulwilf. They murdered the whole—well, *almost* the whole abbey."

"How did you survive?"

"I hid in the broken chimney of the refectory."

"Were there other survivors?"

"Yes."

"How many?"

"Four." Ortto sighed. "Four others survived—at least for a time."

"Who?"

"Morumus, Oethur, Donnach . . . and my brother, Silgram."

"Of those four, how many still live?"

"Two, I hope."

"You hope?"

"I don't know for certain. I have not seen Oethur for months, but when I last saw Morumus, he told me that he and Oethur were returning to their homeland. So I have hope that they may yet live."

"And the other two?"

"Both Donnach and my brother are dead." Ortto's voice was flat, his tone bitter.

"Which of the two died in Naud?"

The mention of the cursed port city hit Ortto like a blow, and it took him a moment to recover. When he again found his voice, it cracked.

"Donnach."

"You were there when it happened." This was not a question.

"Yes."

"Explain."

"Please . . ." Ortto could not bear the shame, and his head drooped. "Please, no . . . please do not make me relive it."

Something ice cold touched beneath his chin and lifted his head. Ortto found himself looking up the length of the long knife. The cold he had felt was the flat of its tip.

The shadowy captain, standing quite close to him now, leaned down so that their faces were level. "I do not wish to torture you. Do not require me so to do."

Ortto closed his eyes and began his account. His whole frame shook with sobs as he spoke.

The Lunumbir stared down at the sobbing monk. It had taken some time for Ortto to tell his tale—and what a tale it had been.

The Lunumbir turned to one of his men. "Prepare the draft."

"Already prepared, sir."

"Good." He took the proffered cup and turned toward the bound monk.

"What is that?" The monk's voice sounded more weary than wary.

"It is *droelum*. It will erase a portion of your memory."

"How much?"

"That is impossible to say. It begins from the present and works backward. We have dosed you for a day, but the potion works differently in different people. Open your mouth."

To the Lunumbir's surprise, the monk cooperated without protest, drinking the droelum with what almost seemed . . . eagerness. When it was gone, Ortto looked up.

"Could you give me more?"

"What?"

"Could you give me more than a day's worth?"

"Why?"

"My sin is more than I can bear." Despite the dim light, the Lunumbir saw agony glistening in Ortto's tear-stained face. "Day after day it grinds me like a great millstone. I betrayed my friends to save my brother, and I failed. My brother died anyway. If you can make me forget it all—forget everything— please, have pity."

The Lunumbir paused. He glanced at the Lumana who had mixed the draft, but the man shook his head, drawing one finger across his throat.

"I'm afraid I cannot. To give you that much would kill you."

"I would be happy for it . . ." As the potion began to take effect, Ortto's voice tapered to a hoarse whisper.

"Perhaps you would—perhaps you even deserve it. But I will not strike where Morumus spared."

"I beg—" But the droelum took Ortto before he could complete the sentence.

The Lunumbir turned to the four Lumanae under his command. "Make him comfortable for when he wakes."

Alone outside, the Lunumbir looked to the full moon, once again unveiled. What wouldn't he give to be able to hang high above the earth, observing all the secret machinations of the emperor's enemies?

The monk's revelations troubled him. He knew already that the Red Order was responsible for murdering the bishop of Aevor, but he had never imagined they were also behind the butchery at Lorudin Abbey. Or that one of their legates— Ulwilf—had died trying to murder Morumus, one of the few escaping Lorudin monks. Like a bloody sunset over the ocean, the Red Order was the storm behind all the Lunumbir's recent headaches.

The emperor had never fully trusted the Red Order. He had invested them with great powers, it was true. But this was not because he believed in their inherent righteousness, but rather because they had proven themselves efficient in extending his authority. And no sooner had the emperor given the red monks their lead than he had ordered the Lumanae to keep them under close surveillance. From the first, he had suspected that they might attempt to go beyond their brief.

A well-founded suspicion, as it turned out.

Powers of inquisition were one thing. Authority to assassinate bishops appointed by the emperor, or burn abbeys under his protection, was something wholly other. What would His Excellency say when he received tonight's report?

The Lunumbir took a deep, pensive breath.

Am I ready to report?

The task of a Shadow of the Moon was not simply to gather information, but to analyze it. And though he now knew *who* was behind events, the Lunumbir did not yet understand *why*. Why had the Red Order taken such a stark risk in murdering Anathadus, the bishop of a prominent Caeldoran city? Why had they compounded that wild venture by burning and slaughtering an entire monastery?

The Lunumbir possessed two clues. First, he knew that Anathadus and some men from Lorudin had been involved in a plot at the Court of Saint Cephan several months back—a plot in which they had helped two bishops from northern Aeld Gowan evade capture by the Red Order. Second, the Lunumbir knew that all the men involved in this intrigue had held one thing in common: they were all committed to what was called the "old order" of the Church.

The Lunumbir was well acquainted with the old order of the Church. It was a sliver-thin minority at the Court of Saint

Cephan. It carried no influence and curried no favor with the emperor. As a spiritual movement, the old order was known for its devotion and integrity. But as a political force, it was known for . . . nothing.

How then had it managed to arouse such reckless malice from the Red Order?

The Lunumbir shook his head in the moonlight. Until he could answer this question to his own satisfaction, he was not ready to make his report. But how would he get the answer?

There was only one thing for it. Though it would carry him well beyond the borders of the empire, though it would push the limits of his authority, he must learn more. In matters spiritual, the Lunumbir could not pretend to be particularly advanced. Yet even from a mundane perspective, the threat was apparent. Many years ago, a letter to His Excellency had expressed the matter quite well:

> The Church is not simply the conscience of the kingdom. She is also her soul. Thus it cannot fail to be true that as goes the Church, so goes the kingdom. But if this be so, then it is further true that as goes the kingdom, so goes her king. Therefore let the king ever take care how he protects her in whose welfare is bound up his own . . .

Emperor Arechon had not been emperor of the Vilgurans when he had received this letter. He had not yet even been King of Caeldora, but he had never forgotten those words— nor had the Lunumbir, to whom he had shown the letter. Though penned by a mere monk from an unknown family, the letter had so impressed Arechon that he had later persuaded his father to make that monk a bishop.

That bishop had been Anathadus—now, on account of the Red Order, the *late* bishop of Aevor.

The Lunumbir nodded. It was settled. The Red Order had overreached—perhaps fatally. But he must understand why. And the only people who could tell him were the two monks who had escaped from Naud: Morumus and Oethur.

No, there was nothing for it.

He must travel to Aeld Gowan.

orches shuddered in their wall sconces as the great figure stalked past them. With every other step the tall man winced, yet despite the pain he carried on with enough haste that his tail wind threatened the corridor's lamps. His worn features were set in a brooding grimace.

Duke Stonoric was in no great mood. Over a month had passed since the royal wedding. The assassination attempt had failed . . . but so far, things were not looking up.

Despite the passage of time, his injuries yet bothered him. Those assassins had been no amateurs. Their weapons had been powerful and well aimed. Had Stonoric leapt but a moment later, the bolts from the two crossbows would have pierced the hearts of the king and queen. As it was, both had lodged deep in him—one in his left shoulder blade, and the other partially through his left arm. The healers had done what they could, but it would be a long time—if ever—before that arm would lift a shield. Moreover, he suspected that the pain lancing his shoulder with every step would never go away.

Thankfully, I am right-handed.

Beyond the physical pain, Stonoric was plagued with personal frustration. Though his gallantry in saving the king and queen had earned him official honors, the duke found his actual influence at court waning. The king seemed to confide in him far less now than he had before the wedding. Stonoric blamed this change of tide on two ill currents.

The first was the fact that the assassins remained at large. Wodic had given the task of apprehending them to "my most trusted and proven duke." Yet to this point, Stonoric had failed to produce results.

He had lived long enough to know how these things *ought* to work. As Duke of Hoccaster, he had a handful of thief-takers in his service. Thief-takers knew all the right places to check: the dankest alleys, the darkest hiding-holes, and the dingiest pubs. Under normal circumstances, such capable men—and he had no doubts regarding their abilities—would get to the bottom of things in a matter of days. The reason for this was simple: most criminals had two habitual flaws. The first was that they liked to drink. The second was that they liked to talk, especially if they had been drinking.

Yet in this case, things were different. Stonoric had procured the services of a small group of thief-takers local to Mereclestour, in addition to his own men summoned from home. But so far, the combined efforts of all these men had produced nothing.

If the assassins were still in the city, they were lying very low.

And here I go again to the king . . . another week without progress.

The thought made Stonoric growl, and he quickened his pace. His footfalls clapped like thunder upon the stones of the corridor. He hated failure. But more than this, he hated how every bad report seemed to push his cousin farther away from him . . .

. . . and right into the waiting arms of Simnor.

The Archbishop of Mereclestour was the second reason for Stonoric's decline at court. The plan to unite Mersex and Dyfann by marriage had originated with Simnor, and it had been he who carefully had arranged and facilitated its every motion. Now that the plan was commenced, it was to the archbishop that the king turned for counsel in its execution.

To the archbishop . . . and the Red Order.

The thought of the red monks only soured Stonoric further. The king might be confident that his patronage ensured their loyalty. But Stonoric was far from certain . . .

"My Lord Duke."

The voice broke Stonoric's dark reverie and brought him up short. He looked up.

Without realizing it, the duke had rounded a corner and now stood halfway down the final passage to the royal audience chamber. He could see the great doors not too far distant from where he stood, their great oak engravings polished and gleaming in the lamplight. Two sentries stood watch beside them. But between these and Stonoric stood an all-too-familiar figure.

Archbishop Simnor.

"Your Grace." The duke did not grind his teeth, though he sorely felt the urge.

"Would you walk with me, my lord?"

"I am on my way to see the king."

"The king is taking his midday meal with the queen. I myself intended to see him just now, but the sentries are under strict orders from the chamberlain that Their Majesties are not to be disturbed. It may be best not to interrupt, my lord . . ."

"I will wait."

Simnor nodded. "Then will you walk with me?"

Nothing would please me less. But he knew protocol forbade a refusal of the archbishop's request without good reason. "As Your Grace wishes."

"Let us go to the chapel, then. There is a matter I wish to discuss with you, Duke."

Saint Eohan's Chapel was a quiet, semicircular chamber situated at the southeastern corner of the Tower of Luca. Though not large in terms of its length or width, the chapel had a high ceiling that gave it an elevated, spacious feel. Two tiers of stone arches encircled the room, and a handful of narrow windows provided it with ample illumination. Unlike most Mersian churches, the chapel's decorations were sparse: the altar was of simple cut stone, and the lectern, rails, and pews were of unpainted wood.

The only person present when Simnor and Stonoric entered was a young servant. He was polishing the rails between the altar and the pews with an oilcloth. When he looked up and recognized them, the cloth stilled and his eyes widened.

"My lords." He touched one hand—still holding the oilcloth—to his forehead. It came away leaving a dull gleam.

Stonoric permitted himself a small smile and waved the man out. "Leave us—and shut the door behind you."

Bobbing in obeisance, the servant scurried out.

When the latch clicked shut, the archbishop turned to Stonoric.

"The matter I wish to discuss with you requires considerable . . . discretion." His black, unblinking eyes regarded Stonoric. "Will you keep a confidence, Duke?"

Stonoric returned the man an even gaze. "I am able to keep confidence, Your Grace. But I should never do so if it meant treason to my king."

"Of course not, my lord." Simnor's eyes flashed with obsidian fire. "That word is as abhorrent to my office as its suggestion is offensive to my honor."

Stonoric did not flinch at the challenge. He still did not trust the archbishop. Yet his words had been strong, and possibly overreaching. His answer must now be . . . measured.

"I intend no accusation, Your Grace. I only wish to be clear. Who knows whether a question such as yours might be a secret test of loyalty?"

For a moment, the archbishop did not reply.

"Well answered, Duke," he said at last. The fire subsided. "You may rest assured: the confidence of which I speak involves no such betrayal of His Majesty."

"Very well. Under such terms I will agree to keep Your Grace's confidence."

The archbishop nodded.

"The matter of which I must speak with you concerns those assassins who attempted to murder His Majesty."

"What of them?"

"I take it you have not yet found them?"

"No."

"I have."

"What?" The smoldering anger that had begun to rise in Stonoric's breast at the mention of his failure now turned cold as ice. *Could it be?*

"We have them."

"Who?"

"The assassins."

"No, I know—" Stonoric pushed the irritation out of his voice. "*Who* has them?"

"My order."

"The Red Order?"

"The Order of the Saving Blood, yes."

"You are sure it is them?" If it was, then Stonoric's influence at court was finished.

"Yes. They have confessed."

"When?"

"Last night."

"Where?"

"A tavern along the riverfront, The Nail and Banner. They were trying to buy passage away from Mereclestour by sea."

"Who are they?"

"I do not know. They have yet to be interrogated."

The Red Order.

It was a bitter draft. *The Red Order has succeeded where I have failed.* He knew how his cousin would respond to this—and he couldn't blame him. *Even I wouldn't trust me after this.*

"That is good news." Stonoric's tone was resigned, and he turned his eyes to the window behind the altar.

I will return to Hoccaster . . .

"Not unless it comes from you, my lord."

"What?" Stonoric turned back to Simnor.

"The news of this capture must come from you, Duke."

"Why should it? The triumph is yours, Archbishop."

"Is it?" The question lingered in the air as Simnor walked to the front of the chapel. Reaching the altar, he placed both hands upon it and bowed his head.

Stonoric did not move. What was the man playing at?

After a long minute, the archbishop turned back. "You misunderstand me, Duke, if you think I aim to undermine you."

And yet you ordered your monks after my quarry.

Though Stonoric had said nothing aloud, Simnor might as well have read his mind. "I set my order to the chase the very day of the attack, just as soon as I was sure that Their Majesties were safe. At that time, your lordship was unconscious. It was not even certain whether you would live. The next day went by very quickly, and I had no opportunity to tell the king about my operation. Then you recovered, and the king gave the task to you. At that point, what was I to do? Call off my order, and lose what advantage our quick response might have gained? Or continue our pursuit in secret, in the hope that more ears and eyes would have a better chance of success?"

"You acted as I would have, and I give you joy of your prize."

"My lord, it is *I* who wish to give *you* the joy of this prize."

"And why should you wish to do that?"

"Because such things are not my duty."

Stonoric grunted. "If you are worried that the king will fault you, Your Grace, be easy. Explain it to him as you have explained it to me. His Majesty is not unreasonable."

"You misunderstand, Duke." Leaving one hand on the altar, Simnor gestured with the other to the rest of the chapel. "*This* is my duty. My responsibility is for the souls of men, not their schemes or their swords. My order is always willing to lend a hand in the affairs of this world, but it must ever be a secret hand. If once it should become known that we were involved in the affairs of the crown, we would lose our credibility with the people of the towns."

"Your Grace, very few priests—and no single Archbishop of Mereclestour—has ever been mistaken for a friend to the Mersian commoners. Besides, it is well known that your order served the emperor on Midgaddan."

"We will always do what is necessary where there are no other capable hands. Yet here in Aeld Gowan I am hopeful that things may be otherwise. Would you yourself not prefer it if my order stayed away from matters of state?"

"I would."

"Then let us be frank. There is much work to do to bring the message of the Saving Blood to Dyfann. I desire to free my order's hands from all other tasks. To do that requires a trustworthy man at the king's side who is competent in matters of state. I believe you are a competent man, Duke, and your injuries prove your loyalty to Their Majesties. Though you may not trust me, I am willing to trust you. To prove my goodwill, I offer you these assassins. Interrogate them yourself, and report to the king what you find."

"It is treason to lie to the king. How can I represent this capture as my own, when I did not in fact accomplish it?"

"If servants prepare food for a guest in anticipation of their master's request, is it not still the master who is credited the host?"

49

"It is."

"Then if you will but consider me your servant, and will but consider the capture of these assassins an anticipated service, there need be no question of lying to the king."

Simnor reached into the fold of his robe and withdrew a large bronze key. This he proffered to Stonoric.

"They are in the dungeons below, my lord, awaiting your attention."

Several hours later, Stonoric again walked the corridors approaching the royal audience hall. Yet this time, the flames in the wall torches did not tremble at his passage. This time, his throbbing injuries were forgotten. Nevertheless, his brow was still furrowed, and if possible, his expression was even more brooding than it had been earlier in the day.

As he rounded the last corner and the polished oak doors came into view, he paused. He reached into his pocket, and his hand came out clenched. Opening his palm, he took a final look at the object by the flickering light of a wall lamp.

Such a small thing. How could it be so deadly?

He had found the prisoners exactly where Archbishop Simnor had left them. He had put them to the question—put them to the question *severely*—but with little effect. The two would-be assassins had confessed that they had fired the crossbows. Yet even under excruciating pain, they had said nothing else. In his frustration, Stonoric had broken off the questioning and gone through their belongings. The men possessed little enough, to be sure. Yet upon careful examination, he had found something significant sewn into the lining of one of their coats—something that made further questioning unnecessary.

In his open palm was a small wooden disc. He recognized the material at once.

Brer. The disc was a bishop's token, and his hackles had risen when he had read the inscription.

COLBALVS.

It was written in Vilguran, of course, but the name was unmistakable.

Ciolbail.

The bishop of Lothair.

The weight of the revelation was staggering. The bishop of Lothair . . . implicated in an attempt on the life of the king and queen! Could it really be?

Stonoric looked up toward the doors. The sentries had noticed him by now and stood waiting to push them open. He could not delay any longer. The king must know.

Such a small thing . . .

But it might well be a token of war.

Far away from Mereclestour, all was ready for the Feast of Bhru Muthad—the Feast of Mother's Belly. It was a high holy day for the Old Faith of Dyfann. From time immemorial, the children of the Mother had celebrated the first signs of spring with a special, fresh sacrifice. As the Source of all things, it was the Mother herself who carried spring within her womb. And a pregnant Mother must be fed.

From within his cowl, Somnadh smiled at his companion. "I am delighted that you are here with us, brother."

"The pleasure is mine." Like all the *Mordruui* at the feast, Somnadh's companion wore a long red robe with the hood covering his face. Yet unlike the others, his accent was foreign. "For years I have longed to attend the Mother at her table. Finally, after so long, I am here!"

Somnadh's spirit soared as the two of them joined the line of worshipers winding up a steep slope. His heart thrilled at the thought of the approaching sacrifice, and his lips curved in a silent smile at his brother's heavily accented attempts to join in with the traditional chants and choruses.

He does try his best—and it is not his fault he had the misfortune to be born in the North.

As they climbed higher, Somnadh looked out over the *Mutha-dannach*. The Mother Glen was a deep dale hidden fast within the interior of Dyfann. A wide stream ran through its center, and surrounding it on all sides was a dark, ancient forest. At the center of the valley, the water curved around the bulge of a high, narrow hill. It was this hill that Somnadh and his brethren now ascended.

"Almost there." Somnadh could not hide the enthusiasm in his voice, even as he labored up the inclined path.

"Soon," panted his companion beside him. "Soon, I will behold her for the first time." The joy in his tone was unmistakable.

Crowning the top of the hill was a circle of tall standing stones. The monoliths themselves were huge, dark masses—almost black. They were grouped by twos, with the top of each two bridged by another heavy slab.

"How, brother . . . how did these come to be here?"

Somnadh shook his head. How often had he wondered the very same thing?

"Nobody knows. Llanubys says the goddess herself gathered them."

As the two men entered through the ring of stones, they saw that the surfaces were etched deep with intricate patterns and runes. These etchings were inlaid with a white, chalky substance—creating a stark contrast.

"What is the purpose of these, brother?" Somnadh's companion motioned to the numerous patterns, lines of script, and interwoven whorls.

"Some of them tell the history of our people. We use others to read the stars."

"How far back does the history go?"

"Far." Somnadh paused, pointing to a worn etching near the top of one of the stones. "That, brother, tells the story of how the Mother came to Dyfann."

"Truly?"

"Truly."

"So those drawings . . . and that person . . . ?" His voice trailed off in awe.

"Yes, they represent Tham's wife saving the holy seed from Eolas, goddess of the First Garden, and secreting it away on the Great Ark—frustrating the jealous god Yeho's attempt to murder his Mother by flooding the world."

"Amazing."

"Yes."

"The Aesusian holy book says nothing of this."

"That's because it was written by the servants of Yeho." Somnadh turned toward his companion. "But when we have achieved our victory, brother, we will rewrite the holy books and expunge the lies."

The conversation came to an abrupt halt as the two men passed through the standing stones and joined their Mordruui brethren. Here, in the inner heart of the Old Faith, there could be no thought of talking aloud. For now they stood assembled before *her*.

Beside him, Somnadh's brother gasped. "*Genna ma'guad ma'muthad ma'rophed.*"

Genna, my goddess, my mother, my salvation.

Genna, the great Mother tree, the Source of all things. It was from Genna that all life came, and it was to her that all life returned at death.

"Amen." Somnadh drew a deep breath. No matter how many times he came here, he never failed to be overwhelmed . . .

The ground upon which I now stand is no mere hill. It is the axis of the universe.

So long as Genna endured, the world would endure. The heavens would continue to turn, and the cycle of life and death would continue . . .

So long as the Mother is protected.

A pang pierced Somnadh's memory, and he looked up.

The Goddess Tree was beautiful and glorious. Her skin was a perfect, spotless white: unblemished, unbroken, and impeccably sublime. The curve of her boughs and the delicate balance of her limbs were more gracious than that of any mortal lady, and her fulsome leaves—each spread like a welcoming hand—were a deep, luxuriant red. Within the center of these leaves, as though held in the palm, were the clusters of precious *nomergenna* herb.

Tears filled Somnadh's eyes as he contemplated the vision. *How lovely you are, Mother! How singularly beautiful!*

Sadly, *singularly* was the key word. With her sapling in Caeldora gone, Genna was now not just the oldest of her kind . . .

She was the last.

Somnadh bowed his head, the silent tears streaking down his hidden face. *Urien, Urien. . . . Oh, sister, what have you done?*

"My dear ones," a thin voice called from somewhere above them.

Somnadh looked up again.

Climbing down from the Mother's high branches was an old woman. Her skin was very pale—almost the color of the Mother's. It stretched mottled and thin over her skull. Long white hair streamed down her back, falling in wispy tresses over her scarlet robe. Of all those standing within the stone circle, only she was hoodless.

"Llanubys!"

The assembly hailed their matron in unison.

Llanubys was older than any living man. According to Somnadh's father Comnadh, Llanubys had been old when *he* had been a boy. For longer than anyone could remember, she had dwelt at the Muthadannach, serving as the Heart of Genna.

Yet for Somnadh, Llanubys was far more than a spiritual guide. It was she who had introduced him to his Northern brother. And it was she who had inducted them both into the secret at the heart of the Old Faith . . .

Though all Dyfanni reverenced the Mother, it was only the Mordruui—the Hands of the Mother—who knew the secret of nomergenna. Only the Mordruui harvested the

Mother's herb, and only they knew the ancient arts by which to call forth its power. For generations, the Mordruui had dwelt hidden within the shadows of the Old Faith—known only to Llanubys and to each other. Few among the Circle of the Holy Groves knew the power of nomergenna—not Somnadh's father Comnadh, not even Seanguth the Eldest!

Descending through the Mother's boughs, Llanubys reached the bottom and dropped to the earth. Moving with a fluidity that defied her age, Llanubys took up a position behind a low stone table. Facing the assembly, she raised her arms. In one hand she held a long knife, and in the other a large goblet. Like the table, both were cut of stone.

"Bring the sacrifice!"

The victim was brought in. She was a young girl, dressed in white. Her feet and hands were bound fast, there was a gag in her mouth, and she was blindfolded. As she came, the song of the Mordruui—a hymn of praise to Genna— rose from the scarlet hoods to drown out the sounds of her resistance.

The song swelled as the girl was bound to the table, and Llanubys raised the knife.

The song reached its zenith, then broke like a wave as the knife came down.

For several moments, the assembly fell silent . . .

"Life!" Llanubys lifted the steaming goblet to her mouth. When she took it away again, the crimson stained her lips and ran gleaming down her white chin.

"New life!" called the assembly in response.

No wind swept down through the dale of the Muthadann-ach that day, and no breeze penetrated the circle of standing stones from without. Nevertheless, the leaves of the white tree seemed to undulate in an unseen current as Llanubys completed the sacrifice.

"Genna ma'guad ma'muthad ma'rophed," chanted the assembled Mordruui as the crone's hands poured each fresh goblet onto the roots of the Mother.

"Genna, my goddess, my mother, my salvation."

Some time later, Somnadh and his fellow walked together down the slope—the last two droplets in the long, bloody line of hooded Mordruui. Behind them, silence once again prevailed within the stone circle. The sacrifice was finished.

"As I said earlier, I am glad you could be with us this year." Somnadh smiled at his companion. "For the spring that now comes is our time, brother. Before the next Bhru Muthad, the Mother will be exalted across all Aeld Gowan!"

"Do you think we will really see it this time, brother? Ten years ago we thought . . . "

"Ten years ago we were not ready. Ten years ago we had to move by night. Now is different. Now the Church protects us. We can move freely across this island."

"In Mersex and Dyfann, yes. But there is still the North—"

"Where you are well placed." Somnadh shook his head. "Do not fear, my brother. Today, the Mother's exaltation is still in the womb. But in seven weeks comes the equinox. On that day, we will see our triumph born into the world."

"The new Feast of the Cross-Tree?"

"That is what the Mersians call it, yes. Here it will be known as the Feast of the Sacred Tree. But the name is not important. What is important, brother, is this: on that day, Dyfanni and Mersians will celebrate side by side in the new cathedral at Banr Cluidan. On the same hill where once they warred as enemies, they will now join in worship as friends. The Old Faith of Dyfann will merge forever with the New Faith of

Aesus. The Dyfanni will receive the Son, and the Mersians will reverence his Mother. At long last, spiritual balance will be restored to Aeld Gowan. A new golden age will dawn!"

"Do you think all will accept it?"

"Some may be skeptical, but the Archbishop of Merecles-tour will preside over the ceremony personally. He will show them the Miracle. Few will doubt after that."

"It is the Mother's power that makes all the difference."

"Truly, her power never fail—" But Somnadh's voice died out as a single word once again flashed to the forefront of his thoughts—

Urien.

His companion stopped, putting a hand upon his arm.

"Is it your sister, brother?"

Somnadh nodded. "I still don't know what to do. She has done great evil, I know. But she was pushed. Weakened by my neglect, she fell under the influence of those two monks."

"Be at peace, brother. One of those two monks is now dead."

"Yes, but the other killed Ulwilf. Now he and another monk have taken Urien. . . . I don't know where."

"But I do."

"What?" Somnadh's heart skipped a beat.

"I know where the other two monks have taken your sister."

"Where?"

"Urras Monastery, off the coast of Lothair."

Somnadh stared at the man beside him. "How do you know this?"

"I have received certain information from the island. And I have a plan, brother."

For the next several minutes, Somnadh listened as his brother from the North related the details. He said nothing until the other man had almost finished.

". . . and thus I will avenge our brother Ulwilf's blood."

"No!"

59

The man started at Somnadh's response. "What?"

"No, brother, you must not kill them." Somnadh shook his hooded head. "You must take them alive. Please!"

"Alive? Why?"

"Because"—a new possibility opened in Somnadh's thoughts—"once they are in our hands, I will take them to Llanubys. Perhaps their blood can restore my sister."

"As you wish. I will take them alive."

"Thank you, brother." For the first time in several weeks, Somnadh felt a pang of hope for his sister. "You are certain this will work?"

"For your sister? I don't know—"

"No, not that." *Leave that to me.* "I mean, you are certain you will take the monks?"

Within his cowl, the Northman laughed. "Oh yes, brother. Already the trap is closing in on them. They suspect nothing."

"Only you, Morumus, could possibly think this is a good idea."

Morumus turned back to Oethur and grinned. With every heaving step the bigger man took, his breath escaped him like the jets of the mythical ice dragon. They condensed to mist as soon as they hit the cold air and covered his straw-colored beard with a sheen of frost.

Like Oethur, Morumus had grown a short beard—permitted to the monks of Urras in winter. He didn't try to hide his amusement. "Exercise is good for you, Oethur."

"So is a warm fire!"

"Is it customary in Nornindaal for a king's son to complain thus?"

Oethur glared up the hill. "In my country, even the peasants are wise enough to stay indoors when it is this cold. None of them would be foolish enough to go climbing in this weather."

"Bah! It's a fine winter day, and we've been indoors far too long. That is why you're having so much trouble. We've done precious little *but* sit by warm fires for the past month!"

Oethur relented. "You are right, even if you are hopeless." He shook his head. "I cannot see past that bend ahead. How much farther?"

"Just a few dozen more."

"A few *dozen?*"

"Only a *few*. Come on . . ."

The two monks concentrated their efforts on finishing their climb. Long ago, the first monks of Urras had cut a great flight of stone steps into the side of the rocky tor overlooking their island. From its top, one would possess a commanding view of the island and the surrounding sea.

Morumus reached the summit about a minute ahead of his companion. As he waited, the gusting wind off the sea caused the heat of his climb to dissipate. The sweat beneath his habit began to cool. Despite the thick wool, he shivered.

A moment later, the huskier Norn joined him on the summit.

"You were right, Oethur," said Morumus as his friend caught his breath. "It is cold up here!"

A merry light flashed in Oethur's grey eyes. "Is it customary in Lothair for a lord's son to complain thus?"

"Only when he's cold."

"Ha!"

After this, both peered out across the ocean in silence.

"Don't let it go to your head, Morumus," said Oethur after a minute or so, "but you too were right about one thing. What a view!"

" 'The sea be his, for he made it himself . . .' "

"Indeed. And 'let him rule from sea to sea!' "

"Just so. . . . You know that's from a different psalm, right?"

"And you know that I can throw you down this hill . . ."

"Just so."

Both men laughed—and shivered.

"If it is this cold on land," observed Oethur, "imagine how cold it must be under sail."

"Just another reason why we probably won't see any ships for at least several weeks."

"You don't think so?"

"No. You remember that ship the week before the Mid-winter Feast?"

"Of course. I sent a letter to my father in the care of her captain."

"That's right." Morumus remembered the letter—a full account of events in Caeldora to which he himself had contributed. "Well, I reckon we won't see another like it until close to the equinox."

"Are you certain, brother?"

"Reasonably so."

"Are you very certain?"

"Very certain? All I'm saying is that it's sensible to think—" Morumus frowned. "Wait, why do you ask?"

Oethur pointed. "Because I think there is a ship approaching."
So there is!

Although it was still quite a way off, there could be no mistake. A great longship, propelled by sweeping oars and a single rectangular sail surged through the high swell out of the east. It was headed straight for Urras.

Morumus shook his head. "I confess, I am amazed."

"So you're not a prophet. Don't be too hard on yourself."

This time it was Oethur who received a glare. "For a ship to sail this time of year, there must be some urgency. Unless . . ."

Oethur's eyes widened. "Unless it is a raiding party."

"Right."

"Should we warn the others?"

Morumus studied the ship again. "It is coming in fast. . . . We'll have to run."

"*Down* the steps?"

"I know." Morumus gathered up the hem of his robe and turned toward the stairs. "But we must try!"

The flight down the ancient, steep, and winding steps of the tor was a precarious blur. Being a bit lighter and more agile, Morumus led the way—attempting to select the safest

63

footing for both of them. Several times his feet slipped, and once he nearly tumbled out over the edge. He would have, too, had Oethur not pulled him back from the brink at just the last moment. By the time they reached the base of the hill, both men's hearts were beating at double speed—and not merely from the exertion of the run.

The stairs ended at the southeast corner of the tor, and from the bottom the men could see both the monastery and the ship. The monastery was a dark mass in the southern distance. As for the ship . . .

"It's too close, Oethur. We'll never make it."

Oethur was peering out at the ship. "We may not need to, brother. Look! Above the sail!"

Morumus looked. Sure enough, there was something flying from the ship's mast—a long, streaming pennant. The bright color was unmistakable.

Orange!

"That is your king's banner, is it not?"

Morumus nodded, releasing a breath he hadn't realized he was holding. The ship approaching Urras was not a band of sea raiders.

It was a king's ship of Lothair.

With the immediate threat gone, the remainder of their return walk to the monastery was unhurried. The terrain was devoid of any large hills, and there was a broad path beneath their feet. The only uncomfortable thing about the journey was the wind. The afternoon was wearing on, and consequently the breeze was growing. Morumus was glad he had worked up a sweat tearing down the hill. Though there was no longer need to hurry, he and Oethur trotted along at a brisk jog.

The simple harbor stood a short distance up the coast from the monastery and, hastened by the wind, Morumus and Oethur reached it in far less time than they would have otherwise. There they found the Lothairin longship, tied to the wharf and unguarded.

A closer look confirmed Morumus's thoughts. "It is a king's ship."

"You think your king himself is here?"

"No, not with only one ship. I wonder who he's sent—and why?"

"I don't know, but it's a bit trusting of them to leave the ship unguarded."

Morumus looked at Oethur. "Who would steal it? Abbot Nerias?"

"Other raiders might."

"They might, but as we've both observed today, this is miserable weather for being outdoors aground, let alone at sea."

As if to underscore the sentiment, the breeze picked up at that moment—sending a fresh chill through Morumus even as it caused the boat's pennant to snap and unfurl.

Looking up, Oethur frowned. "You know, Morumus, I have never understood your king's banner. My own father's standard carries the helmet and spear of our legendary ancestor, Nuorn the Valiant. But what do these lines mean?"

He pointed to the three arcing curves centered on the orange field of the Lothairin banner. The ends of each arc curved away from the other two. Moreover, each was a different color: red, green, and black.

"Those are cords. They come from our own legends—the legend of the threefold cord. I take it you have never heard it?"

"No."

Morumus shivered. "Let's keep walking, and I'll tell you."

The distance from the harbor to the monastery was less than half a mile up a gentle incline, and the sun was nearing the horizon as they made the trek.

"According to our history, three ancestral peoples once lived north of the Deasmor. For many generations, they were constantly at war—with each other and with invaders. There was no peace. Then one day, a king arrived from across the sea. With his strong arms and wise spirit, he united all three peoples under his gracious rule. As a symbol of his kingdom he devised a threefold cord. Each arc was a different color to stand for the different peoples, yet the three were interwoven at the center and connected at their ends to symbolize the unity of the kingdom."

"But on the flag above the boat, the three arcs were not connected," Oethur observed.

"No, they were not. Treachery destroyed the great kingdom, and the threefold cord unraveled. But the ancestor of my people, Lothair the Wise, believed that a new king would someday arise who would reunite the peoples of the north. And so, to keep both hope and memory alive, he placed the three cords—separated at present—on his banner. And yet, if you draw them together from the center"—Morumus paused, picked up a rock, and drew in the dust—"they will connect once again. You see?"

Oethur nodded. "I see it. But it might not need a great king."

Morumus looked up at him, eyebrows raised. "What do you mean?"

"You said your ancestor believed a great king could unite the peoples by drawing them together."

"That's right."

"Yet it strikes me that a sufficient threat might just as easily push all three together from the outside."

66

Morumus's brow furrowed. It was a perceptive insight. "I'd never thought of that before, Oethur."

Oethur grinned. "Try not to think too much about it now, Morumus. The more you think, the slower you walk. It's getting dark, and I'm hungry."

A bell tolled high overhead as the two monks entered Urras Monastery. A wave of warmth greeted them as they passed through the doors, and Morumus felt a last shiver as the chill lost its grip. Both men exhaled—and for the first time in several hours, Morumus did not see a cloud form before their faces.

Oethur tried it again just to make sure. Then he smiled. "Warmer."

"And that was the bell for supper."

"I think I can smell it. Let's go and—"

"Halt! In the name of the king, go no farther!"

The command boomed through the entrance hall of the monastery. Stunned, both monks stopped short and looked around. But the echo from the stone walls made it impossible to tell from which direction the shout had come.

Morumus looked at Oethur, who shrugged—but stayed where he was.

Then, in the silence, they heard perhaps the most unexpected sound . . .

Is that laughing?

It was.

A few paces down the hall from them, a tall man stepped out from the concealment of a shallow alcove. He was tall—taller than Morumus, and perhaps even taller than Oethur. He had dark red hair that ran to his shoulders, and his green eyes shone bright in the light of the wall lamps.

For a moment, Morumus could not speak. There could be no mistaking that face.

But could he really be . . . here?

Then he remembered the ship. Of course. Nerias's words came floating back to him: *". . . much like your father. Yet he is the king's ward, not yours."*

"Haedorn?"

The green eyes locked onto Morumus.

"Hello, little brother!"

Two hours later, four men sat around a comfortable fire in Abbot Nerias's chamber. All of them had enjoyed a robust abbey supper, followed by Vespers in the monastery chapel. With the day's public duties thus finished, Haedorn, Morumus, Oethur, and Nerias had retired for a private conference.

"One hardly knows where to begin such a meeting," said Nerias. "There is so much to tell. But since our news is perhaps the longest and most grim"—here he gestured to himself, Morumus, and Oethur—"it might be best if you go first, Haedorn. Tell us, nephew: why have you come to Urras?"

"My warrant for undertaking this crossing is simple: the king seeks the whereabouts of Bishop Ciolbail."

"Ciolbail?" Nerias frowned. "He is not in Dunross?"

"No, Uncle. He has not been in Dunross these past seven months."

"Seven months? But that goes back to the Court of Saint Cephan!"

"Yes, precisely. We have not seen the bishop in Dunross since he departed for the Court."

Nerias was trembling. "You mean he never returned?"

"Never."

"That doesn't make any sense." Morumus looked at his uncle. "You and Bishop Ciolbail and Bishop Treowin fled Caeldora together. How could you have arrived—?"

"*Fled?*" Haedorn's heavy brows arched.

Nerias put up a hand, and both brothers fell silent.

"This is most disturbing news you bring, Nephew." He sighed. "And I cannot help but fear the worst."

"What do you mean?"

"I did indeed sail from Caeldora with the bishops. We knew we would have no time to provision our ship in Naud, and so we touched at Tratharan to resupply. While in port, Treowin learned of a crew of Trathari preparing to sail for Toberstan. Rather than sail with Ciolbail and I to Dunross and cross by land, he resolved to go with them."

Oethur drew a sharp breath. "But the Trathari and my people . . ."

"Do not get along. Precisely. Ciolbail and I tried to dissuade Treowin, but he was implacable. In the end, Ciolbail resolved to sail with him and make the overland journey from Grindangled to Dunross. The Trathari regard Lothairins as distant kin, and the chances of there being trouble for Treowin with Ciolbail present were—well, we *thought* they were—very small indeed. But it appears we were mistaken."

"I do not think it is that simple," said Haedorn.

"No?"

"No, Uncle. Two days ago, King Heclaid received a letter from Wodic of Mersex demanding the surrender of Bishop Ciolbail."

"Surrender? Whatever for?"

"To be tried for plotting the attempted assassination of Wodic and his new Dyfanni queen."

"*What?*"

"It is true. Our sources in Mersex confirm that an attempt was made upon the king and queen on their wedding day—at

Mereclestour Cathedral, no less!" Haedorn reached into his pocket and withdrew something small. He opened his hand and held it forth. "They found this on one of the would-be assassins."

The brer disc gleamed in the firelight, the "COLBALVS" inscription plain on its surface.

"Oh no." Nerias's concern was clear in his features. "This is bad."

"Very bad." Haedorn nodded. "We have to find Bishop Ciolbail before the Mersians or the Dyfanni."

"Agreed. But why have you come *here*, nephew? Surely you do not think he is here!"

"No, Uncle. But you sent a letter to Ciolbail a week before the Midwinter Feast. Do you remember it?"

"Yes."

"Well, the king remembered it, too. For a long time he left it sealed to wait for the bishop's return. But after receiving Wodic's letter, he ordered that your letter be opened—thinking that if you were writing to Ciolbail, expecting him to be in Dunross, you might have some idea of his last whereabouts."

"And when the king read in my letter about Morumus, he sent you."

"Yes." Haedorn turned to look at his brother. "None of us had any idea you were alive, brother. All these years, it was assumed that you had perished with Father." He turned back to Nerias. "Why the secrecy, Uncle?"

Nerias looked from Haedorn to Morumus.

"Tell him, lad."

"Tell him . . . ?"

"Everything."

Oethur stood. "We're going to need more logs for the fire."

6

In his dream that night, Morumus found himself standing beside a pool of water. It was a fine spring day, and he was standing in a mountain vale of the high country of southern Lothair. Looking around, he knew exactly where he was.

The Mathway Vale.

The vale got its name from the river born in its heights and cradled down its descent. By the time it reached the lowlands, the Mathway was a strong river that flowed north from the Deasmor to Dunross by the sea. But here in the heights, it was but a series of tributary pools and streams—such as the one beside which he now stood.

But this is not just any pool.

Even after more than ten years, Morumus recognized it immediately. This was no mere pool among the hundreds of the Mathway Vale. It was *the* pool—the same smooth, stream-fed pond beside which the Mordruui had butchered his father and his father's men.

He would never forget that night. Even after so long, the memory felt like raw flesh.

Wake up. Oh please, God, let me wake up!

Nothing happened.

So be it . . . but even in a dream, I don't have to lie down.

Morumus hated this place. If he could not leave it by shutting his eyes, he would leave it by foot. Turning away from the pool, he began to walk north. If the rest of his dream was as close to reality as this place, then far away down the vale he would find Aban-Tur, his family's ancestral holding.

Morumus had not taken more than a dozen steps when he felt the fingers of a cold wind rake the back of his neck. A sudden foreboding gripped him, and he turned.

Behind him to the south, high up in the peaks of the Deasmor, he saw . . .

What is that?

At first it looked like little more than a thick fog, spilling slowly down from the hills into the vale. But the longer he looked, the more apprehensive Morumus felt. For one thing, the fog was not grey—not even dark grey—but rather solid black. It did not diffuse light; it absorbed it. And even more than this, there was an unnatural character to the movement of the fog as it spilled out of the heights. The thick tendrils seemed almost alive as they crept down the sides of the ridge, like headless serpents seeking prey.

At the same moment that he saw this, the wind that pushed the fog gave a sudden gust. And in its rush he heard an inhuman, hissing song.

The Dark Speech!

Morumus turned to flee, but as he took his first step something happened.

Though he could not explain how it happened, Morumus *changed*. One moment he was Morumus the monk, lifting the hem of his robe to flee. The next moment he had become a mouse—a red mouse—bounding and leaping over the turf, almost flying away downcountry to the north. And somehow, though it made no sense, he was able to see himself in this form.

What is happening?

As if the wind too could see, its hissing became angrier, and the advance of the black fog increased in speed.

The chase was on.

As he sped along down the vale in mouse form—at times almost seeming to fly—a conversation between him and his uncle Nerias rose from the depths of Morumus's memory:

"I found the yard empty—except for a mouse. . . . It was red."

"What about the mouse?"

"Your name, Morumus. . . . 'Morumus' means 'root mouse' in Dyfanni . . ."

The full import struck Morumus. His uncle had not been describing to him a mere dream. This flight in which Morumus was now engaged was no mere dream.

It was a *tidusangan.* Nerias had explained the difference:

"It means 'time-song.' It is simply a glimpse of what has happened—or what is to come."

"But do such things not come from God?"

"Only in the most common sense."

"Are they magic, then?"

"No more than possessing sharp wits or a strong arm. Some people see tidusanganim, while others—most—do not. Nothing more. It is a gift, son, but not a spiritual—or magical—endowment. How could it be anything more, when even the pagans saw the dreams?"

Morumus had experienced a tidusangan only once before in his life—a horrible glimpse of dark things to come. If he was in the midst of a tidusangan now, what did it portend?

Morumus shuddered—a very odd sensation as a mouse!—and willed himself to move faster. The ground beneath him began to pass by at an even greater rate. Rock, heather, and river became nothing but a blur beneath the gliding red mouse.

But the darkness was just as determined. As the mouse increased his pace, so likewise the ill wind gusted stronger and the black cloud flowed faster in the vale. Again, though he could not explain *how*, Morumus was able to see this happening behind him.

Then he saw something else.

One of the tendrils of the black fog detached itself from the main body. For a moment, the limb seemed to be disintegrating as it broke into a cluster of small pieces. But a moment later, these shards condensed . . .

A flight of crows!

Cawing their malevolence, the wicked birds darted after Morumus. With sinking dread, he realized that these were moving with greater speed than either the fog or the mouse could muster.

Am I doomed then?

But no sooner had the question occurred to Morumus than he heard a new sound—this time from the direction in which he fled.

From the north, another storm was gathering. Morumus was sure the sky in that direction had been clear when his dream had begun. Now, however, great heaps of white clouds were gathering into tall thunderheads. And what was that emerging from their midst?

More birds!

Yet even before he could identify them, Morumus somehow knew that these birds were his allies. But what were they? As the mouse looked toward them, his vision grew to prodigious strength.

Yes! Those are no crows! Those are eagles!

A formation of eagles was racing out of northern sky on a direct path to intercept the enemy. Though fewer in number than the horde of crows, the eagles were of far greater strength. As they flew, the terrific beating of their wings caused the storm clouds behind them to shift and swirl until they had assumed a new shape.

Morumus could not believe his tiny eyes. *Could it truly be?*

Though it defied all natural formation, the thunderhead had taken a legendary form.

The threefold cord!

The pursuit was fast approaching its climax. Behind Morumus, the crows had almost closed the distance. He could feel the air of their wings, and their rasping caw filled his ears. Yet the eagles too were now above him, diving like lightning toward the black cloud. Who would get to him first?

Morumus never found out, for in the very next instant the mouse missed a delicate landing on the edge of a precipice and tumbled over the brink.

With a desperate squeak, Morumus fell into a deep abyss.

Am I dead?

Morumus woke in a cold sweat, his heart racing and his lungs panting for air.

Dead men don't breathe. But where am I?

Bit by bit, the disorientation passed. He was sitting up on a rough pallet. The pallet was tucked into the corner of a small room. The room had three stone walls and an old wooden door. In the far corner, illuminated by the rays of a full moon streaming through the window, he saw a single book sitting on a crude table. He recognized it.

Donnach's volume of Holy Writ.

Morumus exhaled.

He was in his room at Urras Monastery.

Just a dream.

No. It was a tidusangan.

What did it mean?

Unwilling to relive the dream by closing his eyes, Morumus resolved to get up. But he did not immediately rise. His heart was still racing, and another full minute passed before it resumed a normal rhythm. While he waited, he listened.

Silence.

Urras Monastery was asleep.

After what had passed in his earlier conference, Morumus was surprised that he had managed to fall off. Haedorn had accepted the truth about their father's death with remarkable ease. A decade of smoldering anger at the Norns melted off him as Morumus and Oethur had related the truth about Raudorn's and Alfered's murders. But when he had learned that those responsible now walked as monks in Mersex—yea, that one of their number sat upon the Chair of Saint Aucantia as Archbishop of Mereclestour!—his rage boiled over with terrible ferocity. Once he had recomposed himself, Haedorn had winced when Morumus related the death of Donnach.

"King Heclaid will be most vexed by this, brother—a personal tragedy and a diplomatic disaster."

Following this, Haedorn and Oethur had almost fallen into an altercation over their next move. Oethur had been convinced he should return to Nornindaal at once to seek news of Bishop Ciolbail. Haedorn had insisted—in the name of the king—that both Morumus *and* Oethur accompany him to Dunross to repeat their account. Oethur had stiffened at the imperative, insisting that *he* was no Lothairin subject and would do as he thought best for *his* king.

In the end, only Nerias's quick intervention had resolved the matter. Oethur might not have been a Lothairin subject, but he had taken vows of monastic obedience. Oethur would go first to Dunross with Haedorn and Morumus. After that, both Morumus and Oethur should go together to Grindangled. The Mordruui might have had a hand in Ciolbail's disappearance—they knew all about brer tokens—and if so, it was too dangerous for Oethur to travel alone.

As his thoughts drifted back to Oethur, Morumus heard a creak. It was not loud, but in the otherwise perfect silence of the monastery it stood out. He recognized it at once. Somebody was lifting the latch of the room adjacent to his—a latch in need of some oil.

Oethur's room.

Perfect.

The thought of returning to sleep still held little appeal for Morumus. But if Oethur was also awake, then perhaps the two of them could walk together. He got up.

Opening his own door, Morumus peered into the corridor. Nothing. Yet Oethur's door was ajar.

"Brother," he called in a whisper. "Oethur, are you awake?"

No reply.

Strange.

Morumus stepped into the corridor and pushed open Oethur's door.

He was just in time. In the full moon's light coming through the single window, two forms were visible. The first was that of Oethur, lying on his back fast asleep on his pallet. The second was a figure draped all in black, standing over Oethur with one arm raised.

The raised fist clenched a long knife, aimed straight for Oethur's heart.

"Stop!" Morumus burst through the doorway into Oethur's cell.

The shadowy figure turned as Morumus came at him. It tried to slash at him with the blade, but Morumus dodged the first swing as well as the subsequent backslash. When the arm came back up, he grabbed at the wrist and twisted.

"Augh!"

The knife clattered to the floor.

Retaliation was swift and painful. Robbed of his blade, the hooded man swung his free arm full-force into Morumus's middle.

"Oof!"

While Morumus reeled backward into the side wall, his adversary cast about for the dropped weapon.

"Hey!" Oethur was awake.

With surprising awareness, the Norn sighted the dropped weapon in the same moment as his would-be assassin. Both lunged for it, colliding at a spot halfway between the pallet and the door. There were muffled grunts and a brief scuffle.

The two figures separated less than a minute later. Oethur came to his feet near the pallet. The hooded man stood with his back to the open door.

Black spots still flecked Morumus's vision, and for the second time that night his heart was racing.

Who has the knife?

Oethur had it!

After this there was a momentary pause. As his vision cleared, Morumus looked from the hooded man to Oethur. Both were breathing heavily, but unharmed.

The latter, without taking his eyes off his opponent, spoke sideways to Morumus. "Are you hurt?"

"No."

"Good."

The Norn addressed the enemy. "Who are you?"

The hooded figure held up both hands as though he meant to surrender. Then he turned and fled.

Passing but the barest nod of consent between them, Morumus and Oethur were after him—shouting as they went.

"Awake!"

"Murderer afoot!"

The long corridor of the men's dormitory flowed into the central passage leading to Saint Calum's Hall. The hooded man was fast on his feet, and he reached the hall a half minute ahead of his pursuers. There he overturned several benches and a short side table in his wake before dashing toward the abbey's entrance.

Morumus was a few seconds ahead of Oethur, and he called back a warning. "Hall's a mess!"

Both men leapt the obstructions without incident, but the delay allowed their quarry to open a wider lead. By the time they reached the front doors, the would-be assassin was through them.

"And you thought it was cold earlier!" laughed Oethur as they burst into the frigid night.

Morumus shook his head. Oethur had almost been murdered . . .

Now he's laughing?

Yet despite his wonder, Morumus found himself joining in. "Is it customary in Nornindaal for a king's son to complain thus?"

We're not dead. Just mad.

Outside, the landscape of Urras gleamed with pale iridescence under the rays of the full moon. Consequently, it took them only a moment to spot their foe. He was running south—away from the tor, away from the harbor.

"He's headed toward the cliffs!"

"Good!" shouted Oethur. "If we can hem him in, he'll either have to surrender—or swim!"

Oethur was right. The cliffs south of the monastery were jagged and sheer. There could be no climbing down, for there were no gentle grades between the turf above and the rocky surf below. Morumus frowned.

Why would anybody flee this way?

Everybody on Urras knew about the cliffs.

But that's just it! He must not be one of us.

This left only one possibility.

One of Haedorn's men?

As the cliffs drew nearer, the sound of crashing waves reached Morumus's ears. "We're getting close!"

"He's already there!" Oethur pointed. "Let's slow down and spread out."

The enemy had reached the precipice and realized his mistake. Now, as the two monks slowed to a trot and separated, he turned to face them—jerking his hooded face first one way and then the other, looking for a way of escape.

"Give it up!" Oethur still carried the assassin's knife, which he now held forth for the latter to see. The blade gleamed in the moonlight. Whether or not the man understood Oethur's words, there could be no mistaking this gesture.

As the noose tightened, the hooded villain backed up to the edge of the cliffs. He reached into his cloak and withdrew another knife. Its blade was shorter than the first, but still long enough to deal death. He brandished it at each of them in turn—with particular emphasis toward Morumus, who was unarmed.

"There is no escape." Morumus circled to the right, speaking in Northspeech.

With a serpent's swiftness, the man flipped the knife in his hand and threw it at Morumus. At the same time, he stepped backward—over the brink!

The knife was well aimed, but Morumus lunged when he saw the man leap. As a result, the blade took him in the left shoulder rather than the heart. But it was a heavy knife, and it knocked him to the ground nonetheless.

Oethur was there in an instant, concern etched in moonlight on his features. "Morumus! Brother! How bad is it?"

"I'll live," gasped Morumus. "What about him?"

Oethur disappeared for a few seconds, then came back. "Gone."

An hour later, Morumus and Oethur once again found themselves before the fire with Haedorn and Nerias in the latter's study. Abbess Nahenna was there, too. She had removed the knife from Morumus's shoulder and was now dressing the wound.

"I'm afraid this is going to cause more than a little pain." She applied a cloth soaked in spirits.

"I understa—" But as the cloth touched the wound, Morumus had to clamp his mouth shut to avoid yelling. He clenched his teeth as the abbess—his aunt—probed the wound deeper. After what seemed an eternity, she withdrew the cloth and looked at him.

"There."

"*More than a little pain?*" He shook his head. "My dear aunt, you have a gift for understatement."

"Is it customary in Lothair for a lord's son to complain thus?" Oethur was standing behind him, holding him still while the abbess worked. He looked down and frowned. "It is a deep wound, Morumus. If you hadn't moved, the knife might have pierced your heart."

Standing beside the fire and staring deep into its depths, Haedorn shook his head. A quick search upon their return had revealed that one of his men-at-arms was missing.

"I cannot believe that a member of the king's own guard . . ." He turned to Oethur. "My lord, on behalf of King Heclaid, please allow me to express extreme disapprobation and beg you will accept his disavowal. The man who attacked you was new to His Majesty's service. That was the reason he came with me to Urras. He had never sailed before, and I intended the crossing as a rather forceful baptism. So far as I had observed, he was an honest soldier. Had I known otherwise, I would have never—" His face was grave. "Nevertheless, it was I who brought him hence. I bear the responsibility and give myself over to your mercy."

Looking up, Morumus half-expected his friend to make a dismissive jest. But he was wrong. The gleam of jocularity

81

had vanished from Oethur's visage with such completeness that Morumus found himself wondering if it had ever existed at all. Not for the first time he was reminded that his friend and fellow monk was, in the end, still the son of a king.

Yet if Oethur's expression was sober, his words were soft. He inclined his head. "My lord's assurances are accepted with goodwill. Our people have lived at peace for generations, and have withstood greater attempts than these to disrupt our fraternity."

Haedorn bowed. "Thank you, my lord."

After a silence appropriate to the exchange, Nerias spoke. "Surprise of the issue aside, the intent of this attack was clear. Oethur's death in a Lothairin monastery would have resulted in a war with Nornindaal. I doubt whether all the fraternity and goodwill in the world could have prevented it."

"It must have been the Mordruui," said Morumus. "They have tried before."

Oethur nodded, looking at him and Haedorn in turn. "Your father and my brother."

Another long pause.

"We must sail tomorrow," Haedorn said finally. "No longer is our concern simply to find Bishop Ciolbail. If the Mordruui have managed to place one traitor in the king's service, they may have another. The life of King Heclaid himself may be in danger!"

The steady crash of the surf swallowed up the gasps and grunts of the man in black. Hand over hand on the tar-dyed rope, he labored to pull himself up the cliff face. Despite the difficulty of his exertions, he was smiling.

His plan had worked.

Perfectly.

The intent had not been to *kill* Morumus or Oethur. The original plan had changed on that point. That particular pleasure now belonged to another. His revised instructions, delivered by bird but a week prior, had been simple: ensure that they leave Urras as soon as possible, and cast the blame elsewhere.

Until the ship had arrived from Dunross, he had not known how he could comply. But considering that he had had but a handful of hours to execute his stratagem, he was especially pleased.

Everything had fallen into place like pieces in a game of *cynnig* . . .

The murder of the man-at-arms had been his opening move.

Every victory requires the sacrifice of a few pawns.

Fleeing south was the ruse.

Now nobody would search the dormitories!

Wounding Morumus protected his escape.

With his friend down, Oethur took but a glance over the brink.

With a last great pull, the man reached the top and heaved himself onto the turf. His master would deliver the fatal move once the monks reached the mainland.

After that, his reward would be guaranteed.

The knight will become a bishop.

PART II

UNRAVELED PATHS

The Bone Codex.

Urien had never seen a more revolting book.

It wasn't just the fact that the book was bound to a spine of human bone.

It wasn't just because there was an image of the Mother inlaid on the cover.

More than anything else, it was the *contents* of the book that appalled her.

She had breezed through the first section containing Eolas lore. She had heard those stories from childhood. She no longer believed them to be true, yet of all the book's material they were the least sickening.

The second section had made Urien ill. There were designs for the ritual basins and knives, complete with the appropriate runes to be inscribed upon them. Then, lest any blood be lost or wasted, there were exsanguination sketches showing where to cut and how best to hold the victim while so doing. The annotations in this section made it clear that harvesting a victim was a practiced art. The more one prolonged the victim's life during exsanguination, the longer the heart beat, the less the blood would coagulate in the body and be lost to the Mother.

Every ghastly ritual was diagramed and described in meticulous detail and with shameless delight.

Urien almost quit at this point. Though she had poured the Mother's offerings for years in Caeldora, never before had she been forced to come to terms with the enormity of what it all meant.

I have collaborated in one of the most inhuman, wicked forms of worship ever devised.

Almost as bad was the third section—the section she was beginning today. This was the book of cantilations. Besides regular hymns of adoration to the Mother, there were special verses of praise to be sung when offering fresh sacrifices . . .

The whole thing made her sick.

But she had promised to translate all of it.

For Morumus.

She had told Morumus of the existence of the other Muthadannach—the original Mother Glen. She had told him, too, of the nomergenna she had harvested from the Mother. She did not know what it was used for, only that it was valued by the Mordruui above all else. Hearing this, Morumus had grown determined to learn more about nomergenna and, if possible, find and destroy the last Muthadannach. But neither he, nor even she, had any idea of its location. And so she had undertaken the translation in the hope of finding a clue.

In fact, Urien was the only one on Urras who *could* translate the Bone Codex. The script of the book was Vilguran, but the language was a very old dialect of Dyfanni known today only by the priests of the Old Faith. It was the language of the Mother's incantations, not the common speech of Dyfann. For all his familiarity with the latter, the former was a language unknown even to Morumus.

Morumus.

Putting down her pen, Urien stood up and walked to her window. Through the glass, she had a clear view of the harbor.

Empty.

Morumus and Oethur had left Urras yesterday, sailing east for Lothair in a ship captained by Morumus's brother. Something awful had happened the night before they had left. She was not sure of all the details, but it seemed that somebody had tried to kill one—or both—of them. Morumus and Oethur had given chase, but in the end the man had thrown himself off the southern cliffs.

Urien had been sorry to see her friends leave, but thankful that they had survived.

Thankful to whom?

She looked back to the two books on the table beside her door. Lying closed beside the open Bone Codex was Morumus's copy of Holy Writ—the copy made by his friend Donnach, the monk who had come with Morumus to the Muthadannach in Caeldora. The three of them had escaped together after Urien had burned the Mother, but Donnach had died in Naud.

Murdered by Ulwilf, one of her brother's Mordruui captains.

Donnach had saved Morumus's life, and Urien knew that there was nothing Morumus valued more than this copy of Holy Writ—"Donnach's Volume," he called it.

Yet he had left it with her!

"I don't know how long I'll be gone, or what I'll be facing once we reach the mainland. I cannot risk taking Donnach's Volume with me. Will you keep it for me, Urien?"

"Aren't you afraid I might destroy it?"

"Will you?"

"No."

"Then I'm not afraid. Are you afraid to keep it?"

"No."

"Good. Then that's settled. You will keep it until I return."

But Urien hadn't just been *keeping* Donnach's Volume.

She had been *reading* it. After completing the hideous second section of the Bone Codex translation yesterday, she had been unable to sleep last night. So she had stayed up and read Donnach's Volume. She couldn't read the Grendannathi column, of course—this was incomplete anyway. But the Volume contained a complete copy of Holy Writ in Vilguran, written in a clear, fine hand in a parallel column on each page. She had read the two books she most often heard the monks recommend to new catechumens—the accounts of Aesus titled *According to Maerc* and *According to Iowan*.

Reading these books had been an unsettling experience for Urien. It was not the presence of the supernatural that produced her disquiet, for she had read the ancestral tales of her own people many times. No. What unsettled her was the fact that the authors of Holy Writ wrote like *historians*.

These books were not the mythic accounts of Dyfanni bards. Rather, they were *testimonials*. There could be no question that both Maerc and Iowan believed that what they recorded about the life, death, and resurrection of Aesus was actual fact. And it was clear from the way they wrote that they intended to confront their readers with a single, burning question:

Do you believe that Aesus is the Son of God?

At present, Urien did not. Yet in reading these books she sensed . . . *something*.

What it was she could not tell. But it felt clean. And after spending hours mired in the filth of the Bone Codex, she felt a desperate need for cleansing.

It was only after reading Holy Writ that she had managed to drift off into a dreamless sleep—shortly before dawn. Yet if what she had read helped her sleep, it only increased her waking turmoil.

There was no longer any question of which faith she *wished* to be true. The Old Faith, especially as expounded without restraint in the Bone Codex, was hideous. Morumus was more than right to call it the Dark Faith. Indeed, from what she now knew, Urien thought he might be guilty of understatement!

By contrast, the Aesusian faith as explained in Holy Writ was a beautiful alternative. Here there was no Mother goddess with an unyielding appetite for human blood. On the contrary, Holy Writ presented a loving Father God whose Son agreed to give his own blood. Why? So that humans didn't have to die forever. Indeed, the Son had died so that even the most wicked humans, if they would but receive it and repent, might be forgiven—and *live* forever!

The difference was day and night. The Old Faith made voracious demands. The Aesusian faith offered gracious accomplishments.

But it was just at this point that Urien experienced so much turmoil! For though she knew what she *wanted* to be true, she realized that the verity or falsity of the Aesusian faith could not be a mere matter of her desire. Not if it were true.

Real truth could not be a matter of human preference. On his own, nobody was qualified to make the determination. Urien was but a single woman—she could not see all things, nor did she have the power to ordain all things.

In short, Urien was no goddess.

This being the case, she had no authority to decide what was true—no matter how great her desire.

But then how can I ever know if the Aesusian faith is true?

This was the point that she could not seem to pass. And it was killing her.

I need to clear my head.

Urien walked across the room. She took her heavy cloak down from its peg, opened her door—and looked down.

There, on her table, were the two opposing books.

Desire might not settle her dilemma. But might it not echo some basic, reliable *sense*—however faint, however tenuous?

Perhaps.

That was some comfort—something she could carry with her.

Happy to leave the Bone Codex gaping behind her, Urien picked up Donnach's Volume and walked out.

A blast of icy wind struck Urien as she stepped through the monastery doors, sending a shiver skipping up her back. It was a reminder that spring was still a month away. Clutching her cloak tighter, she strolled west through the abbey grounds. The sky overhead was thick with clouds, and the threat of rain was looming.

Maybe this wasn't such a good idea . . .

About a half mile in the distance ahead, she saw the ruins of the first Urras Monastery. According to Abbess Nahenna, sea-raiders had burned them over a century prior. Amidst the clusters of crumbling stone she could pick out the various buildings. There in the center was the old main hall, its roofless outline reduced to half-walls by the effects of weather and the need for stone to build the current monastery. Near to it were the shells of two dormitories, a refectory, and the chapel.

Striding across the washed-out landscape beneath the leaden clouds, Urien let her thoughts drift. Even at the end of winter, Urras Island was such a beautiful place. Well could she understand why Aesusian monks had come to settle here. Aside from the tor away to the north, the green turf was gentle and lilting, with plenty of space for the necessary garden patches. And although the island lacked any great forests or even a modest sweeping wood, there were trees enough to provide for fires and timber. At the same time, Urras was small enough—and far enough away—to protect it from becoming an extension of the mainland. Life here was challenging, but comfortable. The monks and their families were isolated, but not alone.

In short, it was the perfect atmosphere for a monastic community. As she looked around, Urien smiled. She could be very happy here, if only . . .

But her thoughts had no time to sour, for in the next moment it began to rain—a cold, pelting drizzle that gathered strength as it came. Even with the extra layer of wool provided by her cloak, it would not take her long to be soaked. Time to get out of the wet.

Besides, there was Donnach's Volume. Upon reflection, carrying it outside in this weather had been unwise.

That's as may be. What's necessary is that I get it indoors as soon as possible!

Urien looked around. Her walk had carried her quite a distance, and she was now much closer to the ruins of the old monastery than to its current successor. If she hurried, she could be amidst the old ruins in but a few minutes. It would take at least twice as long to get back to her room.

She looked back to the ruins. Could she find a dry place among them until the rain passed? She scanned the various stone husks, finding nothing until—

There!

Most of the old chapel, like the rest of the buildings, was exposed to the sky. Yet there was one small side wing that still possessed its roof.

Perfect.

Urien hurried on. No sooner had she crossed the threshold than the drizzle gave way to a torrent.

Just in time! Relief escaped her with a sigh.

The interior of the old chapel was very dark. Urien didn't mind this, however, for it was out of the cold and there were no windows to let in the blowing rain. A pungent scent reached her nose as she entered, and she looked down. The floor was bare earth. Kneeling to touch it, she found it somewhat damp.

Water always finds a way . . .

Coming back to her feet, she looked around for a dry place to set her parcel. In the near corner of the wall, barely visible in the thick dimness, she saw a recessed niche.

"This will do." She yielded to a yawn as she placed Donnach's Volume on the high, protected ledge. She next cast about for a place to rest. She could not expect to find anything very comfortable—but maybe an old pew?

Yes. There, against the wall near the front.

Despite the decades, the wooden bench remained quite sturdy. What's more, it was nice and wide—wide enough, in fact, for Urien to lie down.

The sight made her yawn again as she remembered how little rest she had managed the previous night.

As the rain continued to pour outside, Urien stretched out on the old pew and closed her eyes.

She was a little girl again, picking her way up the path at Banr Cluidan. As she recognized where she was, she gave a delighted little skip. Urien remembered what she would find within the hill fort at the top of the winding track. Not only her father waited for her there, but her brother too!

But it is never wise to skip up a muddy path, particularly not one that is wet with the blood of the slain. Young Urien slipped and fell.

She was back on her feet in a moment, but now she had mud all over her. She wiped it off her face and spit out the bit that was in her mouth. It left a foul, metallic aftertaste.

She tried picking the clumps off her nice dress, but the muck left a ruddy smear in its wake.

Urien began to cry.

Somewhere close by, another voice picked up the lament. Horrified, she looked around.

She was surrounded by the bodies of slain warriors! There had been a great battle with the Mersians at Banr Cluidan, and many proud Dyfanni warriors had died defending the hill fort. She saw them now: young and old, smooth-faced newlings and seasoned warriors. Some wore nothing but Dyfanni battle paint. Others wore soiled Mersian tunics. But all of them were dead.

And dead men don't cry. Do they?

A dozen yards away, she saw something stir amidst the slain. It was a child—a little girl, just like her! She had a pretty face framed with black hair, and it was she who joined in Urien's cry. The tears were still visible at the corners of her blue eyes.

But something was horribly wrong.

The little girl had a deep gash along the side of her neck. But it didn't bleed. In fact, there was no color in her skin whatsoever.

She was dead.

And yet she was standing!

Urien screamed—and again heard her own voice echoed across the hilltop.

There were more voices now, and as Urien cast about in rising panic she saw other bodies rising out of the mounds of dead warriors. Most of them were children. All of them had the same blood-drained white skin and telltale incisions on their throats.

Exsanguinated.

The victims of the Mother.

Moaning and wailing, they began to move toward her. Urien tried to turn and run, but she kept stumbling in the red-tinged mud. In fact, the more she struggled the deeper and redder the mud around her became. Soon the path had vanished altogether, and she was sinking in a thick mire of blood.

The Well of Souls.

The Mother's victims had reached her by now, but they did not reach *for* her. Instead, they simply watched her sink—tears running from their lifeless eyes, a lament rising from their breathless, ruined throats . . .

Urien jolted awake to find herself lying facedown on the floor of the old chapel. In the violent struggle of her dream, she had rolled off the pew.

Remembering that the floor was damp earth, she pushed herself up.

She sat back down on the pew and shuddered. She could still see those faces, hear the cries, taste the blood . . .

Blood. Why is there still a taste of blood in my mouth, even after waking?

Urien scrubbed her mouth with the back of her sleeve, then sniffed. Sure enough, there had been blood on her mouth.

Did I bite my lip or tongue?

No, she felt no pain in her mouth.

But I smell it, too. The odor is very strong . . .

The realization dawned on her. The pungent smell she had noticed when she had entered the old chapel was not the musty smell of damp earth.

It was the smell of death.

In the next moment, she saw it.

On the wall opposite her there was another pew like the one upon which she sat. She had not seen it when she first had entered the chapel, because her eyes had not been used to the deep gloom. But now she saw it.

And there was something lying on that pew, reposed as she herself had lain but a few minutes before . . .

Urien's hackles stood on end, and she screamed.

It was a corpse.

Ignoring the still-beating rain outside, she fled.

"**W**ell," said the deep bass voice after Morumus finished his account. "Well."

There was a moment's ponderous silence before the voice resumed.

"You cannot imagine how glad it makes me to see you again, my dear boy. I had believed you dead these last ten years, and it does my heart good to have you here before me now in the flesh. Your father was one of my best thanes while he lived, and your brother has taken his place with distinction and honor."

"Thank you, sire." Morumus bowed.

"Yet notwithstanding"—King Heclaid's lined face turned to etched steel—"you bring very dark tidings. The only good news in the whole pile is that the Norns were, after all, innocent of your father's death. We dropped that axe long ago, but it is still good to know—and I look forward to meeting Oethur at dinner."

The king blew out his whiskers and stroked his grey-streaked beard. "But by my honor, Morumus! My gran used to tell stories of the walking Shadows to frighten me as a boy. Now you tell me these—what do you call them?"

"Mordruui, sire—or just *Dree*."

"Just so. Now you are telling me these Dree are real?"

"Yes, sire."

"And not only real, but moving openly in Mersex and on Midgaddan as a religious order—this Red Order?"

"The Order of the Saving Blood. Yes, sire."

"*And* that one of their number is now Archbishop of Mereclestour?"

"Yes, sire. I saw the markings on his wrists at his consecration."

"By my honor!" The king shook his head. "And if all this were not enough . . . these Dree have killed Donnach mac Toercanth, the son of one of our most important allies among the Grendannathi!"

"I am so sorry about that, sire." Morumus felt a stinging at the corners of his eyes.

"So am I, son. So am I. It puts all our efforts with the Grendannathi at serious risk." He sighed, then waved his arm. "But that is a trouble for another day. For now, we have a more pressing matter. Wodic of Mersex has demanded that I surrender Bishop Ciolbail. I take it Haedorn has told you why?"

"Yes, sire."

"Good. Then you understand that this is a matter of some urgency." The king leaned forward in his chair. "Where is Bishop Ciolbail, Morumus? What did Nerias say?"

As Morumus gave his report to the king, Oethur looked out the windows of the palace library. Dunross Castle stood atop a great black mound of rock near the mouth of the Mathway River, and from his vantage point Oethur could see both city and sea spread out below him. The sun had been at its zenith when he had entered the library. It was now halfway toward the western horizon.

Morumus has been with the king for a long time.

A click echoed through the cavernous chamber, and Oethur turned to see the library door opening. He was expecting Morumus, or possibly Haedorn. He was wrong.

A young woman entered the room, dressed in servant's livery.

Oethur studied her. "May I help you?"

"Are you Lord Oethur, my lord?"

Lord Oethur! The title, which he had left behind when he had left Nornindaal last year, gave Oethur a bit of a jolt. Nornish law granted the title of 'highness' only to the king—but all the king's sons were automatically styled 'lord.' But he managed to recover with good grace.

"I am."

"Her Royal Highness Princess Rhianwyn invites your lordship to a game of cynnig."

Oethur smiled. So Rhianwyn had learned he was here.

"Will your lordship come?"

"Does she still play?"

"Quite well, my lord."

"What?"

The girl flushed. "I'm sorry, my lord. I thought you asked me a question."

"Well"—Oethur grinned as he realized he had spoken aloud—"I suppose I did. Yes, I will accept Her Highness's invitation to cynnig—and I thank you, young miss, for the warning!"

The servant hid her embarrassment by turning toward the door. "This way, my lord."

Leaving the library, she led him through a series of corridors and up a long flight of stairs. The servant was quick on her feet, and Oethur had little leisure to dawdle.

Yet as they went, he admired the interior of Dunross Castle. The palace was well decorated, to be sure: the kings of Lothair must needs live above their people to some extent. Royal rank required *some* visible degree of separation. But there was nothing in the way of ostentation about Dunross Castle. This left a tremendous impression on Oethur. It bespoke a monarch who controlled wealth, but was not himself controlled thereby. Oethur had not yet met King Heclaid, but he respected him already.

After a few minutes, the servant girl stopped before a broad set of doors. "Wait here." She disappeared through one of the doors. Less than a minute later, she returned. "Her Highness will receive you now."

The girl ushered Oethur through the doors into a sitting room, where she directed him to a chair. Princess Rhianwyn waited until the servant had joined another behind her own chair before she stood.

Oethur bowed. "Your Highness. It is good to see you."

And it was.

Oethur had known Rhianwyn a long time. She was the only child of King Heclaid, and thus Crown Princess of Lothair. He had first met her a dozen years ago, at the ceremony where she was engaged formally to his eldest brother Alfered. Over the next months, during visits in Dunross and Grindangled, when various affairs of state had called Alfered away, her entertainment had often fallen to Oethur. As the future king of both realms, Alfered had had much to learn in those days.

Then, a year later, Alfered had been murdered. His death had crushed Rhianwyn.

At the same time, Morumus's father, Raudorn, and his men had been butchered in Mathway Vale. And though it had not come to open war, the ensuing tension had frozen relations between Lothair and Nornindaal for two whole years.

"It is good to see you, too, Oethur. But please, call me Rhianwyn. We will be as good as siblings this summer."

It had taken another three years before the courtiers of both kingdoms of the North had begun the inevitable talks of a succession engagement between Rhianywn and Aeldred, the new Nornish Crown Prince.

It had taken another two years after that before the engagement had been formalized. This had been almost four years ago. A long time by most accounts, yet King Heclaid had insisted that his daughter wait to be married until her twenty-fifth birthday.

Rhianwyn had come of age at the beginning of this month.

The years have been good to her. Soft brown hair, eyes like the sky . . .

She would marry Oethur's brother this year, at midsummer.

"As you wish, sister."

"Shall we sit?"

They did, and Rhianwyn sent one of her ladies to fetch the cynnig board.

"It has been a long time since you wrote, Oethur." There was just a hint of reproach in the princess's voice.

Shortly after Alfered's death, Rhianwyn and Oethur had maintained a regular correspondence. The princess loved his eldest brother as much as Oethur had, and they had found solace in pouring out their grief to one another. The communication had continued until Oethur had left Nornindaal for Caeldora last year.

"I have been overseas."

"Tucked away in a monastery, I know. Do they not have paper and ink in Lorudin?"

Oethur flinched at the mention of Lorudin as though it were a present reality.

But she couldn't know . . .

Rhianywn might not have known about Lorudin, but she saw his expression. "Oethur, what is it? Have I given offense, brother?"

"You have not."

The conversation paused as the servant returned, and they set up the cynnig board.

"Then why do you look so grim?"

He looked down at the board. "It's nothing. Why don't you take the first move?"

Rhianwyn slid a pawn forward two spaces—with a bit more than the necessary force. "You're lying. Are you aware that it's a crime in Lothair to lie to the king or his heir?"

Oethur looked up. Rhianwyn's beautiful, sky-blue eyes bored into him.

"It is not a happy tale, sister."

"Have either of us ever known one? Please, tell me."

As the game unfolded over the next half hour, Oethur relayed the account of what had happened in Caeldora and how it had ended with the sacking of Lorudin Abbey. Rhianwyn was a strong woman, but by the time he finished she was in tears.

"Your brother's murderers . . . are these red monks?"

"Yes. The Mordruui and the Order of the Saving Blood are the same."

"And now they rule the Church in Mersex?"

Oethur nodded.

"And this all came to a head . . . when?"

"Four weeks before the Midwinter Feast."

Rhianwyn's tone was urgent. "You must warn your brother as soon as possible. He could be in danger, if he's not already been . . ."

Oethur sat up straight. "What?"

"I'm sure it's only a coincidence."

"What's only a coincidence?"

"I have not received any letter from Aeldred these past two months."

"Is that unusual?"

"He has never been as avid a correspondent as some." She smiled, a trace of tension in her features. "But we have corresponded at least monthly from our engagement up until now. But perhaps it is not related, Oethur. After all, your father *has* been very ill."

Oethur's heart skipped a beat. "What?"

"You don't know?" She shook her head. "No, but of course you wouldn't. You've only just arrived."

"Know what, Rhianwyn? What's wrong with my father?"

The princess put down the piece she had been about to play. "Your father took suddenly ill this past autumn. Nobody is sure what's wrong, but he has been abed for months."

"But my father is no older than your own." Oethur was stunned. "He was well when I left."

Rhianwyn put her hand upon his arm. "Oh Oethur, will we ever know a happy tale between us?"

Oethur looked away. He would not have his doubts read by those piercing eyes.

9

Urien ran as though pursued by ghouls.

The rain tore across the open turf of Urras in long, drenching sheets. She disregarded it. The only thing that mattered now was getting away from the old chapel.

For the next several minutes, Urien's experience took on a surreal quality. She knew that she was running—running very hard, in fact. She knew, too, that she was screaming. Yet as she went, her awareness of both receded—almost as though she were a passenger in her own body. A single thought dominated what portion of her consciousness remained connected:

I must get away from them . . .

It wasn't just the body in the chapel from which she had to escape. There were also those in her nightmare.

All the victims whose blood still lies buried in the Well of Souls in Caeldora.

Despite the roar of the rain, Urien was sure she could still hear their wailing voices. And she was more than a little afraid that if she looked back, she might see them pursuing her. She dared not even look too closely to the left or to the right, lest she see them rising out of the ground.

I must reach the monastery. That is the only safe place.

Urien ran as though pursued by ghouls—which, in a way, she was.

The doors of the monastery swung inward before Urien's extended arms, then crashed into the walls behind them with a boom that resounded through the entrance hall.

Urien barreled through them, bowling over a monk who had the misfortune to be standing too close. His backward tumbling form registered but the barest note in her mind as she stood there in the open doors, heaving for air, soaking wet, and screaming in between her sobs.

But at least I'm safe. Safe at last.

The monk recovered his feet and was now standing close. "Urien! Urien, what is wrong?"

The living human voice brought her back to herself.

"Landu." For once, Urien was not unhappy to see him.

For his own part, concern etched Landu's dark features. "Urien, what is it?"

But though she was returned to earth, Urien found she had little control of her faculties. Something was wrong with her eyes, and she was shivering uncontrollably. Her teeth chattered as she spoke.

"Abbot Nerias . . . get . . . abbot."

"Urien, you must sit down." Landu's tone would brook no dissent, and she did not offer any. Taking her arm, he led her to a chair.

"You are in shock, Urien. Do not move. I will go and fetch the abbot."

A few minutes later—Urien had no notion of time passing, but some time must have passed—three figures came rushing into the entrance hall. She saw them as dim outlines.

Landu reached her first.

"Here, let me cover you with this." He wrapped her in a thick, dry blanket.

Abbess Nahenna was close behind him. "Here, dear, you must drink something warm."

Urien felt a mug press against her lips and tasted hot cider.

Her vision was going in and out, but she recognized Abbot Nerias's voice.

"Urien, what is wrong? Has something happened?"

Urien made an effort to collect herself, but she was numb all over. "The ruins of the old monastery . . ."

"What about them?"

"The old chapel . . . still has a roof."

"Yes, Urien. What of it?"

"Body . . ."

"*What?*"

With the last of her strength, Urien forced herself to form a complete sentence. "There . . . there is a body . . . dead."

The last thing Urien heard before she collapsed were gasps.

Urien drifted in and out of consciousness, with no sense of the passage of time. Her robe was dry. Several thick blankets swaddled her. Opening her eyes—but only halfway, because of the brightness—she found herself tucked into a high-backed double bench next to a fire. Somewhere close by, she heard voices speaking in low tones.

"Is she all right, Nahenna?"

"Yes, I've gotten her into dry clothes and fresh blankets. She just needs to rest."

"Good."

There was a pause, then:

"What is wrong, Nerias? I've never seen you so grave."

"The body . . . it was a man. But not just any man, Nahenna. He's the missing Lothairin soldier."

"What? Are you sure?"

"Yes. Besides the tunic, I recognized the face as belonging to one of those who arrived with Haedorn."

"But I thought the man who tried to kill Oethur jumped from the cliffs."

"He did."

"So . . . what happened? He somehow survived and then later died in the chapel?"

"If only."

"I don't understand."

"This man never jumped from a cliff, Nahenna. The body of the soldier was bound . . ."

"Tied up?"

"Yes. He couldn't have been our assassin."

"But all the other soldiers were accounted for that night."

"I know."

"But that means"—here there was a gasp—"one of our own?"

"Exactly. But that's not the worst."

"There's more?"

"Yes. Besides his soldiers—who were all accounted for— the only people who left with Haedorn were Morumus and Oethur. Do you realize what that means, Nahenna?"

Another long, dreadful pause.

"The culprit is still among us."

Four days passed.

Urien was sitting in Abbess Nahenna's chamber. Her voice was steady again, and her vision had returned, but there were dark lines under her eyes.

"You look tired, dear."

"I haven't been sleeping well."

"It has been a hard week. Have you slept at all?"

"Not since that first night. And even that . . ."

Abbess Nahenna nodded. Her eyes, which of late had twinkled but little of their characteristic joy, glistened with compassion. "We've all had a horrible shock, Urien. You more than anybody. It may take some time."

"But that's just it, Abbess. It's getting worse—for everybody."

News of the murdered soldier and what it meant had put the entire Urras community on edge. Nobody would venture anywhere alone. The sense of fellowship had vanished from mealtimes, and the worship services were strained and tortuous. How could it be otherwise, when a community based on mutual trust *knew* that one of their members was a murderer?

"I know."

"What will happen to us?"

"Either the guilty party will come forward, or he will be found." The abbess paused, clearly relunctant to admit another possibility. "Or he will not."

"And what will happen if he is *not* found?"

"Our community will disband."

Despite the strain, the monastery had managed to hold together thus far. But it was a tenuous thing. Cracks were beginning to appear. Tempers were short, and tongues were quicker. If things had degenerated this far in but four days, how much longer before they fell apart entirely?

"Oh, Abbess . . ."

A hint of a smile touched the older woman's cheek. "It is touching to see your concern, Urien. I wonder, dear, that you have come to possess such a common feeling for us—without also having come to embrace our common faith."

Urien looked down. "I want to believe, Abbess."

"You do?"

"I do. It's just . . . for years I was convinced that the Old Faith—the *Dark* Faith—was true. I don't believe that anymore, but I've had to face the fact that for years I was convinced of a lie." Tears welled in her eyes. "For years I *served* a lie, Abbess—and you cannot imagine the horrible things I've done."

"Aesus's death will pay for them all, my dear."

"I know what your book says. I've read it for myself. I want to believe it."

"Then why do you not?"

"Because I don't know *how* to know if it's all true. I *want* it to be true. But for years I wanted the Dark Faith to be true, too—and it's not. What I want makes nothing true. So what does? How can I *know* that your Aesusian faith is true? Does my question make any sense?"

"I think so. You realize that you don't possess the authority to establish truth."

"Yes, exactly."

"And so you are looking for One who does."

"*Is* there such a person?"

"Only God himself, my dear."

Urien frowned. "You mean the God of Holy Writ?"

"Of course. And there, my dear, is your answer."

"I don't understand."

"Holy Writ is God's own Word. He breathed it out himself. The authority to believe it comes from itself."

"I still don't see."

"It is God the Spirit who speaks in Holy Writ, Urien. It is God's voice that you hear every single time you read or hear Holy Writ. If you are honest with yourself, you know this is true."

"How can you be so sure?"

"Because God made us, and in making us he made us able to recognize his voice—whether in the dim whisper of conscience or the clear words of Holy Writ. His law is written on our hearts and revealed in his Word. We may suppress the former and deny the latter, but we cannot eradicate or silence either. This is what makes all people guilty before God. We see his signature not just in the fabric of creation, but upon the very fibers of our being. All of us know that God is there, and all of us know that he is speaking. Faith is born when we stop denying this truth and entrust ourselves to it."

"I'm still not sure . . ."

"There is nothing more to it, Urien. But you *are* very tired."

"Yes."

"Get some rest, dear. We'll talk more another day."

"But that's just it. I cannot sleep. Every time I close my eyes, I see the vict—" Urien's heart skipped a beat. She had been about to say *victims!* "I have horrible nightmares."

"No wonder, considering what has happened. But you may be making it worse. Are you still working on that awful book, the Bone Codex?"

"I'll be finished with the translation in a few days."

Nahenna pursed her lips. "I know how important this work is, Urien, but why don't you give it a rest—just for this afternoon? It may help with the nightmares, and if you don't get some sleep soon you won't be able to translate anything."

Urien nodded. "Yes, Abbess."

Landu was waiting for her when she came out.

"Hello, Landu. Thank you for coming back."

"Did you have a good visit?"

"Yes, but I am very tired. Will you walk me to the dormitory?"

"Certainly."

Since the day she had knocked him over, Urien had come to a reassessment of Landu. She possessed no romantic feeling for him—that had *not* changed. Yet he had shown genuine compassion on the day she had found the body. By comparison, she found her former treatment of him quite lacking. Now, with a murderer on the loose in the monastery, she was more than willing to accept his frequent offers of an escort.

"I am glad you had a pleasant time with the abbess, Urien. I wish things were as pleasant among the rest of the brethren."

"I know. Things are bad."

"Worse than you know."

Landu stopped, looking before and behind them. The two of them stood alone in the central corridor between Saint Calum's Hall and the sisters' dormitory wing. When he turned to Urien, there was a troubled cast to his countenance. "There are whispers, Urien."

"Whispers? What are you talking about?"

"I overheard a few monks talking. They didn't see me."

"It's an unseemly thing to go skulking about."

"I know, I know, but listen. If a few are saying it aloud, then more than a few are whispering it in corners."

"Whispering *what*? Would you just come out and say it?"

"It's a bit . . . awkward to say."

"I've seen more than you would believe, Landu. I'm not a little girl."

"You're not an Aesusian either," he said quietly.

"What?"

"People are looking for somebody to blame. Of all the people on Urras, you are the only non-Aesusian—and you've not been here that long."

A chill crawled up Urien's spine as she realized what Landu was saying.

"They think . . . *I* am the killer?"

"They're scared, Urien. It is only natural. You mustn't blame them for it."

"But it's nonsense . . ."

"I know."

"I was the one who found the body! Do they know what that was like?" Rage boiled until Urien trembled. "Do they know that I fell face down in his blood? *Do* they, Landu?"

"I believe you, Urien."

Her anger subsided. "Thank you."

The monk touched her arm. "I will protect you."

"That's very kind of you, Landu." Urien offered a faint smile as she pulled away. "But I am not afraid of whispers." She turned in the direction of the dormitory. "I think I can make it the rest of the way on my own. Thank you for walking with me."

"And the killer?"

"What of him?"

"Are you not afraid?"

Urien shook her head. "As I told you, Landu, I've seen more than you'd believe."

"I will always believe you, Urien, but I urge you to believe me when I say that it is different here. On a small island, whispers can be more dangerous than you imagine."

t its zenith, the shadow of the Vilguran Imperium had stretched far across the western world. Its civilizing and efficient—not to say *ruthless*—hand had extended even across the breadth and height of Mersex. Yet for all their legendary might, the imperial legions had never established a foothold beyond the Deasmor. Consequently, the road from Dunross to Grindangled was not a straight highway, but rather a Northman's winding track.

Morumus and Oethur had traveled this road for three days. From Dunross they had followed it south along the banks of the Mathway, then east along the lower skirt of the Deasmor. Today they had reached the upper course of the River Fersk. In another day, following the road northeast along the river, they would reach Grindangled.

What will we find?

Morumus's thoughts ran back to Dunross, to the dinner he and Oethur had shared with King Heclaid before leaving:

"The murder of Donnach mac Toercanth is a disaster," the king had said, "and I will soon require your aid, Morumus, in explaining it to the Grendannathi. But the disappearance of Bishop Ciolbail and the machinations of the Mordruui are even more pressing." Here he had turned to Oethur. "I cannot command you, Lord Oethur, yet I strongly urge you to carry warning to your father."

"I concur, Your Majesty. I sent my father a letter from Urras, but I have since learned that he is taken very ill and that my brother is quite taken up. Between Father's care and the cares of Father's kingdom, Aeldred—or one of his secretaries—may have assumed my letter to be mere personal correspondence and laid it aside unread."

"So you will go then?"

"I will."

"Good. Along with your warning, please convey to your brother my desire to consult on these matters."

"With pleasure, Your Majesty."

"Thank you." Here Heclaid had turned back to Morumus. "And I want you to go with Oethur, Morumus. Your task is to search for Ciolbail. Speak to Bishop Treowin, and send me whatever news he may have—along with whatever else you can learn."

"Yes, sire."

"It has been years since I came this way," said Oethur as they started their horses up a sloping rise on the river's east bank. A cold breeze gusting down out of the Deasmor, a looming presence on their right, rippled the hem of his heavy riding cloak. "Yet if I am not mistaken, there is a village on the other side of this hill."

"I hope you are right." Morumus cast a wary eye behind them at the sun, now low on the western horizon. "I think it is going to be cold tonight."

"All the more reason to be indoors. Isn't that why God made fire?"

"In part, no doubt."

The horses did not exactly hurry. It had been far too long a day for that. Yet as they ascended the hill, the beasts did seem to draw on some untapped reserves.

Do they sense that their labors are approaching an intermission?

Morumus's pondering was cut short, however, as they reached the crest of the rise and a familiar scent reached their nostrils.

Oethur looked at Morumus and smiled. "Do you smell that, brother?"

"You were right, Oethur."

Below them, about a half mile in the distance, they saw a small village. There were no lights visible in the growing twilight, yet the smell of wood smoke was unmistakable.

"You needn't sound so surprised, Morumus."

"You're right. There *is* a first time for everything."

The Norn opened his mouth to reply but came up with nothing. "Come on." He urged his mount down the grade. "The village is called Dorslaan."

But as they drew closer to the village, good humor turned to apprehension.

"Dusk is settling," observed Morumus, "and still no lights."

"And that smell of fire." Oethur wrinkled his noise. "It is too strong."

"Something is wrong here, brother."

Riding into the village, they found their fears confirmed. Most of the dozen or so homes clustered around the main green had been burned.

"Fire." Oethur gave a deep sigh. His breath turned to mist in the growing chill.

Some of the fires were worse than others. In a few places, nothing remained but a few charred wooden posts and smoldering piles of rubble. Yet even where the damage was less extensive, it was no less irreversible.

"I wonder if there are any survivors?" Morumus looked around, but his heart held little hope.

"Over there."

"Where?"

"The far side of the square—that bigger building."

Morumus peered hard. It was almost dark, and visibility was dropping. "Is that the village church?"

"Looks like it may have been. Looks, too, like somebody is standing in the door."

"Your eyes must be better than mine." Morumus could make out a vague shape, but he could not tell if it was a man.

"Hello!" Oethur waved an arm. "You there!"

No reply.

"Maybe it isn't a man?"

"I'm sure I saw somebody moving."

Oethur nudged his horse forward, and Morumus followed.

"Oh!" exclaimed the Norn when they were close enough to see. "Oh, no!"

"Not again," whispered Morumus.

Most of the village church had succumbed. The roof had vanished, and the ravaging fire had reduced the wall studs to a line of black, jagged, and uneven teeth protruding at various intervals from the stone foundation. Smoking logs of charcoal lay resting on the earthen floor, marking the ordered layout of the lost pews. Of all the small chapel, the only portion that remained intact was its stout doorframe. Even here, however, the door itself was missing. Yet the doorway was not empty . . .

A man's body sat slumped against the side of the frame. The skin of his face was blackened and blistered, and his eye sockets were empty holes. Worse still, there was a telltale gaping wound in his middle.

"Disemboweled," growled Oethur.

"*Dree.*" Morumus's tone was quiet fury.

Before either man could say more, however, a voice spoke behind them.

"Turn around slowly, if you want to live."

Startled, Morumus nearly fell out of his saddle. Yet recovering himself, he obeyed the order. Beside him, Oethur did the same.

There, standing before them in the growing dark, was a lad at least ten years their junior. He was on foot—but he held a crofter's pitchfork in front of him and wore a serious expression.

"Who are you, youngster?" asked Oethur.

"My name is Colba," replied the lad.

"Do you intend to kill us, Colba?"

The lad's grip tightened on his weapon. "I don't know if I can, sir. But if you are enemies, I am bound to try."

"We are not your enemies, son." Oethur dismounted, motioning for Morumus to do the same. He pushed back the hood of his cloak and stepped toward Colba, holding both hands empty before him. "My name is Oethur son of Ulfered, and this is Morumus son of Raudorn."

"Son of *King* Ulfered?"

"The same."

Colba's eyes widened—white saucers in the near dark—and he dropped the pitchfork almost as fast as he dropped to one knee.

"My lord, please forgive me! I had no idea—"

"Be calm, son. Your ignorance is pardoned, even as your foolish courage is commended. Please rise."

Colba struggled to comply, and Morumus saw that he had a club foot.

"Here, let me help you." He helped the young man to his feet, then retrieved the pitchfork and handed it to him. "Tell us, Colba. Do you have shelter, somewhere under a roof? It's going to get cold tonight."

Colba led them away from the chapel and the green to a tiny cottage on the very outskirts of the settlement. Compared to the rest of the village, it was unscathed—only a bit of burnt thatch at one end of the roof. He knocked on the door, then pushed it open.

"It's all right, Mother. They aren't enemies."

A few minutes later, Morumus and Oethur were sitting in front of a meager fire with Colba and his mother—an older woman named Wyris. The two monks provided food from their travel stores, and the four of them now shared a humble meal over a horrid tale.

"It all started a fortnight ago, my lord," Wyris addressed herself to Oethur, "when a monk dressed all in red descended out of the hills."

"Out of the Deasmor?"

Wyris glanced at Morumus. "What other hills are there, sir?" She paused before continuing. "Anyway, he was a strange monk. Never lowered his hood, and spoke with a strange accent."

"What language did he speak?"

Wyris gave Morumus a patient look. "Not ours. The only one who could understand him was Friar."

Oethur addressed Morumus in Vilguran. "Let her finish her tale, brother. These village matrons do not like to be interrupted in their yarns. We can ask questions when she's done."

"That's it," Colba piped up. "That's just how the red monk talked!"

"*Anyway.*" Wyris laid great emphasis upon the word, and her son wilted under her gaze. "Anyway, the monk demanded to preach to the village. He claimed to bring glad tidings of . . . what was it your father said, Colba?"

"Saving blood."

"That's it. He claimed to bring glad tidings of 'the saving blood.' But our friar and the village elders, my husband among them, refused him. For one thing, he was unknown to us. We'd never even met this man before, and he thought we should let him preach? For another thing, my husband said that what this man seemed to mean by 'saving blood' sounded like something else besides the blood of Aesus. But besides all this, the man lacked any credentials from Bishop Treowin of Grindangled. I trust you know our bishop, my lord?"

"I do." Oethur nodded.

"Well, this monk had nothing to show he met our bishop's approval. So our men refused him." Wyris leaned back and looked into the fire. "And despite all this coming upon us, I still believe it was the right decision."

"What happened then?"

Wyris started to resume, but tears welled in her eyes and she could not continue. She motioned to her son.

"The monk got very angry. He told our friar—who told my father and the other elders—that our village would be cursed for refusing this 'saving blood.' Then he left. This was over a week ago. Then, last night . . ." Colba's face took on a haunted expression.

"Go on, son."

"Last night, the whole village awoke to the sound of scream-ing. The chapel was on fire, and the body of our friar hung in the doorway. Every man in the village tried to put out the fire, but while they strove the chapel exploded!"

"Exploded?"

"Yes, my lord. I cannot explain it, but I saw it with my own eyes. The chapel exploded. The explosion itself sent burn-ing fragments raining down upon our village, and there was a great cloud of glowing smoke. The fragments set most of our homes ablaze, and the smoke engulfed our men, nearly choking them." His voice dropped to a whisper. "Then the Shadows came."

A knowing chill stood Morumus's hackles on end. "The Shadows?"

"Yes, sir. People from other villages in these parts have seen them moving these past few years. Black, hooded creatures the size of men. They move like wraiths, murder like wolves, and sing like serpents."

Oethur interjected. "People have been seeing them *for sev-eral years?*"

"Yes, my lord."

The Norn sounded astonished. "Why has this never been reported to the king?"

"Reports were sent, my lord." Wyris's voice remained respectful, but she looked away as she spoke. "Nobody ever came."

Oethur's voice shook with regal authority. "On my honor as the king's son, this is the first I have ever heard of it. When I leave here, I shall carry the word personally to my brother and father at Grindangled."

Morumus looked at Colba. "What happened next?" He asked more to change the subject than to obtain information. He *knew* what happened when the Dree appeared. He knew all too well.

"It was awful, sir. Some of our men grabbed staves and weapons, but the Shadows paralyzed most with their dark song. There was a battle. We wounded one of theirs, but they killed a half-dozen of ours and carried away three of our youth—two girls and a boy. This morning, one of the elders led the remaining women and children to a neighboring village. My father led the rest of our men in pursuit of the Shadows. But because my mother would not leave—and because of my foot—my father left me to care for her and to bury the dead."

Though Colba spoke with a quiet, measured gravity, his mother did not.

She broke down and wailed through her sobs, "My little girl was among those taken!"

Two hours later, Morumus and Oethur kept watch as the exhausted Colba and Wyris slept. The two friends were arguing in hushed tones.

"We will go *together*, brother."

"No, Oethur. You must go on to Grindangled. Deliver the warning and King Heclaid's request to your father. Send soldiers to help us and speak to Bishop Treowin. Send word to Dunross if you learn anything of Ciolbail."

Oethur stiffened. "*You* do not give the orders in my country, Morumus."

"I know, brother." Morumus spoke in a deferential tone, remembering his friend's royal lineage as well as the proverb about a soft answer. "But did you not give your word to these people that you would personally carry their warning?"

Oethur's face darkened, and for a moment he made no reply. "There is that, I suppose. But I still think splitting up is a bad idea."

"I don't like it much either, Oethur. But if the Dree have another Muthadannach in the Deasmor, we need to find it. If we don't, those children are dead—along with who knows how many others. Both the Dree and their pursuers are on foot. I will be on horse. With Colba to guide me, we can catch up to his father and his men within a day."

Oethur's eyes were granite. "There are dark places in the Deasmor, brother. You might be walking into a trap."

"Maybe. But I would rather walk into Shadow than permit the Shadows to walk free."

he next day, Oethur rode alone across the first bridge of Grindangled Castle. The stronghold of the Nornish kings was quite unlike that of their Lothairin brothers to the west. Whereas King Heclaid's castle in Dunross overlooked the sea from atop a great mound of rock, Grindangled Castle squatted upon a long island near the mouth of the Fersk estuary. The first bridge that Oethur crossed, then, was the long bridge from the mainland to the castle gate.

There had been no little surprise among the men of the watch at his appearance. So far as any of them knew, King Ulfered's second son had gone to Caeldora over a year prior. Oethur's arrival now without warning—and the fact that he wore the garb of a monk—made many men-at-arms uneasy. A messenger was sent running to the keep as the great gates swung open to admit him.

Oethur smiled as he passed beneath the gatehouse into the great bailey. The sprawling courtyard was filled with bustling life. The squeaking trundle of cart wheels as they passed, the barking orders of sergeants to men-at-arms, and the echoing clang of the hammers in the distant forge: all these were familiar sounds to him. He rode through it all overcome with a comfortable sense of *home*.

Despite the darkness of these days, it is good to be back.

Ahead of him, Malduorn's Keep rose upon its high mound, surrounded by a moat that connected to the outer sea by an artificial channel. The large structure was named for the king who had built it. Grandson of Nuorn the Valiant, it was Malduorn who had led the Nornish people across the sea to Aeld Gowan. During the long years of his reign, the Keep *was* the castle. The great bailey, with its sheer walls that surrounded the entire island, had not been added until the reigns of his successors.

Oethur was about to take his horse across the moat bridge when he saw a rider crossing toward him. Recognizing the man, he drew up, dismounted, and waited. The rider waited until he was within a dozen paces to do the same, then ran to embrace Oethur.

"My brother!"

Though three years his elder, Aeldred stood no taller than Oethur. Indeed, the two men looked almost identical. Both were tall and thick-chested. Both had the same grey eyes—eyes they had inherited from their mother. The only difference between them was the color of their hair. Whereas Oethur's was yellow, like that of his father and late eldest brother, Aeldred had his mother's dark brown hair.

"Aeldred," said Oethur as they parted. "It is good to see you, my lord."

"And you, brother. And you can stuff all this 'my lord' nonsense right now."

Oethur smiled. "But you *are* my lord, you know." He adopted a formal, paternal tone. "You are going to be *king* someday, Aeldred. Then you will be 'Your Majesty.' You must learn to act the part!"

This had been a long-standing jest, but for once Aeldred did not smile. "I'm afraid that day is coming sooner than either of us expected, brother. Father—"

"—is not well, I know. Rhianwyn told me."

Aeldred frowned. "You saw Rhianwyn?"

"Yes, in Dunross."

"How came you—" He shook his head. "But we'll get to all that in due course, I'm sure."

"How is Father, Aeldred?"

"Rhianwyn's information is old. He was 'not well' when I last wrote her. Today he is . . . near death, Oethur. The physicians do not expect him to last much longer."

Oethur felt as though a forge hammer had struck him in the middle. "What? But this can't be right. When I left for Caeldora last summer, he was not even sick!"

"I know, Oethur, and I'm sorry. I wish I had an explanation."

"What is wrong with him?'"

"Nobody knows. A high fever of some sort. It struck him suddenly last fall, and he has been abed ever since."

"But surely, Aeldred . . . surely *something* can be done?"

"Everything has been tried, brother. Nothing works." Aeldred gave a heavy sigh. "The fever is incurable."

"How much longer?"

"He stopped eating almost a week ago."

Oethur could not believe his ears. *This cannot be happening!*

"It could be another day or two, or it could be less."

"Can you take me to him?"

Aeldred nodded. "That is why I came to meet you."

"Wait . . ." In midst of his shock, Oethur remembered the village. "Before we go to Father, we must dispatch a company of men to Dorslaan."

"Dorslaan? The little hamlet in the hills?"

"The same."

"Why—?" But again Aeldred stopped himself. "No, we don't have the time. I will send the company as soon as we get back to the Keep. What is your order for them?"

"Thank you, brother. I'll explain the whole thing to you soon. For now, just tell the captain to take his men to Dorslaan and follow the instructions of a monk named Morumus."

The two princes had just dismounted in front of the Keep when the grey-faced chamberlain met them at a run.

"My lords, you must come quickly. Your father is dying—now!"

Forgetting all else, Aeldred and Oethur sprinted into the Keep. Neither needed to be led to their father's chambers. Both had grown up in this hold, and both were well practiced in racing one another down its halls and up its stairs. Yet on this day, both ran faster than they had ever run as youths.

They crashed through the door of their father's chamber in time to see a physician turn from the bedside.

"Is he—?"

"Not yet, my lords." The physician's eyes were red-rimmed. He had served the royal household since Ulfered's childhood. "But he has fallen asleep, and he will not wake again. I am sorry."

"You have served him well, Lildas," said Aeldred. "Go and rest. Oethur and I will stay with Father until the end."

As the door shut behind Lildas, Aeldred and Oethur took up positions on either side of their father's bed. Between them, the king lay half-buried amidst a raft of pillows and a mound of blankets. His face looked skeletal, and his skin stretched thin over it, yet the expression of his visage remained untroubled.

Despite his manful years, Oethur felt little more than a boy as he watched his father's breathing grow shallower and slower. He and Aeldred wept, and they each cried out to their father in turn—begging him to open his eyes, pleading that they might say good-bye in person.

But their father didn't wake. And after about a half hour, they could no longer hear any breath pass his lips.

"To stand at the final cusp without fear, to take the eternal step without terror," Oethur whispered. "It is a gift given to few."

He looked at Aeldred through tear-fogged eyes. Aeldred looked back at him, silent, his face mottled, red.

"You must go now," Oethur said in a low voice.

"But . . . I cannot leave him alone."

"He is no longer here, brother. But I will wait with the body."

"Are you certain?" Aeldred sounded anything but.

"The household must be informed. Arrangements must be made. It is your duty now . . . *sire*."

Aeldred looked pale as he got to his feet. But after only a moment's further hesitation, he went out.

For another minute, Oethur remained motionless. Though the door had shut behind his brother, he imagined that he could see through it.

How must it feel for you, brother, as the weight of a kingdom settles on your shoulders?

Oethur turned back to look at his father . . .

. . . and found his father looking at him!

"Father!"

"Oethur, my son." Ulfered's breath was still faint, but there was a wide smile on his thin face. "Can you hear them, Oethur?"

"Hear them, Father?" Oethur's heart thumped in his chest. "Hear who?"

"The voices." The king's eyes, though half-glazed, were bright. "I hear voices singing, Oethur. A vast, ancient chorus. So many languages, yet I can understand them all. They are singing praise to God. Do you hear them, Oethur?"

Oethur strained his ears but heard nothing. "Tell me, Father," he said through a heavy knot in his throat, "tell me what they are saying."

"Ah, Oethur." Ulfered's voice grew warm, even as it faded. "You ever were the jester. If you cannot hear them for yourself, then I cannot tell you what they are saying. Not yet. Someday we will sing the words together. But for now, take my hand, son." With surprising strength, the king drew his arm from beneath the covers.

Oethur took his father's hand. "I love you, Father."

"I love you too, son." Ulfered drew a final, rasping breath. "I think I can hear your mother. Yes, it is her—she is singing among the chorus. I am going to join her."

With these words, Ulfered exhaled and shut his eyes.

He was gone.

A final tear rolled down his lifeless cheek, but Oethur knew it was a tear of joy.

12

Urien replaced her pen and stood up.

On the table below lay two books separated by an oil lamp. Both books lay open to their ends. The lines of text in the first were aged and faded. The lines in the second were fresh, and the last of these dried on the page as the pen that had inked them stood quivering in its pot.

The translation of the Bone Codex was complete.

But Urien took no joy in the accomplishment. She had finished the translation, to be sure. Yet in so doing, the translation had finished something in her, too.

Urien sighed.

Her time on Urras had begun with such pleasure. Now, just over two months later, pain defined her experience.

In the past week, Urras Monastery had gone from uncomfortable to intolerable. Landu's warning had proved prophetic, and over the last several days Urien's alienation from the brothers and sisters—always felt because of her creed, but once minimal because of their grace—had grown chill and palpable. Nobody had made a direct accusation, but two days prior she had heard two of them whispering around a corner:

"Who else could it be, but her?"

"But the abbot and abbess . . ."

"I know, I know. . . . She must have bewitched them."

"Bewitched? Do you really think so?"

"She is Dyfanni. . . . Who knows the sort of sorcery of which she might be capable?"

Urien had not remained for the speculations almost certain to ensue. Nor had she rounded the corner to identify and confront her accusers. What good would it have done? She knew they were not the only ones.

The overheard conversation had settled the matter for Urien: she must leave Urras. And she must do so soon. The whispers had already grown dangerous. She must not wait for them to draw swords. She did not want to be the cause of any additional bloodshed—least of all her own.

"But where will you go? What will you do?"

Landu had raised both questions yesterday when she had told him of her decision.

Until today, she had not known.

But now she had finished translating the Bone Codex, and in so doing, she had identified a destination for her looming departure.

Somnadh.

The Bone Codex had destroyed everything she had thought she knew about her brother.

Forever.

She should have seen it coming long ago. Why had her father never spoken of harvesting the Mother's herb? Why had Seanguth the Eldest never spoken of a Well of Souls?

Because they didn't know of either!

Today, Urien had finished translating the final section of the Bone Codex. And in so doing, she had learned the last of its secrets. It was a horrible revelation.

The Mordruui were a sect—a secret circle within the Circle of the Holy Groves.

This did not make the Old Faith any less a Dark Faith. Every Dyfanni who bowed to the Mother still worshiped an idol. Whatever their sincerity, all the faithful of the Dark Faith gave praise to a fiendish tree that fed on human blood. Ignorance was no excuse.

But it did make the Mordruui much worse. *They* were not deceived.

Somnadh had not received the custom of exsanguination from their father Comnadh. He had not merely participated in an ancestral evil. He had not simply perpetuated an ancient wickedness. Complicity was not his crime . . .

No.

Complicity was *Urien's* sin. And it was bad enough . . .

But not for Somnadh.

Her brother had not been deceived, as she had. He had embraced the darkness with open eyes. Somnadh hadn't fallen into the Well of Souls, as Urien once had.

He had jumped.

Her brother—her whole world for so many years—was a monster. The realization shattered whatever pleasant picture of him Urien had tried to hold in her mind since leaving Caeldora. It cast a more sinister shadow upon everything . . .

Upon him.

And yet, though she hated all that he had done, Urien still loved *him*.

Which was why she must confront him. It was *because* she loved Somnadh that Urien so *hated* what he had become and what he had done. Her hatred for his conduct flowed out of her love for his person.

But was there any hope? Was Somnadh beyond redemption?

Something that Abbess Nahenna had said the other day came back to her now:

"God made us, and in making us he made us able to recognize his voice—whether in the dim whisper of conscience or the clear words

of Holy Writ. His law is written on our hearts and revealed in his Word. We may suppress the former and deny the latter, but we cannot eradicate or silence either. This is what makes all people guilty before God. We see his signature not just in the fabric of creation, but upon the very fibers of our being. All of us know that God is there, and all of us know that he is speaking. Faith is born when we stop denying this truth and entrust ourselves to it."

Urien was still not sure that she believed all this, but if just part of it was true, then even Somnadh might still possess a conscience. And if so, he was not beyond hope.

Nor am I.

It was a comforting thought. A faint glimmer, to be sure, but it was the only light Urien now possessed. Her last candle against the darkness.

Would it last?

Today she would begin the journey to find out.

Yesterday morning, the first trading ship had arrived. It was quite unlike the Lothairin longship that had carried Morumus and Oethur to Dunross more than a week past. For one thing, it was sailed by Trathari. This meant that it not only stopped at Urras, but would also call at Mersian ports. For another, it was a larger merchant vessel. This meant it had plenty of space for goods—and, for a fare, the odd passenger. The Trathari had finished their business with the monks and intended to cast off from Urras this afternoon.

Urien intended to go with them.

She had carried few coins and no possessions with her from Caeldora. There was no baggage over which to fuss. The only things she had to carry with her were a few dry biscuits, a small purse of money, and a spare grey robe. The former two she wrapped in the latter—withholding from the purse only those coins necessary to pay for her passage—to create a tight roll that she bound with twine. It was a very modest kit.

There was but one decision that remained to be made: *Do I take the Bone Codex with me?*

The translation would stay, of course, for she intended it for the abbot and Morumus. But what of the original? Should she carry it with her for her confrontation with Somnadh?

She was still standing beside her table, looking down at the two volumes, when a distant bell tolled. The bell signaled the end of the midday convocation and the beginning of Afternoon Solitude. It was just the signal for which she had waited.

Because of the mounting tension with the others, Urien had not attended the common meals or convocations for the last three days. In place of the former, she had resorted to sneaking down to the refectory at odd times and asking for leftovers from a gentle old sister who was too aged to hear or heed the rumors about Urien. With respect to the latter—the various devotional services—she doubted any grieved her absence.

Now that the bell had tolled, it would not be long before she could abscond to the ship. Within minutes, the corridor would fill as the sisters returned to their chambers. Then, like a wave receding into the depths, all would fall silent. It would be much the same in the men's dormitory, for Afternoon Solitude was a ubiquitous practice on Urras. Soon every monk and monkess—including the abbot and abbess—would be reposing in his or her chamber for a few hours' private meditation.

There would not be a better time for her to slip away unnoticed.

As expected, Urien began to hear the sound of shuffling feet beyond her door. Along with the movement were the murmurs of muffled conversation. There was always a burst of chatter before Afternoon Solitude—a couple minutes' binge before the few hours' fast. Yet today the voices sounded particularly excited and seemed to take longer to dissipate.

Silence had just fallen without when there was a sharp knock at her door.

Urien jumped—but she did not open the door.

The knock came again, its rap insistent.

"Please come back after Solitude, sister!" Urien had little interest in abbey gossip, and even less in being chided for absenting herself from convocation.

"Urien, open the door. It's me, Landu."

"Landu?" She opened the door a crack, peering out. "What are you doing here?"

"Please, Urien, may I come in?"

"Landu, this is the *women's* dormitory. You are not even allowed in our corridor unescorted, let alone in my chamber!"

"I know, Urien. But this is urgent."

Poking her head out, Urien scanned the corridor in either direction. Nobody. "It better be."

Securing the door behind her, Urien turned to find Landu peering down at the books on her table.

"What are these?" He reached as though to turn the pages in one.

"Leave those be." Urien's tone was sharper than she had intended, yet Landu's arrival was not only irregular, it was an interruption. Afternoon Solitude was begun, and she was keen to execute her escape. "Tell me what was so urgent that it could not wait."

For a brief moment Landu gave her a bruised look. But this vanished almost as soon as it had appeared, replaced by a broad, beaming smile. "You don't know, do you?"

"Know what?"

"They've caught the assassin, Urien!"

"What!"

"It's true! The man who murdered the Lothairin soldier and who tried to murder Morumus and Oethur—they've caught him!"

138

Dumbfounded, it took Urien a moment to recover herself. "Who, Landu?"

"A Lothairin monk. Abbot Nerias announced it during the midday meal. His name was Feindir—"

Urien gasped. "The silent monk? The one without a tongue?"

"The same."

"But if he can't speak, how do they know that it was he?"

Landu's dark eyebrows arched. "Are you sure you want to know?"

"Yes."

"He wrote a confession, before . . ." Landu made a small gesture as though the rest were plain.

"Before what?"

"Before he took his own life."

Urien made a sound somewhere between a groan and a sigh. "That's horrible."

"I know."

"Why would Feindir have wanted to kill Morumus and Oethur?"

"It wasn't Morumus he was after. Just Oethur."

"How do you know?"

"His confession . . . Abbot Nerias read part of it at the midday convocation."

"But why?"

"Revenge."

"Revenge for what?"

"Apparently the men who cut out his tongue when he was a boy—and killed his family, as he revealed for the first time in his confession—were Norns."

Urien struggled to believe what she was hearing. Feindir had always seemed so sweet and kind. "But why now? Oethur came to Urras months ago—he and Morumus and I came by the same ship. If revenge was in Feindir's heart, why did he wait so long?"

"He didn't say."

"And why wait until a shipful of Lothairins arrived? If this was just a private vendetta, why try to frame somebody else? Why try to start a war?"

"You're asking the wrong person, Urien." Landu spread his hands against the volley of her questions. "Brother Feindir had many years to nurture his grudge. Perhaps during those years his hatred for a few grew to encompass all Norns."

"It just doesn't make sense."

"Does sin ever?"

"No." Urien shook her head, and a few tears came loose. "No, I suppose not. But it is sad, Landu. I'll be glad to leave it all behind."

"It is sad—wait, you still intend to leave?"

"Yes."

"But—" Landu stammered. "But—you cannot leave now! You must not even consider it, Urien!"

"I have considered it already, Landu. And I must leave."

"I don't understand. You've been vindicated."

"That's not why."

"Then what is?"

Urien stole a glance at the Bone Codex. "It's complicated."

Landu's tone soured. "You mean you won't tell me."

Urien sighed with a mix of frustration and sympathy. She was losing time. "There are things about me you don't know, Landu—things in my past you could not possibly imagine. I must leave here to deal with them."

"I will come with you."

"No. You don't even know where I'm going."

"It doesn't matter!" Landu's tone brightened, and his eyes lit up as though already glimpsing unseen vistas. "Whatever these things may be that haunt you, or wherever they may lurk, I will accompany you."

"No."

"But how else can I protect you, Urien?"

"I never asked for your protection, Landu."

"But I am in love with you."

Taken aback by the abruptness of his words, Urien stared at him. "What?" she managed after a long pause.

Landu's face reddened. "Must I say it again?"

"No. Please don't." Urien felt her own face flush. "You have been a faithful friend, Landu, but—"

"But I would be more than friend, Urien."

"But I do not *wish* for more than a friend. What I must do I must do alone."

"But Urien, I—"

She held up one hand. "There is no more time. I must go soon, Landu, if I am to make the boat. Please, you must leave now." Urien turned and stooped to pick up her bundle, not wishing to watch his face as he departed.

"No."

The vehemence in Landu's voice whirled Urien about. The monk's face had darkened, and he now stood squarely in front of her door. There was no way out. "I will not lose you, Urien."

"Move out of my way, Landu."

"Not unless you marry me."

The embarrassment Urien had felt a moment prior flashed hot. "If you will not go, I will." She moved to walk past him—but Landu grabbed her wrist.

"You're not going anywhere until you agree."

Urien's anger flared. "Unhand me this moment!" She tried to yank her wrist free.

Urien did not succeed in freeing her hand. Landu's grip was too strong. Yet as she attempted to wrench her arm free, something worse happened. The sleeve of her robe fell back, revealing the ornate tattoo on the back of her forearm.

Landu gasped, his eyes going wide as he clenched her wrist tighter and held it up to the light of the lamp on her table. "What is this sign?"

The mark of the Queen's Heart.

Urien's patience was exhausted. She was no girl to be handled thus, and she was losing valuable time. Uncovering the mark of her shame was the last straw.

With her free hand, Urien reached for the only thing to hand that approached a weapon: the original Bone Codex. Landu saw her going for it, and he tried to jerk her away from the table. Yet even as she spun, Urien snatched up the book and closed it with a single motion. Then, when the motion stopped and Landu stood between her and the table, she thrust the heavy Bone Codex edge-on with all of her strength—straight at his throat!

There was a horrible crushing sound as the book made contact. Stunned, Landu released her and clutched at his neck with both hands. As he did so he staggered backward into her table.

The dark monk hit the table with an ugly grunt, his arms flailing. One of them missed the edge of the table entirely, and Landu tumbled sideways to the floor. As he fell, the other hand struck the still-lit oil lamp atop the table and knocked it over.

Time seemed to slow as lamp oil gushed from the overturned vessel onto the open pages of the Bone Codex translation. Urien watched in horror as the lamp's flame ignited the oil. A moment later, burning oil engulfed her work as time returned to normal.

"*No!*"

Urien leapt over Landu. Ignoring the monk as he choked on the floor, she attempted to beat out the flames with the closed leather volume in her hands. But by the time she vanquished them, most of the translation was ruined, consumed by the fire or shattered by the attempts to quench it.

Urien put down the original Bone Codex—still quite intact—next to the smoldering cadaver of her translation.

Months of excruciating labor. Gone.

At her feet, Landu's voice sounded broken and hoarse. "I'm sorry, Urien," he croaked.

"Sorry?" She wheeled on him with sudden ferocity. "*Sorry, Landu?*" Urien was incensed. How would she explain *this*—all this—to the abbot and abbess? And what of the lost translation? The prospect of starting over . . .

No. I must confront Somnadh.

Further delay was unacceptable. It was time for drastic action.

With a determined calm, she put her foot on Landu's throat. The monk's eyes widened. "Don't worry, I'm not going to kill you, but I cannot have you following me—or reporting my departure."

When she was sure he was unconscious, Urien removed Landu's brown robe and donned it herself. She bound his arms behind his back with his own belt and gagged him with straw from her pallet. Then she picked up the Bone Codex and walked out of her cell, leaving him trussed on the floor.

Let him explain what happened!

Some time later, a brown-robed monk stood at the aft rail of the trading vessel. The island of Urras was little more than a receding speck on the western horizon. Within the raised cowl, the monk wore a pensive expression.

"There looks to be a bit of a squall coming on from the north, brother," said a cheerful voice from somewhere close by. "Nothing to give us too much trouble, but you may wish to go below."

"Thank you, captain," replied the monk in a whisper, turning from the rail.

"Not at all," said the captain, his Tratharan accent giving his Vilguran a peculiar, lilting quality. "Not at all, Brother Urien."

"Brother Morumus!"

Morumus turned. He had been standing apart, casting long, pensive looks back across the way they had come. But the sound of the voice snapped him out of his reverie. Looking toward the others, he saw a scout sliding down the scree from the ridge above. Even had he not heard the urgency in the man's tone, there could be no mistaking it in his movements.

Morumus and the scout rejoined the main body of village men at the same time.

"Brother Morumus!" panted the scout, a quick young man with keen eyes.

"What is it, Skeit?"

"I think I've sighted them!"

"At last!" growled several voices in close succession.

Three days had passed since Morumus had ridden into Dorslaan with Oethur. Three times the sun had sunk in the west since the two monks had separated—Oethur racing northeast to Grindangled, and Morumus riding south, climbing into the Deasmor in pursuit of the Dree. Morumus had never experienced days so tense—or so tiring.

The Deasmor was a beautiful place. A thick range of mountains stretching east to west across the neck of Aeld Gowan, it formed the natural boundary between Lothair and Norn-indaal in the north and Mersex in the south. The mountains themselves were old and low, full of winding trails with pre-cipitous drops. Nestled among the mountains' skirts, a vast collection of lochs and glens lay hidden and untamed. The Deasmor was beautiful, but its ways were wild and dangerous.

With Colba to guide him, Morumus had caught up to the villagers early on the second day. Morumus was glad to have had the boy with him then. Apparently the larger company of Dree had split into several bands once they had entered the Deasmor, and the villagers had pursued the band whose trail indicated the presence of children. Without Colba's vouching, Morumus was almost certain that the men of Dorslaan—on edge and suspicious—would have taken him for an enemy.

But later that same day, Colba had had to turn back. Moru-mus's horse, on which the club-footed lad had ridden, could no long traverse the dangerous trails of the high Deasmor. So the youth had returned home with the animal, while Morumus remained with the villagers to pursue the enemy on foot. It was a tiring, treacherous endeavor.

"How far, Skeit?" asked a middle-aged man with fierce eyes. His name was Mulcan, and he was Colba's father.

"They are on the next ridge."

"Which fork did they take? The south or the west?"

"They went south."

A dark murmur passed through the men.

Mulcan ignored the others. "Are you certain?"

"Yes."

From the tone of this exchange, as well as from the furtive looks that passed between the men, Morumus could tell that Skeit's report boded ill. But he had no idea why.

He turned to the village elder. "What's wrong, Mulcan?"

"The Dree"—the villagers had taken to using Morumus's name for the enemy—"are headed for Fheil's Delf."

The murmur rippled again through the men like a sea serpent breaching the water's surface.

"I do not know that name," Morumus confessed.

"I will explain as we go." Mulcan turned to one of the other villagers. "Jun, I remember that story you told at the Midwinter Feast."

Jun, a barrel-chested, sandy-haired fellow of about Mulcan's age, nodded.

"Do you think you can find the tunnel again?"

"I believe I can."

"Good. If we reach the tunnel, we may reach the Delf before the Dree. But it will be a near thing, even with one of them injured. Let's move out. Jun, you take the lead. There's no time to lose."

The pursuers lost no time. Within minutes they had crested the hill from which Skeit had sighted the Dree. As they moved down its far side, it became apparent to Morumus what Mulcan had meant when he had mentioned forks in the trail. Ahead of them, a long sheer ridge reared up against the sky. Its multiple peaks were joined at the shoulders, forming a wall of stone that blocked the southern horizon and appeared impregnable. At its base, the path on which they now trod split in two. One branch skirted west under the lee of the high cliffs. The other climbed by switchbacks up the face of the cliffs until it disappeared south in a shoulder between two of the peaks.

One of the men pointed. "There they are."

It was true. About halfway up the southern switchbacks, dark shapes were moving—with some smaller shapes strung between them.

"There is a third path, beyond the two you can see from here," Mulcan said to Morumus as they descended toward the fork. "To reach it, we must climb a narrow runoff stream almost straight up the face of that ridge. About a third of the way up, the stream pours from the mouth of a small cavern. At the back of that cavern is a tunnel that—according to Jun—will take us through the heart of the mountain. Its far side opens just above where the southern path dips down to Fheil's Delf."

"What is Fheil's Delf?"

"The name comes from the old speech of my people. It means 'Shadow's Digging.'"

"A curious name."

"Indeed. My people are accustomed to sheer mountains and sharp ravines, Morumus. Nornshaam across the sea, from whence we came so long ago, was a land hammered out of height and depth—with precious little left between. But Fheil's Delf set even my ancestors whistling." Mulcan glanced sideways. "Truly you have never heard of it?"

Morumus shook his head.

"It is a vast black chasm, wreathed in perpetual mist. None has ever seen its bottom. Those who try to descend its side never return alive. Those who fall into it . . . well, it is said that their screams do not stop. They simply fade into the depths."

"And it is close?"

Mulcan pointed to the cliff wall, now looming above as well as ahead of them. "It lies just beyond this ridge."

"And the Dree are heading straight for it."

"Yes. They must intend to cross the Delf."

"Is there a way across?"

"There is a bridge—an old rope bridge."

Morumus nodded. Now he understood why the men had murmured. "If the Dree get across before we catch them . . ."

"They will cut the bridge, and our children will be lost." Mulcan's face was flint. "That is why we must cut them off."

"You are sure of this tunnel?"

"I have never seen it myself, but Jun has. His grandfather was the one who found it."

By this point the men had reached the base of the towering ridge. They turned right, following the western fork for a short distance until they found the place where the runoff stream crossed it. At this time of year and in these heights, there was no flowing water—only a dry trough crossing the path with a narrow strand of ice at its bottom. Morumus would never have marked it for a trailhead.

"This is the place." Jun pointed to where the ice threaded up among the rocks on their left.

"It's a steep ascent, brothers," said Mulcan. "Mind your holds as we climb."

They minded them with great care. Not a man among the pursuers permitted his attention to wander as they picked their way up the face of the cliff. The runoff stream had cut a true course down through the rock, but it was a narrow way, and there was plenty of loose stone on which their feet might slip. Yet they could not afford to take too much time. With the Dree so far ahead, any unnecessary delay could prove fatal. Thus the climb proceeded with all haste—despite the precarious path.

They had a brief rest when at last they reached the top. There they found the cave, just as Jun had said—and while he and Mulcan stooped to strike a torch, the rest resorted to their waterskins and scant provisions. Morumus stood by the men striking flint and steel, peering into the cave's gloom.

What will we find on the other side?

"Here we are." Mulcan spoke with grim triumph as he stood, holding a lit torch, and stepped forward into the cave.

The shadows fled before the flame, and for the first time they had a clear view of the cave's interior. It was wide, but not more than a half-dozen paces deep. Most of the wall surface glistened with the dull sheen of ice. But there was one place in the far corner where no light reflected.

Morumus pointed. "There's our tunnel."

"God be praised." Mulcan strode toward it. "Come on, then, brothers! We pass this way!"

How long they walked in shadow through the heart of the mountain, Morumus could not say. The small torch at their head was bright, yet the passage was narrow and the surrounding darkness palpable. Thick gloom stalked hard on their heels, swallowing up the path behind and snatching away their sense of time.

A sense of deep foreboding settled upon the men as they went. Nobody spoke. Yet the longer they trod through the lightless space, the more sinister doubts began to rise in Morumus's mind. His was the last position in the line, and dark suggestions seemed to whisper to him out of the blackness behind . . .

What if Jun is wrong? What if this passage is a dead end?
Or what if the far end of the tunnel has collapsed?
Or what if the passage behind us should . . . ?
No.

With a severe inward reproach, Morumus forced himself to stop. What did he think he was doing, allowing himself to start down that path? He was a trained monk, not a mewling child. And he had an obligation—both to God and to the others.

"The Lord is my shepherd, I shall not lack," he said aloud.

No response from the others. Morumus waited for several long moments.

Nothing.

He continued. "In pastures green he makes me lie, to restful waters me he guides."

Silence again, until . . .

"He brings back my life," called a voice from near the front.

"To ways which are right," said another.

"For his own name's delight," called a third.

Morumus smiled.

"Yea, though I walk through the death-shadow valley," he called out.

"I need fear no evil, for thou art my ally." This time Morumus recognized Mulcan's voice, carrying back from the head of the line.

"Thou orderest my table before my foes."

"Thou anointest me with oil—my cup overflows."

Back and forth it went, the men picking up a verse in turn.

"Surely goodness and faithfulness pursue all my days . . ."

"And I will dwell in the house of the Lord always."

At the conclusion of the psalm, the voices joined together in a corporate 'Amen.'

After this, though Morumus could see no change in the darkness around them, he sensed a change in the men. He sensed it in himself, too. It was not an immediate relief from disquieting circumstances. Rather, it was an inner rest *despite* their circumstances. They still walked amidst the inky blackness of the mountain. But now they remembered that they did not walk alone.

Several more minutes passed in silence. Then, finally, they reached the end.

"Light ahead!"

At Mulcan's cry, the men pressed forward, and within moments even Morumus could see the rectangle of light in the forward distance. It was small, but sure—and growing!

At last!

Along with the relief returned the anxiety of their pursuit.

Are we in time?

The question seemed to strike the others at the same time as it struck Morumus. Without a word, they all picked up their pace. Mulcan dropped the torch—there was no need of it now they could see daylight—and as one man the pursuers raced toward the exit.

They emerged onto a broad shelf bathed in a bright sun. After a few moments' squinting, they realized where they were. The ledge upon which they had emerged stood about two hundred yards up-slope from the edge of the Delf. Below them they saw the path join to the near end of the bridge.

Two things struck Morumus as his eyes adjusted.

The first was the Delf itself. Everything Mulcan had reported about it was true. The gorge spread away as far as he could see in either direction: a vast, jagged tear in the fabric of the Deasmor. Its width was at least two hundred spans. Its sides were sheer, dark, and damp—for less than fifty yards below the brink they disappeared into a sea of mist. The thick white fog, though it roiled as if stirred by hidden currents, was seamless. Nothing could be seen through its swaddling cover, and nothing emerged from its swallowing depths.

Yet for all the awful grandeur of Fheil's Delf, Morumus's eyes soon fixed upon a second, more terrifying sight.

"Mulcan, look!" He pointed to the bridge. "The Dree! They are already crossing!"

It was true. The Dree had managed to get all their company about a quarter of the way across. The bridge was in good condition—had the Dree been maintaining it?—but their progress was slow. One of the figures was hobbling at the head of their company.

"I can take them from here." Skeit bent his longbow to its string and retrieved a shaft from his quiver.

"Not from this distance." Mulcan shook his head. "You might hit one of the children. See how they fight!"

The children were the second reason for the Dree's slow progress: they were struggling wildly now. Arms were bound motionless, but legs flailed as the captives struck out at their captors. The boy yelled, and the two girls screamed. Those screams drifted up to the men on the ledge.

Seeing the prisoners struggling, the image of the murdered girl in Caeldora came rushing back to Morumus . . .

The dead girl had raven-black hair. Her eyes were blue, like the color of the summer sky. Her skin, however, was very, very pale . . .

no color in it at all. . . . He knew even before he saw it that there was a deep gash in the soft flesh of her throat.

It must not happen again!

Before he knew what he was doing, Morumus had grabbed a stave from the nearest villager. Wordless prayers flew from his soul to heaven as he tore down the slope toward the bridge. Perhaps in answer, he began to feel as he had when cornered in Saint Dreunos's Cathedral in Versaden. His awareness expanded, and it seemed to him that he could perceive every plank in the rope bridge ahead of him.

Behind him, Morumus heard the others following. Though he knew they could not be more than a few paces behind, he heard them as though from a great distance. Some shouted encouragement to the children.

"Give 'em all you've got, son! Da's coming!"

"Hang on, dear one! Papa's almost there!"

Morumus reached the bridge in a warrior's rage that would have made his father smile. The stave was clutched in his hand, and the long years that had passed since his weapons training melted away. He was ready to give battle and even to accept death. The only thing he would not accept was the escape of the Dree with their victims.

But the enemy had heard and seen their pursuers and made preparations of their own. There were six of the black-robed Dree, and these six had now divided their efforts. One of them was attempting to help his injured comrade to the far side of the bridge. Three others had taken a child apiece—one arm around the throat, the other clamped about the middle. The last stood as a rearguard, his faceless cowl facing Morumus. In his hand he clutched a stone knife.

"Stop!" he hissed in Vilguran as Morumus stepped onto the bridge. "One step farther, and we will drop the children into the pit."

Hiss!

Skeit's arrow took the speaker in the chest. The force of the shot knocked the Dree back and spun him sideways. He was dead even before he tumbled over the edge of the bridge.

Seeing his opportunity, Morumus sprang to the attack. The Dree nearest to him tried to heave his child over the edge, but the would-be victim—it was the young boy—gave him such a well-timed backward kick that the maneuver failed. The boy's foot caught the enemy somewhere below the middle, and in the next moment the Dree had dropped him onto the bridge. Morumus's stave crashed into the black-hooded head with a sickening *thud*, and the enemy staggered. In one fluid motion, the other end of Morumus's stave caught him between the legs and heaved him up in the opposite direction.

As the Dree cleared the bridge, his hood fell back. Dark eyes shone wide in a pale face, and thin lips twisted from baleful leer to panicked scream. The scream echoed long after the man vanished beneath the mists.

By the time Morumus looked back, the other two Dree were turning to flee toward the far side of the bridge, forcing the young girls before them at knifepoint. They were about halfway across now—

Hiss.

Another arrow found its mark, this time in the unprotected back of the nearest fleeing Dree. The man fell forward, trying to hold on to the little girl. But Skeit's arrow had been well aimed, and the enemy's strength was broken. Though her arms were still bound, the girl managed to writhe free of the Dree's dying clutches and run toward Morumus.

"*Genna ma'guad ma'muthad ma'rophed,*" croaked the Dree with his last breath.

By this time Morumus heard footsteps on the bridge behind him. He turned and, seeing Malcun, gestured toward the boy and girl. "Get these two clear. I'm going after the last."

Malcun nodded, helping the boy to his feet and scooping up the girl in his arms.

"Papa!" she cried as he lifted her to his shoulders.

A tear moistened the corner of Morumus's eye as he turned toward the last fleeing Dree. The enemy was beyond even Skeit's capable bowshot now. And thanks to Morumus's pause, he had a significant lead.

But I'm not carrying a prisoner.

Morumus dashed after the enemy, stave at the ready.

For several seconds, it seemed that he would succeed. But he mistimed his jump over the body of the second fallen Dree. Morumus's robe snagged on the thick arrow shaft protruding from the back of the corpse, and he fell face first onto the bridge. It was a smacking fall, and he grunted as his face struck the hard planks.

Precious seconds were lost as he distentangled his robe from the arrow shaft.

Come on! Come on!

Finally he got free and back on his feet. He turned to resume his chase . . .

. . . and saw that it had ended.

The three surviving Dree now stood at the far end of the bridge, looking back at him with faceless malice. One of them held the sobbing girl. The other two held long knives, raised to strike.

Twang!

The first blows struck the guide ropes, severing them and sending such a tremor along the length of the bridge that Morumus nearly lost his place.

"Morumus!" Mulcan shouted and gestured vehemently from the other side of the bridge. "They are going for the main ropes! Run for us!"

Morumus's chest heaved, and his heart pounded. The heat of battle still coursed through his veins. But Mulcan was right.

There was no way he could rescue the third girl now.

From the middle of the bridge, he turned back. Behind him, the Dree hacked with ferocious blows at the main ropes. He could feel the tremors beneath his feet as each blow went home.

Hurry!

Ahead of him, safe on the land, he saw the two rescued children and the men of Dorslaan. Foremost among these were Jun, Malcun, and Skeit. The three of them had made a human chain extending out onto the bridge—with the heaviest, Jun, holding on to a bridge post, and the lightest, Skeit, reaching out his hand toward Morumus.

Morumus ran with all his might. Every fiber of his being was bent on reaching that outstretched hand. He forced his body to move faster, imploring his limbs to exceed their limits—if only for a few more moments.

Almost there!

There were less than a dozen paces to go.

Less than half a dozen.

Twang!

Morumus felt the first of the main ropes go, and he lunged forward, desperate to get just a few paces nearer before he leapt.

Twang!

As the second rope went, Morumus gathered what strength remained and jumped, stretching every inch of his frame toward Skeit's hand. The men on the land leaned out, stretching themselves as far as they could go. The two men's hands converged . . .

. . . and fell short.

Passing less than a handbreadth from rescue, Morumus's hands fell to the deck of the bridge. But it was not a hard landing this time, for the bridge was in motion, too.

Pushing off as best he could, Morumus lunged in a final, frantic grab for Skeit's hand . . .

But it was too late.

The bridge of Fheil's Delf fell away beneath him . . .

Morumus plummeted into the open maw of the mist.

PART III

SHADOW'S WEB

ethur dipped his spoon into the soup, watching it sink beneath the opaque surface. He brought it out again after a moment, its thick contents steaming. He brought the spoon toward his lips. Closing them with a silent prayer, he tasted . . .

"Ugh!"

He forced himself to swallow when every instinct urged him to gag. This self-discipline stemmed not from any consideration for company, for Oethur dined alone this night. On the contrary, it arose solely from a desire to avoid spewing any of the odious liquid on the remainder of his dinner. There was no sense in ruining the bread and cheese on account of the soup.

Oethur set down his spoon and glared at his bowl. *Why would anybody in his right mind want to eat pea soup?*

It must have been a villainous soul who first thought to cultivate and eat the pea; of this Oethur was convinced. When he had been a boy, his nurse had tried many things to convince him of the rightness of consuming peas. Her first attempt had been to point out that men had cultivated and eaten peas for thousands of years—thus the practice was of great antiquity.

"So is the practice of sin," he had snarled.

God made peas edible, she had reminded him.

Even now, years later, Oethur remembered his reply: "All things are lawful, but not all things are profitable."

Faced with such retorts, his nurse had finally despaired of teaching him to appreciate peas. But she had made him promise that he would always try at least one bite—just in case his tastes should change. He had kept that promise to this day. And to this day, his taste continued its settled opposition.

No peace with peas.

Oethur permitted himself a weak smile at the memory. It had been a long week. He had possessed little time even to think, let alone reminisce. Thus the stray recollection was most welcome, however fleeting might be its relief.

A minute later the distraction had faded, taking Oethur's smile along with it.

His father's death had overwhelmed Oethur. He had learned of the illness but two weeks ago. But then, to arrive home only to see his father die the same day . . .

Oethur's eyes grew hot, and he shook his head. *When will I stop feeling so raw?*

According to Nornish custom, King Ulfered's body had lain for a week in the House of Mourning, where he might be viewed by any of his people who chose to come. The rite was ancient and inviolable among the Nornish people. Those who had served a man in life had a right to see him at his death. How could they know that their bond of service was fulfilled if they could not confirm that their master was dead? Moreover, in the case of a king, the rite had special significance as the first step in the succession process. How could a new king be named unless it be confirmed that the old king had departed this life?

With the period of mourning now complete, the funeral would take place tomorrow. This promised to be a significant affair of the kingdom. All seven lords of Nornindaal would be present, and presiding over the service would be Bishop Treowin. Oethur had not seen Treowin since returning to Grindangled, but Aeldred had assured him that the bishop was in the city and would officiate at the funeral.

The thought of Aeldred made Oethur frown. He and his brother had found scant time to speak since their father's death. When one or the other was not taken up in attending at the House of Mourning—another ancient custom of the Nornish people—various matters occupied his brother's attentions. Besides the funeral arrangements, Aeldred was now Prince Regent. As such, the daily affairs of the kingdom were in his hands. As if all this were not sufficient, Aeldred must also begin to make preparations for his coronation . . .

Oh brother, what strain you must be under right now.

Only in the matter of the coronation did Aeldred have a bit of respite. It could not occur for another four weeks at the earliest, thanks to yet another inviolable custom. This tradition stipulated that the coronation of a new king must wait until a full lunar cycle after the burial of his predecessor. The idea behind it was to give the lords of Nornindaal time to consider: was the heir truly worthy of the crown, or should they select another?

It had been generations since there had been any serious doubt about succession to the crown. Nevertheless, the custom would be observed. And for his brother's sake, Oethur was glad. Anything that eased Aeldred's burden during this time was most welcome.

Though Oethur hated to add to his brother's strain, he needed to speak to Aeldred soon. His brother—and his future king—must be warned about events unfolding beyond their borders. The plots of the Mordruui needed to be uncovered, the threat of the Red Order could not be ignored, and the disappearance of Bishop Ciolbail called for most pressing atten—

Oethur came up short.

Morumus!

Thoughts of the Lothairin bishop had made him think of his Lothairin brother in Aesus. The realization struck him like the tolling of a deep bell.

It has been a week!

A whole week had passed since Aeldred had dispatched troops to Dorslaan. Seven days had expired since they had sent swords to aid Morumus in chasing the Mordruui. Even if the soldiers had become involved in a protracted tracking operation, there should have been *some* word. They should have sent at least *one* messenger back to Grindangled.

Why has there been no word?

Oethur stood.

Enemies and intrigues could wait, but a brother was a different matter. The Mordruui, the Red Order, Bishop Ciolbail—he would speak of them to Aeldred *after* the funeral tomorrow. But he would go and speak to the officer of the watch about Dorslaan and Morumus tonight.

Right now.

Stepping out of his chamber, Oethur found the corridors of Malduorn's Keep swarming with activity. With several of the seven lords of Nornindaal already present—and the rest threatening to arrive at any hour of the night or morning—servants were scurrying this way and that along every corridor in a veritable army. Some swept, while others dusted behind them. Some carried trays of food, while others carried piles of clean linen. It had been years since the Keep had been this full, and there were innumerable requisite preparations. Even after a week's notice, the household staff looked harried.

"Carry on," Oethur insisted any time his passage was noted. "Go on, I say! A simple nod will do; no need for a full bow or curtsy."

Few could simply carry on, however. With so many nobles present or coming, all the servants—even those Oethur had known for years—were in no mood to show even the slightest hint of familiarity. He couldn't really blame them. Yet the result was an inconvenient nuisance to them all, and he left a trail of disrupted activity in his wake.

Oethur was glad when he emerged at last from the Keep.

Crossing the silent moat bridge in the dark, he looked up at the sky. His breath misted in the crisp air. It was a moonless night, and myriads of stars twinkled in the velvet canopy overhead. Amidst the stars he thought he even saw a faint strand of purple. The sight was so spectacular that he paused.

"What are men, that thou remembrest them?"

The line was from one of Morumus's favorite psalms. Oethur smiled at its recollection. Yet the thought of his friend also reminded Oethur that he was losing time. He lowered his gaze and returned his attention to its terrestrial mission.

Now is a time for focused action, not pensive meditation.

Oethur hurried on across the bridge.

Reaching the great bailey, he was not surprised to find that it too was bustling. Each of the seven lords would come bearing a retinue of men-at-arms, and each of these must have a pallet for his bed and a stall for his horse. From the looks of things, at least four of the lords had arrived today. Thus the whole yard was engaged in a massive operation of shifting and stowing men, beasts, and supplies. It was well managed, as far as these things went—but it was still a great din.

Oethur threaded his way through the mix of flesh and fodder, making for the main gatehouse on the outer wall. He did what he could to avoid notice, and here—in sharp contrast to his indoor passage just a few minutes prior—he succeeded. So long as he was neither help nor hindrance, the busy soldiers were only too glad to ignore him. Unlike household servants, they considered it no part of their job to stand about looking for reasons to bow and curtsy! Oethur passed through their midst without exciting a single comment.

As he drew near to the gatehouse, he looked up. Above him, the stone walls reflected a ruddy gleam from the firelight in the yard, shining like dull embers against the dark night. Yet besides this, Oethur also saw the glow of true lamplight escaping from the gatehouse's high windows. He nodded.

Despite tonight's bustle, he would still find the officer of the watch at his usual post.

It only made sense. Each night the watch officer was charged with the oversight of both interior supervision and external surveillance. Where better to execute both responsibilities than from a location straddling the barrier between the two worlds? From the height of the gatehouse, one could command views of both the great bailey and the outer bridge.

Oethur approached the gate sentry. He had no intention of being ignored now. "You there!"

The sentry saw him coming and stepped forward. "Who approaches?" He spoke in a somewhat crabby, yet circumspect tone. The household servants weren't the only ones wary of an unannounced superior.

"It is I, Lord Oethur. How are you tonight, Orm?"

"Well enough, my lord, considering all this commotion." The veteran sergeant smiled as he gave his duty. "How can I be of service?"

"I wish to speak with the officer of the watch. I take it he is upstairs?"

"Yes, my lord. Shall I fetch him?"

"Who is it tonight, Orm?"

"Dabbin, my lord."

"No need to fetch him down, Orm. I will go up."

"Very good, my lord."

Orm opened the gatehouse door, and Oethur climbed the steps. Reaching the heavy door at their top, he gave it a solid rap. The booming knock resounded on both sides of the door.

"Come!"

Oethur's rank permitted him to enter without knocking, of course, yet he always preferred to give a man warning. He pushed open the door and strode into the room.

"My Lord Oethur!" Dabbin, another veteran, recognized him at once. He and his assistant—a young man Oethur did not recognize—bowed their duty.

"Dabbin. How are you?"

"I am well, my lord. How can I be of service?"

"A word, Lieutenant?"

"Certainly, my lord." Dabbin dismissed his man with a wave. He waited until the door latched shut before turning back to Oethur.

"You look grave, my lord."

"It has been a long week, Dabbin."

The lieutenant nodded. "How can I be of service to you tonight, my lord?"

"A week ago, at my request, a company of men was dispatched to Dorslaan."

"Yes, my lord."

"You know of it?"

"I led the expedition, my lord."

Oethur's heart leapt. "You did?"

"Yes, my lord."

"When did you return?"

"Just this morning, my lord. I made a full report to the Prince Regent this afternoon. You did not know?"

"No, Dabbin. But my brother is overwhelmed these days. Please, be so good as to fill me in yourself. Why are you returned so soon?"

"There was nothing more we could do, my lord."

"What do you mean?"

"We met the men as they returned out of the Deasmor, my lord. The villagers, along with that monk—"

"His name is Morumus."

"Yes, my lord. The villagers, along with the monk Morumus, killed three of the raiders and rescued two of the children. But three others escaped with a third child, and—"

"Escaped? Why did you not pursue them?"

"We could not, my lord. The raiders escaped across the bridge at Fheil's Delf, and—"

"The Black Pit?" Oethur knew the place only by reputation, but both his father and brother had seen it.

Dabbin nodded. "The villager reported that the raiders cut the bridge behind them."

"Well . . . it's a bad business, but it could have been worse. We took three, rescued two, and lost none. I must consult with Morumus immediately. Where is he?"

"You knew this monk Morumus, my lord?"

Knew? What did he mean . . . *knew*? The past tense made his skin crawl. "I *know* him, yes. He is my particular friend."

"My lord . . ." Dabbin's face had gone ashen.

A spider of doom began to creep up Oethur's back, its touch light but foreboding. He knew the look in Dabbin's face, and he dreaded what would come next. But he must ask. "Where is he, Lieutenant? Is he injured?"

"My lord . . . he was on the bridge when the enemy cut it."

The spider struck.

"No!" Oethur reeled backward as if stabbed in the middle. "No, it cannot be!"

Dabbin's tone was pained. "I am so sorry, my lord. From what the villagers . . ."

But Oethur heard no more of the man's words. The news coursed through him like pitiless venom. He staggered from the room and stumbled back down the stairs, past Orm, and across the great bailey in a daze. The starry sky attracted no more of his admiration as he walked back across the moat bridge, and he ignored the various bows and curtsies that greeted him in the corridors of the Keep.

Oethur was numb all over as he returned to his chamber and his dinner. He picked up the spoon and began ladling in the cold pea soup. It tasted even worse cold, but he didn't care. If only it could do more than just *taste* like poison, he might find relief.

But no relief would come. Not in this life.

His friend was gone.

rien strode without fear through the streets of Marfesbury. From within the cowl of her hood, she watched as people of all ranks diverted their gazes as well as their steps. Nobody wanted to be in her way. Everybody moved to give her a wide berth.

Four days had passed since Urien had boarded ship. After departing Urras, the Tratharan vessel had followed a ponderous course south along the Lothairin coast. It had stopped at many fishing villages along the mainland, then struck out to touch at the island of Tyn.

Believing "Brother Urien" to be on a sensitive errand for Abbot Nerias, the Trathari had warned her that Marfesbury—their next stop—would be crawling with red monks. Thus it was that when they had landed at Tyn, she had gone ashore and purchased red dye. Using this, she had turned her spare robe from Urras grey to the blood-toned scarlet of the Order of the Saving Blood.

Now clothed in this red robe, Urien moved unmolested through the streets of Marfesbury. She took no pleasure in the dread she engendered, only a grim satisfaction. The ruse was a necessary part of her plan—and it appeared to be working.

Her plan was simple. Disguised as a red monk, she would enter the cloister of the Red Order in the city cathedral. Once there, she would look for clues to her brother's whereabouts. Before leaving her in Caeldora, he had told her his intentions:

"There is trouble back home. The king of Mersex has died. His son is preparing for war against our people. But there may be a chance for peace. So I must return home to help."

Since that conversation, Urien had learned the truth of her brother's dark faith and his personal deceptions. Yet she believed that he had been telling her the truth about his intentions. And so this was her first clue: her brother was somewhere in Dyfann. Her second clue was the fact that Somnadh's Mordruui were masquerading as an Aesusian religious order. This being the case, it stood to reason that she might expect to find some trace of his movements among the Order of the Saving Blood.

Having never visited Versaden or Mereclestour, Urien had never beheld a greater Aesusian church than Marfesbury Cathedral. The front of the cathedral was dominated by a tall, square tower, and from its base two small wings extended left and right. From the ends of these extended a wall twice the height of a man. This wall ran back along the bulk of the cathedral, enclosing both cloisters and gardens and giving the whole complex the appearance of a fortress. It was toward this fortress that Urien now marched.

The sexton saw her coming and moved to open the door.

"Greetings, brother," he said in Vilguran. There was an eager gleam in the young man's eyes. Like her, he wore a robe of scarlet. Yet unlike her, he wore his cowl down and his head shaved.

"Greetings." To disguise her gender, Urien used a combination of growl and whisper. "I have just arrived from Dyfann. How many of my brothers are in the cloister here?"

"From the Motherland?" The sexton gave a low whistle and touched his forehead in respect. "Ours is a modest cloister, brother. We provide shelter to no more than a dozen of the

Order, along with half as many more catechumens—myself included. But we have plenty of room. If you care to stay with us, I will show you to the cloister."

"That would be excellent, thank you."

"Not at all, brother. Just follow me."

Urien followed the sexton. Together they passed down the long, dim nave of the cathedral. Exiting through a door in the transept, they came out into a spacious rectangular garden. On the far side of the garden, tucked against the outer wall of the cathedral complex, was the cloister—a squat stone structure of two stories.

"It is modest, brother," said the sexton as they entered the cloister, "but we try to make it comfortable."

They were standing inside the antechamber now. On either side of the door were stairs. One flight ascended to a second floor. The other led down . . .

"The common area is on this level. Private chambers are on the level above. Shall I take you up?"

Urien pointed to the descending stairs. "What is down there?"

The sexton coughed. "Below are the cells for . . . guests. You understand, brother, of course."

"Of course." Urien's tone was cold and severe. She understood far better than any novice. "Tell me, how many guests are with us at present?"

"Just one, brother. An orphan girl who used to beg bread from the bishop. The bishop had been wondering for some time how to be rid of her. Now she is to accompany the brothers of our cloister to the great feast in two weeks at Banr Cluidan. We lured her in with the promise of a new Mother." He smiled.

The knowing gleam in that smile revolted Urien, and she felt an almost irresistible impulse to violence. But she forced herself to remain focused.

For now.

"Banr Cluidan?" Urien's voice shook as she repeated the name of the hill fort she had known as a girl, and her disguised tones almost slipped.

"Yes! The archbishop's proclamation arrived last week. In just over two weeks, at the equinox, there is to be a great feast—the Feast of the Sacred Tree!—to dedicate the new cathedral of Banr Cluidan. Every brother is summoned, and even a few novices may attend if—" He frowned. "But surely you know all this already, coming from the Motherland."

Urien made no reply, but she clenched her hands to keep them from trembling. She need look no further.

Two weeks.

She now knew exactly when and where she would find Somnadh. With the help of the Trathari, two weeks should be plenty of time to reach Banr Cluidan. She had to get back to the ship at once, but . . .

What about the girl?

The question rose unbidden in her mind.

Of course I cannot leave her.

Like the question, the answer came to her as though from outside herself. Yet it carried undeniable conviction.

But how?

As if in answer, Urien noticed—for the first time—that an eerie silence hung over the cloister. A sudden hope filled her. "Where are the others?"

"The others?"

"The others of our order."

"Oh! Most will not return until evening, brother. Every day they ride out to the villages to spread the good news of the Saving Blood."

Excellent. "What is your name?"

"Bachul, brother."

"How long have you been a novice, Bachul?"

174

"Four months, brother."

"Four months?" Urien feigned shock. "Four months, and they have not yet raised you to the full brotherhood?"

The sexton looked uncertain, as though trying to determine whether this was a test. "They have not. They say I am not yet ready for the final test."

"What would you say, Bachul, if I told you I disagree?"

The sexton's reserve vanished. "Do you really think so, brother?"

"I do. Furthermore, as a member of the Banr Cluidan cloister, I am empowered by the Hand of the Mother himself to administer the test to whomever I deem worthy. Are you prepared to take this examination today?"

"I would love nothing more, brother." The boy's eyes widened, and his voice quivered with a mix of anticipation and uncertainty. "But I know nothing of this test. How can I know if I am prepared?"

"Do you have here a quantity of nomergenna, as well as the ritual implements?"

"We do."

"Then the final test requires only two things further: a living victim and a willing heart. We have the former in the cells below. Do I have the latter standing before me? Are you ready to yield to the Mother your absolute obedience, Bachul?"

"I am, brother!"

"Good. Then heed my command without deviation. This is what you must bring . . ."

After a few minutes, the sexton returned with the necessaries, and he and Urien descended to the cells. Bachul led her down, offering profuse thanks all the way.

"I am extremely conscious of the honor you do me, brother."

"See to it that you do not disappoint me, Bachul."

"Oh no, brother! Never!"

"Be warned. The final test is so called for a reason. You will not understand everything until afterward, and yet any failure to obey—*any* failure, Bachul, *any* delay or questioning of my order—will result in immediate failure. And you will not get a second chance. Is that clear?"

"I will not disappoint you, brother."

They entered the cell a minute later. In the yellow light from Bachul's lamp, Urien saw the girl curled up against the wall in the far corner. Her hands and feet were bound.

Bachul set his lamp on a small table by the door, then walked over and kicked her. "Get up!"

"Do *not* strike the victim. It bruises the victim, and bruising wastes blood."

"Yes, brother." Bachul backed away from the girl. "My apologies, brother."

"Fill the goblet halfway full with nomergenna. Fill the rest with wine, and mix it using the knife."

Bachul obeyed. From within the cowl of her robe, Urien watched him stir. She saw the wine change color. The mixture was very strong.

Bachul looked at Urien. "It is ready, brother."

"Good. Hand me the basin and the knife, then take the goblet in your own hands."

Again, Bachul obeyed. His hands trembled as he held the full goblet.

"Do *not* spill any of the wine."

"I'm sorry, brother." The goblet steadied.

"Do not be sorry. But *do* pay attention to what I say now. In order for the power of the Mother to come upon you, you must drink all that wine in one draft. I warn you now, it is

176

very strong—but if you spill or spit any, you fail the exam. You will drink upon my word. Are you ready?"

"Yes, brother."

"Drink."

Bachul threw back his head and drank with such eagerness that Urien almost pitied what would become of him.

Almost.

In less than a minute, he had drained the goblet.

"That *is* strong, brother . . ." His speech began to slur.

"Set the goblet on the table."

Bachul obeyed, but his movements were clumsy. The goblet landed hard on the table, toppled, and clattered onto the floor. He looked back to Urien, his expression anxious.

"It is well. You are under the Mother's spell. Do you feel it?"

"I . . . do . . ."

"You are almost ready, then. Close your eyes, and walk toward me. I will give you the basin and the knife."

As she said this, Urien steeled herself. If Bachul made it to her, she would strike him with the stone basin. She did not want to use the knife, if it could be avoided.

But in the event, neither proved necessary. Bachul took one step toward her, staggered, and, with a groan, fell to the floor. Urien stepped sideways and rolled him over with her toe. His eyes had rolled back into his shaved head, but he was still breathing.

Alive. But he won't wake up for a day—at least.

She dropped the basin and turned to the girl, lowering her hood. "There's no time to lose. I'm here to free you."

A look of confusion passed over the girl's face, and she said something in a language Urien did not understand.

"Can you understand me?"

The girl just stared at Urien.

Of course not. How many Mersian orphans speak Vilguran?

Urien pointed to herself. "Urien."

"Lenu," replied the girl.

Still holding the stone knife with one hand, Urien held up the other and gestured as though she were cutting. Then she pointed at the girl's bonds. "I am going to cut you free."

The girl nodded.

Urien knelt, severed the girl's bonds, and helped her up. Then she pointed toward the door. "Go?"

The girl nodded vigorously. "Go."

Urien walked over to where Bachul lay unconscious. She intended to retrieve his key and lock him in. But she had just stooped down to pull the key from his belt when Lenu screamed.

"Urien!"

Urien turned to see a large red monk filling the doorway.

"What are you doing?" he demanded in angry Vilguran. Then as his eyes took in the situation—including Bachul's limp form and Urien's long hair—he cursed. "You are no monk!"

Without another word, he lunged for Urien.

She tried to bring the knife to bear, but the man dodged her hurried thrust. As the blade whisked past, he grabbed her wrist and twisted.

"Aah!" The knife clattered to the floor. Yet in the same moment, Urien lashed out with one foot—and caught the man below the belt.

"Ugh." He released her wrist and staggered back, bent double in agony. But a moment later his anger overcame his pain, and he moved toward her again, his nostrils flaring.

Urien picked up the heavy stone basin from where she had dropped it next to Bachul. As the monk closed in, she swung it at his head. But before the basin could connect, his arms had flung forward and strong hands closed around her neck.

The basin dropped from Urien's hands as the monk lifted her up and pinned her against the cell wall. His grip tightened. She couldn't breathe, and black spots speckled her vision. She struggled, but her strength was fading.

"Ooh!"

The grip released, and Urien fell free to the floor.

As she gathered breath and the spots winked out, she saw the cause of her deliverance. While the monk had occupied himself with strangling Urien, Lenu had retrieved the fallen knife and plunged it up into the side of his stomach. Though the girl did not have the strength of an adult, she possessed a lethal aim born of her determination to escape.

The monk lay on the floor, coughing blood and moaning. Lenu stood over him, looking bewildered but fierce.

"Urien. Go." She pointed to the door.

Urien wasn't going to argue. "Yes, Lenu. Let's go."

Two days later, the sun was dipping below the western horizon as Urien stepped out of the Tratharan ship onto the shores of Dyfann. In the distance, she saw the lights of a small coastal village.

It was now six days since she had left Urras.

She and Lenu had returned to the Tratharan ship without further complication. The captain had taken to the little girl immediately—saying she looked just like his own daughter. And with him to translate the girl's Mersian, Urien and Lenu had been able to converse. Urien had told Lenu about Urras, and the captain had promised Brother Urien that he would see the girl safely set down there before his ship returned home.

Urien turned to look at the departing ship and saw Lenu waving to her from the rail.

She returned the wave and smiled. *Go and live, Lenu! Be free of the Dark Faith!*

After the ship vanished into the dusk, Urien turned inland.

At long last, she had reached the shores of home. What she had desired for so many years of imprisonment had finally come to fruition. Yet as she walked along the surf, her smile faded.

Why do I feel like such a stranger here?

But never mind. Disquieted feelings and uneasy questions could wait. What mattered now was what lay in front of her.

She would reach Banr Cluidan by the equinox. She was sure Somnadh would, too.

You will not escape me this time, my brother.

Urien strode up the beach toward the distant village.

16

Dressed in their finest regalia, Oethur and Aeldred stood side by side at the front of Grindangled Great Church. Shoulder to shoulder they stood as the funeral unfolded, the two great masts of the Nornish longship of state.

Flanking the two princes stood the seven lords of Nornindaal. Four of them—Aberun, Corised, Geraan, and Halbir—stood to Aeldred's left. The remaining three—Jugeim, Meporu, and Yorth—stood to Oethur's right. All of them stood at gravest attention before the bier of their late sovereign, and a few eyes even glistened with tears. Ulfered had been well loved.

Sitting in his chair on the dais above the bier, Bishop Treowin presided in his blackest robe. Standing on the step below him was Aeldred's personal chaplain, Erworn. It was the latter man—not the bishop—who conducted the service.

" 'I myself am the resurrection and the life,' promises our Lord Aesus. 'He that believes in me, even if he should die, he will live; and all who live and believe in me should certainly never die.' "

As the service continued, Oethur could not help but wonder at the bishop's silence. It was not that Erworn was doing poorly, but why would the bishop delegate his responsibilities to a subordinate on this most important occasion? For this reason, as often as he could do so without appearing to ignore Erworn, Oethur stared at Treowin.

Is something wrong with the bishop?

For most of the service, the bishop's expression did not change. His face was the very picture of pain, and his eyes were set straight ahead. But once—and only once during the entire ceremony—those eyes glanced at Oethur. And in that briefest of moments, something very significant passed between Oethur and the bishop.

But what?

The closest comparison Oethur could make was to a look he had seen many times in his father's eyes, the expression that appeared right before Oethur or one of his brothers got in trouble. It wasn't anger—there was no mistaking anger in the face of a Norn. But then what was it?

Was it grief? He knew his father had never enjoyed punishing his sons—though he had done so without hesitation. *Or was it something else? Disappointment? Warning? Paternal affection?*

Try as he might, Oethur could not place the expression.

". . . earth to earth, ashes to ashes, dust to dust."

The words of committal snapped Oethur's attention back to the present.

Erworn had finished speaking, and now liveried servants laid bundles of spices at the king's head and feet.

As they stepped back, a guard of four soldiers took their place. They draped Ulfered's bier in the banner of the Nornish kings: a great warhelm and spear centered on a field of solid black. Then they lifted the bier by its poles and turned.

"Walk behind me, brother," whispered Aeldred as the other nobles peeled off to flank the bier. "We will lead the procession together."

With a last look at the bishop, Oethur turned and followed his brother.

Oethur waited to speak to Aeldred until they were alone. It was late afternoon, and the interment was complete. The other lords had been sent on ahead to the King's Hall. Soon both Aeldred and Oethur would join them, and the reception would begin. But for a few precious minutes as they walked back together, the two sons of Ulfered were alone.

"A very moving service," said Aeldred. "Erworn did well."

"Yes," agreed Oethur. "Though I confess I was surprised that Bishop Treowin did not speak."

"He could not, brother."

"What do you mean, Aeldred?"

"The man can no longer speak."

Oethur tripped and only just caught himself from falling. "What?"

"It happened on his return voyage from Midgaddan last year. For some misguided reason, he took passage on a Tratharan ship. A *Tratharan* ship, brother! Something happened, and they cut out his tongue before casting him off on the wharf at Toberstan."

"It cannot be. . . . He was supposed to have sailed with Bishop Ciolbail of Lothair to prevent this very thing!"

Aeldred gave him a dangerous look. "Do not speak to me of Ciolbail, brother. That man has played us false for years. It was he who persuaded Heclaid of Lothair to delay my marriage to Rhianwyn—this business about her being twenty-five years of age was his invention. And now we know why! He has been delaying the union of the North in the hope of destroying us."

Aeldred's sudden vehemence stunned Oethur. "Surely not, brother . . ."

"You have been away a long time, brother, so you cannot be expected to have heard. Bishop Ciolbail has been implicated in a plot against the life of the Mersian king and queen. They found one of his tokens sewn into the coat of one of the would-be assassins."

"I have heard of this, brother. Before coming here, I was in Dunross. King Heclaid has received a letter demanding Ciolbail's surrender."

"Good. I hope to God he gives him up."

"He cannot, brother! Ciolbail never returned to Dunross."

"Ah! There you have it! Incontrovertible proof!"

"What do you mean?"

"Treowin told me that Ciolbail was put to shore by the Trathari at Laucura. That—"

"He *told* you? But you said he cannot speak."

Aeldred raised his brows. "In *writing*, Oethur. There's nothing wrong with his hand, thank God."

"Sorry, brother. Please continue."

"Ciolbail was put to shore at Laucura—and that is why our bishop was left alone with the pirates who maimed him! Ciolbail never returned to Dunross because he was busy in southern Mersex—busy trying to murder Wodic at Mereclestour!"

Oethur could not believe his ears. "Brother, King Heclaid asked me to convey to you his desire to consult on these matters. From what you have said, the need could not be more dire."

"I agree, brother. Unless we can convince the Mersians that Lothair does not harbor Ciolbail, I fear there will be war."

"I share your fear, brother. Please, let me go see Treowin. Even if he can no longer speak to me, I would speak to him."

Aeldred gave him a quizzical look. "Why do you want to speak to Treowin?"

"I would like to ask him about these things."

Aeldred's dark features clouded. "Do you not believe me, brother?"

"Of course I do, Aeldred. But these are hard tidings, and there are other enemies afoot of which I've not yet told you. They have murdered two of Bishop Treowin's dear friends in Caeldora, and now they have come to our island."

Aeldred relaxed, but he shook his head.

"You must tell me of all this soon, brother. But not tonight. And I say the same about Treowin. You will see him soon. Tomorrow even, if you insist. But tonight I need you beside me." He smiled. "You told me a week ago that I needed to start acting the part of a king. Do you remember?"

"I do."

"Well, I'm going to start now. Treowin and the rest will wait until tomorrow. Tonight your kings—our late father, and your elder brother—require your service. Do you understand?"

Oethur inclined his head. "Yes, sire."

The reception for King Ulfered continued long into the evening. A pair of hearths blazed at each end of the King's Hall, and every pair of eyes shone bright with their reflection. Long tables propped up heaping platters of food, and the spread was anchored at either end by a great vat of mead. The combination had a cheerful effect, and many hearts soared with shared memories of the late king.

Oethur did his duty for the sake of his father and Aeldred. He greeted dozens of guardsmen and spoke to each of the seven lords at length. Yet he could not put his heart into the celebration, and as the night wore on he grew weary.

There was just far too much to consider. To begin, there was the pain of his twin loss: first his father, then Morumus. And then there was what Aeldred had told him about Bishop Ciolbail.

Oethur was not sure which he found more difficult to believe. Could Morumus really be dead? Could Ciolbail truly have betrayed the North? He had no solid reason to doubt either report. If Morumus had fallen into Fheil's Delf, there was no possible way he could have survived. And if Ciolbail had done as Aeldred believed, the case was just as clear.

But why?

Why what?

Why would Ciolbail do it? Why betray the North? Why sell out to the Red Order? What could he hope to gain? He was already a bishop. No commoner in Aeld Gowan—whether in Mersex or the North—could hope to rise higher or to command more wealth.

It didn't make sense.

Try as he might, Oethur could not ignore the matter.

There was a low cough at his shoulder.

"Lord Oethur."

Oethur turned to see a guardsman younger than himself standing at his elbow. The man looked familiar, but he could not place him. "Good evening, corporal. Do I know you?"

"No, my lord. I was with Lieutenant Dabbin in the gate-house last night."

"So you were." Oethur remembered now. "What is your name, corporal?"

"Thornil, my lord."

"It is good to meet you, Thornil."

"And you, my lord." But Thornil looked rather anxious. "My lord, might I have a—that is to say, would you drink with me to the health of the king?"

"Yes, of course I will. Will you fetch us some mead?"

More anxiety flashed across Thornil's face.

"My lord, if it's not too much trouble . . ."

"What it is, corporal?"

"I thought we might—er, I mean to say—I mean, I meant to ask . . ."

Oethur put his arm on the younger man's shoulder. "It's all right, Thornil. Just tell me what you are asking."

Thornil gulped. "Could I beg a private word, my lord?"

Oethur looked around the Hall. He saw his brother near one of the hearths at the far end, in intense conference with two of the seven lords. Corised and Meporu were known to be loquacious, especially when in mead. From the look of it, his brother would be occupied for the foreseeable future.

I won't be missed—not for just a few minutes.

He turned to Thornil. "I am at your disposal, corporal. Lead the way."

After stopping to draw two goblets of mead from the nearest vat, Thornil slipped behind the line of carved wooden columns that held up half the roof. Once out of sight behind them, he made for the nearest exit from the King's Hall. The door he selected led not outdoors, but rather deeper into the Keep.

Per his promise, Oethur followed.

Once they had reached the corridor beyond the Hall, the corporal stopped. He turned, handed Oethur one of the goblets, and raised his own goblet.

"To the memory of King Ulfered."

"To Father."

The goblets *clunked*—they were made of wood—and each man drank. Thornil dashed his off in one draft.

"My lord," he said after lowering his goblet, "thank you for coming. I realize my request was impertinent, but I was told to give my message to you alone."

"A message for me? From whom?"

"Bishop Treowin, my lord. He begs you come to him tonight, if at all possible. He says it is a matter of some urgency."

"He *says?* I am told the bishop is no longer capable of speech."

187

"Begging your pardon, my lord, but he spoke to me himself."

"Who spoke to you?"

"Bishop Treowin, my lord."

"You are certain of this, corporal? It was *the bishop* who spoke to you?"

"Yes, my lord. Had it been anybody else, I would not have come."

"Not one of his servants?"

"No, my lord."

"Not another priest?"

Thornil looked puzzled. "No. My lord, I do not understand . . ."

"Neither do I. You'd better lead me to him at once."

"Yes, my lord. This way."

Oethur kept his eyes sharp as he followed the guardsman down the corridor. If Thornil was lying or deceived, then the odds were that Oethur was walking into a trap. If, however, the guardsman was telling the truth . . .

I'd rather have the trap.

With a silent prayer, Oethur reached down and eased his dagger in its sheath.

After a few minutes' silent passage, they reached the head of the stairs leading down to the Keep's dungeons. Thornil drew up short and turned. The man's face was pale, and it glistened with streaks of sweat. When he spoke, his voice was low.

"My lord, I beg leave to go no farther."

"Why have you brought me to the dungeons, corporal? Is this a trap?"

"If it is a trap, my lord, it is not of my making."

"What do you mean?"

"Please, my lord. Let me go. I have a wife and child . . ."

Oethur had Thornil pinned to the wall in an instant. He pressed the point of his dagger under the man's chin.

188

"If your next words don't make perfect sense, corporal, they will be your last."

Thornil gulped through his words.

"The bishop . . . is being held in the dungeons."

"Held by whom?"

Thornil's eyes widened in fear, and he closed them as he spoke his next words. "Begging your pardon, my lord . . . by the Prince Regent."

Oethur released Thornil and stepped back. *Can this really be happening?*

Much as he wished otherwise, there had been no lie in the corporal's words. As the younger man regained his breath, Oethur scowled.

Worse than a trap.

"Go." He pointed with his dagger down the corridor away from the dungeons. "And if you want to protect your family, speak of this to no one."

"My lord, I cannot."

"What?"

"I cannot go."

"Why not?"

"I was assigned to help guard the bishop, my lord. If I just disappear, they will know it was I who led you here."

Oethur considered. "That is a fair point."

"My lord, if I might make a suggestion?"

"Please."

"The other guard sent me to filch some mead from the reception. If you were to strike me unconscious, leave the goblets, and take my sword . . ."

"They will not suspect you."

"Exactly, my lord."

Oethur frowned. "There has to be another way."

"My lord, there is no time. When the king's reception ends, the Prince Regent will return. Your opportunity to help the bishops will be lost." Thornil's tone was insistent. "Please, my lord, you must strike me. The hilt of your dagger should serve."

Despite the mounting tension, the ghost of a smile found its way to Oethur's expression. "That has to be the strangest request I've ever heard. Very well, Thornil."

"One last thing, my lord."

"Yes?"

"Godspeed, my lord."

"And to you, Thornil."

It was the work of moments. The corporal turned away and shut his eyes. Oethur drew his knife and struck the man on the back of the neck. Hard.

Thornil crumpled to the floor.

Sleep well.

Drawing the man's sword, Oethur descended the steps. They were old and worn—and quite familiar. These dungeons had not been used as a proper prison for generations—not since the expansion of the castle and the subsequent conversion of the Keep into a royal residence. But Oethur and both of his brothers knew these depths well, for they had imprisoned one another on countless occasions as boys.

Yet it was no child's errand that took Oethur to the dungeons now. As the winding stair carried him lower, his mind raced with questions:

Had Treowin committed some secret crime? Why had Aeldred lied about the man's ability to speak? And if he had lied about Treowin, what about his accusations against Ciolbail?

A dark line of reasoning began to form in Oethur's mind. *No, not that. . . . Please, Aesus, anything but that!*

Reaching the bottom of the stairs, he passed down the dank corridor and rounded a corner. At the far end of this passage, he saw a small lamp. As he approached, he saw that it stood before the last door in the corridor—a door flanked by a tall man.

"Is that you, Thornil?" called the man.

"My name is not Thornil." Oethur stepped into the edge of the light, the sword held before him.

In an instant, the guard had his own sword drawn and ready. But as he squinted, recognition dawned.

"Lord Oethur! What are you—?"

"The same." Oethur took a step forward. "Whom do you hold in this cell?"

The guard stepped between Oethur and the door, his sword raised.

Oethur lowered his sword. "I said, whom do you have in this cell? Answer me!"

"You must go back."

Oethur's tone was incredulous. "You forget yourself, guard. Lower your sword and step aside at once."

The guard's grip tightened on his sword. "Go back, my lord. *Now.*"

Before Oethur could respond, footsteps rushed down the corridor behind him.

"What is going on down—Lord Oethur! What are you doing here?"

Oethur turned his head, and two things happened at once.

The first was that he saw Erworn, his brother's chaplain, standing in the corridor behind him. The expression on his face was unreadable, but there was no mistaking the man's scarlet robe.

The second was that he felt the air stir behind him.

The guard!

Oethur wheeled, but he had realized his mistake too late. The gauntleted fist caught him in mid-turn, striking him in the temple.

Everything went black.

rien walked along the narrow road, the morning sun pouring down its benevolent rays upon her back and before her path. Spring was coming to Dyfann. Everywhere she looked, new life was returning to field and forest. Birds sang in the trees beside the road. The gentle breezes stirring their blossoming boughs came away laden with the scent of pollen. On every side, the hills were undergoing a transformation—exchanging their washed-out winter smocks for the verdant garb of spring. New life was making its annual return to western Aeld Gowan.

Urien smiled. Despite her grim errand, she could not help but enjoy this morning. There were so many familiar sights and smells! All around her, her homeland echoed songs of her lost infancy. It made Urien's heart ache.

Why did it all go so sour? Why could I not have grown up here? Why did you ever carry us away from this happy place, Somnadh? Why, brother?

But she knew the answer.

The Dark Faith.

Your heart is darkened, brother—blackened and charred by your service to a false goddess. Somewhere, at some point, you turned against your conscience. As a result, your heart turned wooden. Wooden and wretched, like the Mother herself.

A line from Holy Writ in Donnach's Volume whispered to her from the recesses of memory:

"The idols of the nations, silver and gold, are the work of the hands of men. A mouth have they, but speak they not; eyes have they, but see they not. . . . Just as they, their makers become; those who trust them—every one!"

Urien brushed away a tear from her eye and pulled the red hood up over her head.

It was noon when Urien reached the outskirts of Cyrdol. She had never visited the village before this day. Indeed, she would not even have known its name, but for a passing forester carrying his bundle to the village market.

Yet for all its strangeness, there was also an underlying sameness. First, there were the similar clusters of small homes, built in the traditional Dyfanni style. Then there were the familiar, roving bands of children. The girls sang songs as they gathered flowers and herded animals, while the boys shouted taunts and waved sticks at the girls—and one another. But for the years and distance, Cyrdol might have been the same village below the hill fort at Banr Cluidan, where her father had served as priest—and she had spent her first years.

It was as though she had come home.

Another similarity between Banr Cluidan and Cyrdol was the weekly market. It was into this that Urien now walked. The wide village green had more or less vanished, and in its place there stood a somewhat haphazard collection of temporary booths and parked wagons. Most sellers were offering the results of their indoor winter industry: knit stockings, woven blankets, and the like. A few others, such as the man who passed Urien on the road, sold firewood. With winter still a recent memory, there was nothing like fresh produce. Nevertheless, there was but a modest representation of fruits and vegetables assembled from winter stores.

Urien tried to purchase some of these, but the merchants refused.

"I'll accept no payment from you, brother."

"Please, I want to buy food. I have had a long journey, and—"

"Take whatever you like, but take it as a gift."

"What?" Urien stared. "I cannot do that."

"I know it's meager enough fare. Winter hasn't left much. But what I've got is yours."

"That's not what I mean. How will you feed your family if you give away your wares?"

"This is a test, isn't it?" The merchant eyed her with a wry smile. "To see if we were paying attention at chapel last market day? To see if we are loyal to the New Faith?"

"I don't know what you're talking about."

"Sure you don't, brother. Sure you don't." The merchant winked. "Well, I remember what the preacher said: 'To give to the Order earns the smile of the Son, and to earn the smile of the Son buys the favor of the Mother.'"

"Who said that?"

"One of your own order. It was just last week, in that very chapel!" The merchant pointed.

Following the finger, Urien saw something she had never seen before in Dyfann.

There, at the far end of the village square, stood an Aesusian chapel.

Here? In Dyfann?

It was not a large structure. Not anything like the cathedral at Marfesbury. But there could be no mistake. The thatch-roofed building, with the modest bell tower topped by a cross, was an Aesusian church.

"See, I remember," said the merchant as Urien regarded the chapel in silence. "It's no good trying to pay me. Take as much as you will, and I'll see you there this evening."

"Thank you." Urien's words were absent, distracted. She picked up a carrot and walked toward the chapel.

In some respects, the little church was just like the chapel at Urras Monastery. Entering through the narthex, Urien made sure she was alone before lowering her cowl and looking around. There was a broad center aisle, flanked on both sides by rows of pews. Light entered from small windows near the top of the walls, and at the front of the nave there was a raised platform.

Yet it was at the front of the chapel that the similarities ended. For whereas the back wall of the apse had been bare at Urras, here in Dyfann there hung a large, scarlet banner. On it was embroidered in white an ensign Urien knew all too well: a cross whose bottom divided into the roots of a tree.

The symbol of the Mordruui!

What was *that* doing in an Aesusian church?

Differences continued as Urien lowered her eyes to the dais itself. Whereas a lectern had occupied the central place in the Urras chapel, here in Dyfann there was an altar. And whereas in Urras the central object was a copy of Holy Writ, here there sat upon the altar a strange-looking statuette.

Urien walked forward to get a better look.

The figure on the altar was an image of the Mother, carved from a single thick stump of oak. Urien recognized it at once: a precise replica of the Dyfanni Goddess Tree.

But what is it doing here? And what is that in the lower branches?

Stooping down, Urien saw that the lower branches of the image had been carved to look as though they bent together to form a cradle. In this cradle there was a baby, and above the baby another branch of the Mother formed the shape of a cross.

The words of the merchant in the market came back to her: *"To earn the smile of the Son buys the favor of the Mother."*

Urien gasped, recoiling from the image as though from a serpent.

Regaining her feet, she had just turned toward the back of the nave when she saw the door open. She only had time to pull up her hood before another red monk entered the chapel, leading a troop of children.

Seeing her, the hooded monk paused. "Greetings, my brother!" he said at last, still sounding somewhat startled.

"Greetings." Urien's heart pounded in her chest.

"I am surprised to find another of our Order here in Cyrdol."

"I only just arrived, brother"—Urien had little time for an elaborate ruse—"and am only passing through. I am on my way to Banr Cluidan for the Feast of the Sacred Tree."

The monk nodded. "You have yet a great distance to traverse. But praise the Mother, there is plenty of time for it. I myself intend to make the journey a few days hence."

"Brother Claghul." One of the children was tugging at the monk's robe.

Claghul leaned down. "Yes, dear one?"

"When are we going to *start*?"

"Right now." The monk turned back to Urien. "My brother, I would speak with you further before you depart. There is an important message for Banr Cluidan, and you are traveling thence sooner than I. But first, I must conduct these children through their catechesis. Will you join us?"

Urien nodded. What choice did she have?

She followed as Claghul led the children down the nave, out a door in the transept, and into a small walled garden.

There he and Urien sat on a wide bench, while the children formed a semicircle on the grass around them.

"Would you like to ask the questions?" Claghul turned to Urien. "You will be delighted to see how well they have learned."

Urien shook her head. "I have had a long journey, my brother. I am weary. Please, you go ahead."

Claghul nodded and turned back to the children. "All right, children. Who wants to show Brother—" He turned to Urien. "My apologies, brother. I did not get your name."

"Firin." Now that she was in Dyfann, Urien dared not use her true name. But she doubted anybody would recognize the name of her father's *deaclaid*.

Claghul turned back to the children. "Who wants to show Brother Firin how much they've learned?"

Every hand shot up. Claghul selected one—a little girl—and they began.

"What is your comfort in life and death?"

"That I belong to the Mother and Son."

"Who is the Source of all life and death?"

"The Mother who lives and the Son who died."

"What is the name of your Mother?"

"Genna."

"What is the name of her Son?"

"Aesus."

"Very good." Claghul nodded. "How do we honor the Son?"

"We honor the Son by following his example."

"And what example did he set for us?"

"He showed us how to honor the Mother."

"And how do we honor the Mother?"

"We honor the Mother in life and in death."

"How do we honor the Mother in life?"

"By obeying the priest."

"Exactly!" Claghul clapped his hands. "How do we honor the Mother in death?"

"By a normal or special death."

"What is a normal death?"

"A normal death is part of life, the way we return to the Mother."

"Yes, it is. How many special deaths may honor the Mother?"

"Two."

"Which is the first?"

"To give my blood to protect the Mother."

"A very important and special way." Claghul smiled. "And which is the second?"

"To give my blood to nourish the Mother."

"A rare honor given only to some." Claghul turned his faceless gaze to Urien. "Did I not tell you they have learned well, brother?"

Only too well.

Urien wished she had brought the knife from Marfesbury cloister. *I'd give you a "special death," brother.*

Several hours later, Urien was alone on the road to Banr Cluidan. Cyrdol was a distant speck behind her. As the sun neared the western horizon, she shivered—and not only from the cool air.

What she had witnessed in Cyrdol chilled her blood. The image in the sanctuary had been bad enough, but the catechism...

She shuddered. That sweet little girl reciting "give my blood to nourish the Mother" had made her want to bury Claghul. Even now Urien trembled with rage at the memory.

The teaching of the red monk was not the teaching of Holy Writ. Nor was it a "New Faith." It was the Dark Faith using new words. Aesusian words. Putting it under a roof with a cross was worse than mere fraud ...

It is an affront to Aesus.

18

ethur awoke to a throbbing headache. He tried to put a hand to his temple, but it would not cooperate. Something was weighing it down. There was an odd clanking noise when he tried, but his hand would not budge more than a few inches.

Disoriented, he opened his eyes.

Darkness.

"Where am I?"

"You're not dead, if that's what you're wondering," said a voice from nearby.

"At least, not yet," said a second.

Oethur turned his head toward the sounds. The voices had both come from somewhere to his right.

"Who's there?"

"Oethur, it is Treowin."

Treowin!

At the sound of the bishop's name, Oethur's memory revived. The king's reception. Thornil's message. And then, finally . . .

He groaned.

No wonder his head hurt. And no wonder his hands would not move. They were not weighed down—they were shackled. Which meant only one thing . . .

"I'm in the dungeon."

"We're happy to see you, too," said the second voice.

"Ciolbail, give over." Treowin's voice was gruff. "He got here trying to help us. And besides, we can't *see* anything in this darkness."

Ciolbail!

"Bishop Ciolbail, you are here too?"

"I am."

"Your Graces," Oethur began, the pain in his head increasing, "I do not understand."

"I am sorry, Oethur," said Treowin. "I should not have sent for you."

"Please, Your Grace, do not apologize. Just explain what is going on."

"How much do you know already?"

"I know nothing as to why you are here, Your Grace. But Heclaid of Lothair sent Morumus and me here to look for you and to seek the whereabouts of Bishop Ciolbail."

"Me?" Ciolbail was surprised.

"You have been accused of conspiring against the Mersian king, Your Grace."

"What?"

"An attempt was made upon King Wodic and his bride on their wedding day. The attempt failed, but they found one of your brer tokens sewn into the coat of the would-be assassins."

"Oh no." The Lothairin bishop whispered a prayer. "This is bad."

"It's far worse than you think, Your Grace. Do you know what has happened in Caeldora?"

"We have been locked in this dungeon since our return from the Court of Saint Cephan." This was Treowin. "We have heard nothing of the world beyond this hole."

"Since the Court? But that was months ago!"

"We've noticed." Ciolbail's laugh was bitter.

"What has happened in Caeldora?"

"Abbot Grahem and Bishop Anathadus have been murdered. Lorudin Abbey is destroyed."

Both bishops gasped.

"*No!*"

"*It cannot be!*"

"It is so, Your Graces."

There was a long silence. When Treowin spoke again, his voice was shaking.

"Perhaps you'd better go first, Oethur. Tell us everything."

When Oethur had finished, there was a very long silence.

"These tidings . . . very grave indeed." All the sardonic humor had gone out of Ciolbail's voice.

"Monstrous," Treowin agreed.

"I mourn especially for Donnach and Morumus. Both of them were such promising young churchmen."

"But to die fighting the darkness, and to lay down one's life for another . . ." Treowin's voice nearly broke, and he finished in a whisper. "May we all die as well."

Oethur nodded. His cheeks burned with hot rivulets, and it was several minutes before he could speak. "There is something I still do not understand, Your Graces."

"What is that?"

"Why has my brother imprisoned you both here?"

"As to Ciolbail, it appears that you yourself have brought the answer, Oethur. They are using his token to implicate Lothair. It is the perfect pretext for Mersex to invade the North."

"But that would mean Aeldred is in league . . ."

"Exactly."

"But why?"

There was a heavy sigh. "The answer to that underlies my own imprisonment."

"What do you mean?"

"Your father spoke to me before he fell sick."

"Suspiciously sick," added Ciolbail.

"He did? When, Your Grace? I've been told that Father fell sick last autumn."

"It was around that time, just after the two of us returned from the Court."

"I take it you had no difficulties in your passage, then?"

"None. Why do you ask?"

"My brother said the Trathari cut out your tongue."

"Would that they would cut out his!" snapped Ciolbail.

Bishop Treowin grunted. "They did no such thing, of course. Thanks to Ciolbail, the Trathari treated us with the utmost courtesy. They conducted us to Toberstan without incident and departed. From Toberstan we came overland by horse. All told, I believe that the journey from Versaden here to Grindangled took just over three weeks. A few days after that, your father drew me aside."

"And what did he say?"

"He told me that he had learned something awful about your brother, something so terrible that Aeldred could no longer inherit his crown. He intended to change the succession."

Oethur was shocked. "That hasn't been done in generations."

"A fact of which the king was well aware. He wanted my help in persuading the seven lords."

"Whom did he intend to name? One of them?"

"*You.*"

The sudden, harsh voice came from a different direction. A shaft of light flooded into the dungeon. The cover came off the window in the door, and a moment later the door itself swung open. Four men strode into the chamber, two of them holding bright lamps.

After the total darkness, the lamplight was blinding to Oethur. But though it took several minutes for his eyes to recover, he did not need sight to recognize that voice.

"Aeldred."

"Hello, brother."

"Aeldred, what have you done?"

"Nothing you would not have done to me, brother."

"You're wrong, Aeldred."

"Am I?" The Prince Regent's voice grew angry. "For years you have corresponded with *my* betrothed, intending to steal away her heart. Did you think I did not know?"

"Brother, I never . . . Rhianwyn and I began to write after Alfered's death. I never intended . . . when I met her in Dunross just a fortnight ago, she was talking about your upcoming wedding. She was thinking about *you*, brother—not I. And I might add that she was worried!"

"So you admit you went to her in Dunross," Aeldred snapped. "Your guilt is plain."

Bishop Treowin's voice was harsh. "And what of *your* guilt? Fratricide? Murdering your brother to steal his bride!" The bishop turned to Oethur. "This is what your father learned just before he fell sick."

Oethur was thunderstruck. *No! It cannot . . .*

But by now, Oethur's eyes had adjusted. In the illumination of the lamplight, he could see his brother's cruel face. And standing beside him, he saw Erworn. The chaplain's funeral vestments were gone . . .

Oethur hissed at the sight of the telltale scarlet robe. "Aeldred, you are in league with the Mordruui." It was not a question.

"Yes."

"You murdered Alfered?" It was still hard to believe.

"Yes."

"And the Lothairin lord who died about the same time, Raudorn?"

"A more elaborate ruse, but yes."

Anger flared in Oethur's breast. "And Father? Did you arrange that as well?"

"Of course. A compound of nightshade, delivered in diluted form over a long period. Anything stronger and Lildas would have detected it. That man is too fine a physician."

"But *why?*"

"Why what?"

"Why did you kill them? Your own brother and father."

"Don't be a child, Oethur. So long as Alfered lived, I could never be king. And as Treowin has already told you, Father intended to change the succession."

Aeldred's calculated coldness made Oethur's blood boil. "You have betrayed everything, Brother." His voice shook. "Not just your family, and not just your people. You have betrayed our God."

"God!" Aeldred spat. "This isn't a monastery, Oethur, and I'm not afraid of your religion. Your so-called 'Holy Writ' is nothing but a collection of myths—a fabrication intended to perpetuate the weak by terrifying the strong. I renounced it all long ago! The true Aesus was a servant of the Mother. It is she whom I serve."

"A tree? An idol of wood? You are a fool, Aeldred."

"Am I? Your god would have prevented me from wearing the crown. The Mother has placed it upon my brow. Was that the choice of a fool? Was it the work of an idol?"

"The white tree burned in Caeldora. Is that the power of a god?"

"By the same token you condemn your own Aesus—for he also died."

"That's different. His tomb is empty."

"Just another fraud intended to pervert the truth. Are you so blind, Oethur?" Aeldred shook his head. "There is no resurrection. There is no need! Sons and daughters may die. Seedlings may perish. Yet it matters not, for all return to the same Source. Death brings return to the Mother. It is only she who lives forever."

"You are worse than a fool, Aeldred. If God does not strike you down first, I swear to you that I will."

"You are as weak and pathetic as your god, Oethur—and no more of a threat. No, Brother. Let me tell you what is going to happen. Tonight, the three of you will go south." He turned to the bishops. "The two of you will bow to the Mother and sign allegiance to the Archbishop of Mereclestour. You, Ciolbail, will then be executed for your part in the plot against King Wodic. As for you, Treowin, you will attest that Ciolbail confessed to you that he conspired under the order of King Heclaid, and you will issue an edict calling for God's judgment upon Lothair."

Treowin met Aeldred's gaze without flinching. "Never."

"We fear neither death nor torture," added Ciolbail.

Aeldred ignored them. "By this time I will have been crowned king. And receiving this edict as a faithful son of the Church, I will have no choice but to comply." He smiled. "With the full support of Mersex to the south, Heclaid will be surrounded. He will have no choice but to surrender or perish. I will have my bride with no further delay."

"Rhianwyn will never marry you now!" Oethur hissed.

Aeldred wheeled on him. "With you finally out of the way, Oethur, she will!" His eyes flashed pure malice. "As for you, you too will go south—but only until you can be bound over for Dyfann. You are not going to Mereclestour, but to my true brother—the Hand of the Mother himself. You will look upon the goddess, and you will tremble!"

"Your goddess is a heap of ash, Aeldred.

"No, Oethur. Your friends may have murdered her daughter, but the Mother herself lives. Within the Ring of Stars, she lives forever! I have beheld her beauty myself, not six weeks gone! And you will, too, Oethur. You will look upon the goddess, and then—only then—will you die."

Am I dead?

At first, Morumus was not sure.

After what had seemed an everlasting fall through the mists of Fheil's Delf, he had struck something. Hard. Pain had exploded everywhere in his body, and the world had disappeared . . .

> *"Thou certainly hast pushed me unto falling, but the Lord hast helped me;*
> *"The Lord be my strength and song, and he is become to me salvation."*

The singing woke him. But when he opened his eyes, Morumus found himself suspended in thick mist. He was unable to move, yet felt a gentle rocking motion lulling him . . . back and forth, back and forth.

The singing certainly fit the hypothesis of death. But why was Everlight so grey?

A light!

There was a light next—a hazy orb approaching him through the all-pervasive grey. As it drew nearer, he saw that a man dressed all in brown carried it. His clothes were the same brown Morumus himself had worn at Lorudin Abbey.

Yet it was not until the man's face appeared that Morumus was sure he had died.

Abbot Grahem!

"*I shall not die, for I shall live; and I shall recount the deeds of the Lord!*"

Again, Morumus woke to the sound of singing . . .

I am not dead.

Despite the singing, he was in too much pain to have reached Everlight. His body was sore all over, and chills shook him. Beyond this, he felt a ravenous yawning from the pit of his stomach.

I am hungry.

Morumus opened his eyes. He was definitely not dead. *But then where am I?*

Wherever he was, it was dim. The light, such as there was, was flickering and thin. Yet it was enough to show Morumus a rock ceiling above him.

I am in a cave of some sort. He tried to push himself up on his elbows. He failed.

He sank back down into his bed—soft, whatever it was.

"Hello?"

"Hello!" returned a somewhat distant voice. There was a sound of footsteps, but the owner of the voice seemed to be padding around him, rather than nearer to him. "Welcome back to the land of the living."

"How long have I been asleep?"

"More than a week."

A week!

"What happened?"

"You fell from the upper bridge. Or rather, you fell *with* the upper bridge. The whole thing came crashing down. Thankfully, most of it missed the lower bridge. And thankfully, *you* didn't."

"A lower bridge. Thank God."

"Indeed. You sustained many injuries as it was. How do you feel now?"

"Sore. And hungry. But alive."

The voice chuckled. "I've had some broth waiting all morning, in the hope you might wake. A bit of that should help."

The footsteps receded a short distance, and Morumus could hear liquid being ladled from one container into another.

"So tell me," said the voice as it returned. "What happened? I heard a great din . . ."

"It was the Dree."

The footsteps stopped. "What did you say?"

"I said it was the Dree. We were pursuing them, and they cut the bridge."

"How do you know that name?"

"I learned it from my uncle."

"Who is your uncle?"

"His name is Nerias."

"Nerias . . ." The voice shook as it repeated the name. "I believe I once knew that name." The footsteps picked up again, but now they were quicker.

A moment later, a face appeared over Morumus. It bore an intense frown, and its eyes scrutinized him as though searching for something. It was a face Morumus had seen before.

"Abbot Grahem?" Now Morumus's voice shook. "But how . . . ? You are dead!"

The eyes stopped scanning him. "My name is Gaebroth. But I know the name of Grahem . . ." He looked up and seemed to focus on some distant time or place. "It is connected somehow to the other name you mentioned, Nerias. But I cannot remember how."

Gaebroth. Abbot Grahem's lost brother. Could it really be?

"I know how, sir. If you will help me sit up and hand me that broth, I will tell you what I know."

An hour later, the bowl sat empty. On either side of it sat Gaebroth and Morumus. The older man was shaking his head.

"I don't remember any of it, you know. I remember that I was once a monk, and I can remember long portions of Holy Writ. And the names you mentioned—Anathadus, Nerias, even my brother Grahem—these I can recall, now that you say them. But the events of which you speak might have happened to another man. My memory of them is gone."

"What happened?"

"The other name you mentioned. The Dree. They did it. These many years I had forgotten their name. But I am well acquainted with their works."

"I don't understand."

"You tell me that I once spent years searching far and wide for knowledge of the Dree, do you not?"

"That is what Abbot Grahem told me. He said you were last seen at the monastery in Toberstan."

"And Toberstan is where, in relation to where we are now?"

"We are still in the hill country, I take it?"

Gaebroth chuckled. "Where else?"

"Then Toberstan is somewhere south and east, beside the sea."

"Ah." The older man nodded. "Then I must have learned something in Toberstan that sent me into these mountains. This is only a guess, mind—but it would explain how I got here."

"You don't remember any of it?"

Gaebroth shook his head. "I remember nothing prior to waking up in Cuuranyth."

"Cuuranyth?"

"That's the Dree's name for their mountain stronghold. I call it the Shadow's Nest."

"Where is that?"

"Here, in the high hill country."

"Here?"

"Well, not *right* here. About three days' journey to the west. It lies near the headwaters of a river that runs north, down out of the mountains into Lothair."

"The River Mathway."

"You know it?"

Know it? "My family's holding is at the bottom of that river vale."

"Ah."

A thought struck Morumus. "Is there a white tree in this Shadow's Nest, Gaebroth?"

"A tree? No. There is nothing green in that place. Only darkness and fire . . . and pain." He closed his eyes.

"You were tortured."

Gaebroth nodded, his eyes still shut. "All of us were."

"There were others?"

"Yes. Mostly children, but some adults. They gave us little water, and for food we had only a thick gruel made from their vile herb."

"Their herb?" Morumus's attention caught fast on the word.

"Oh yes. Nomergenna, they call it."

"Nomergenna?" Urien had used the same name for the herb she had described.

"The herb I harvested from the Mother is called nomergenna, Morumus. I do not know how they use it, but there is nothing more valuable to the Mordruui."

"I don't know what it is or where it comes from," answered Gaebroth, "but they have a whole magazine—a dedicated store-room—of it in Cuuranyth. It is the source of their power."

The source of their power!

A chill ran up Morumus's spine. This was the clue he had sought for so many years. But what did it mean? "It comes from the tree they worship. But tell me, Gaebroth, how does it work?"

"Work?"

"How do they use this nomergenna?"

"They don't."

"But you said it is the source of their power."

"It is. But they don't use it on *themselves*, Morumus—at least, not that I could tell. They use it on *us*."

"I don't understand, Gaebroth."

"Nomergenna is what makes you obey the song."

Morumus's heart skipped a beat. "What did you say?"

"I said nomergenna is what makes you obey the song."

"You are certain of this?"

If he was, then Morumus's long quest had just reached a turning point.

"I am. The day I escaped, there was a child who was too sick to eat his gruel. The Dree could not make him see or do anything. They grew so angry that they murdered him on the spot. Under my own severe tortures that day, I didn't make the connection at the time. But I am convinced of it. Unless you ingest nomergenna, the dark song cannot command you."

Morumus nodded. His mind raced . . .

"Oh, how they tortured us with that serpent's song," Gaebroth continued, "that evil, incessant, cacophonous hiss! Under its power we were made to see terrible things." The old man opened his eyes. "We were made to *do* terrible things, too—to ourselves and to one another—things too awful to describe."

"There is no need." Morumus could only manage a hoarse whisper. "I have witnessed the power of the Dark Speech."

As Morumus told Gaebroth what had happened to his father, something clicked in his own memory. Something had happened before the Dree had ever appeared on that infamous night. Early that afternoon, while in pursuit of what they had believed to be Nornish raiders, his father's company had stopped to warn a shepherd about the threat. In seeming gratitude, the shepherd had given Morumus's father two flagons of strangely spiced mead . . .

The 'spice' must have been nomergenna.

Raudorn and his men had been drugged in advance.

It all fit.

Gaebroth agreed. "It is just as I said."

For a few minutes after this, neither man spoke.

"How did you escape Cuuranyth, Gaebroth?"

"I tried to take my own life."

"What?"

"I do not excuse it, mind, but I was desperate. You see, the Dree would not kill me. They killed everybody else, in due course. But not me. Oh no, not me. They had other plans for me."

"What other plans?"

"They were trying to convert me."

"They meant to persuade you of the Dark Faith? By torture?"

"Persuade me?" Gaebroth shook his head. "No, Morumus. They meant to force me by their dark power. And they were unremitting. Day after day, night after night, there was no respite. They put me through everything—even erasing my memory in the hope of erasing my faith. But it didn't work."

"Do you think it could have worked?"

"I hope not, but I do not know. To my shame, I decided to take my own life instead of waiting to find out."

"But instead you survived. How?"

"In Cuuranyth there is a deep pool of water that acts as a sort of cistern for the place. We had to walk past it every day as we went between our cells and their torture chambers. It was here that they watered us when they felt we needed it to survive. Well, it was one such day when I escaped. My tortures had been excruciating that day. As I knelt down and stared into the water's surface, I saw my opportunity to end it. I threw myself into the water."

"You tried to drown yourself."

"Yes. And I would have succeeded, too. The shackles on our ankles and wrists were iron and sank me to the bottom just as I expected."

"But then how did you survive?"

Gaebroth smiled. "At the very bottom of the pool there is a small tunnel."

"A tunnel? In a cistern?"

"It was not a stone cistern, Morumus. It was a natural pool. Cuuranyth is a network of caves."

"But still, would not such a tunnel have caused the pool to drain?"

"No, because it led through the rock to another, hidden pool—in a cavern unknown to the Dree. From there I found a way out."

"So you escaped Cuuranyth. But why remain in the Deasmor all these years?"

"Where else would I go? Until you woke up an hour ago, the only things I knew about my past were my name and some passages from Holy Writ. I know nothing of the surrounding lands or peoples. Besides, if I stayed here I could surveil the Dree. I could learn their paths, track their movements, and even slay the few of them who dared travel alone. This I have done these many years, waiting and watching against the day when I might find help to storm Cuuranyth and burn the magazine of nomergenna. Without it, they are powerless—at least until they harvest more."

"Will nomergenna burn?"

"Oh yes. It is rather volatile around fire."

Which explained the speed with which the white tree in Caeldora had burned. And then there was what the boy Colba had told them in Dorslaan . . .

"I cannot explain it, but I saw it with my own eyes. The chapel exploded. The explosion itself sent burning fragments raining down upon our village, and there was a great cloud of glowing smoke."

"Perhaps the day to storm Cuuranyth has finally come."

Gaebroth looked at him. "I had hoped it might come *soon*, little brother. But you have just returned from the brink of death and need time to mend."

"Three days' journey is plenty of time."

"Three days?" Gaebroth scoffed. "More like three weeks."

"There is no time for such delay."

"Why do you say that?"

"The Dree whom we were chasing at Fheil's Delf kidnapped three children. We managed to rescue two before they cut the bridge, but the Dree got away with the third. The longer we wait to strike the Shadow's Nest, the longer we leave her to the mercy of those who have none."

Gaebroth stood up, wrath clouding his gracious face. "You will eat broth while I make preparations. We leave in the morning."

20

"Riders approaching, sir!"

The Lumana's exclamation came in a low, urgent tone.

Beside him, lying belly down just below the lip of the hill, the Lunumbir trained his spyglass north. Through the glass, a little more than half a league's distance away, he saw three riders on horseback, approaching his position at a trot. Two of the riders were guardsmen. Likewise, there could be no mistaking the third.

"Signal the others. Move to intercept. First two expendable, the third not. On my order. Acknowledge."

His subordinate pulled a small mirror from a messenger bag and lifted it above the rim of the hill. Being careful not to point it north, he aimed it toward the hill opposite them. One slow flash, two fast, another slow, then two more in quick succession.

The road over which the Lumanae kept watch this afternoon was the road between Toberstan—the southernmost city of Nornindaal—and Noppenham, one of the five royal cities of Mersex. At this location, about a day's journey south of the former, the terrain swelled like an aggravated sea and the road was forced to pass through many tight squeezes and uncomfortable twists.

It was the perfect place for an ambush.

The Lunumbir saw the return signal from the far side of the road. Four quick flashes, then two slower.

Acknowledged. Await mark. Two and one. Moving to intercept.

"This is it." The Lunumbir and his attendant slid backward, dropping below the brink of the hill before standing. Once out of sight of the road, they crept along the back slope with all possible haste. Their targets would arrive within minutes.

The intercept point was a natural trench. There the road passed through a miniature canyon created by the near juncture of two lumpish hills. This trench was at least a hundred yards long, with walls of sheer rock on both sides—walls about a dozen yards high, but no more than ten across at the widest point.

The Lunumbir waited until the riders entered the trench. The two soldiers seemed to tense as they approached its mouth, almost as if they could sense his presence. They looked about them with palpable unease, and the lead man called a halt.

"Junior, ride to the far end and make sure all's well."

Though he looked none too pleased with the order, the younger soldier complied. "All's clear!" he called when he had reached the far end.

The remaining soldier gestured at his charge. "You first, if you please, sir. Just in case."

They resumed their forward pace.

Crouched behind some half-buried boulders near the entrance to the canyon, the Lunumbir and his assistant watched the men enter the trench.

"Now."

At the Lunumbir's imperative whisper, the Lumana grabbed his bag and scrabbled up to the near rim of the trench.

As his assistant flashed the signal, the Lunumbir raised his crossbow and began counting backward . . .

Ten . . . nine . . . eight . . . seven . . .

The riders were well within the canyon now.

Five . . . four . . . three . . .

He stepped into the open behind them. The soldier waiting at the far end caught a glimpse of him and shouted to his fellows. But it was too late.

Two . . . one . . .

The bolt raced from the Lunumbir's crossbow. It took the soldier riding sweep right between his unprotected shoulder blades. The man arched his back with a harsh grunt, then slumped onto the neck of his mount. The horse rushed forward.

At the far end of the trench, the Lunumbir's men gave similar quick treatment to the man riding post.

The third man, seeing the lead soldier fall, wheeled his horse.

In that exact moment, the horse carrying his other escort— who was now dead—ran past him the opposite direction. Yet his mount was well disciplined and did not rear. He squared it off and advanced on the Lunumbir.

The Lunumbir stared at the mounted man.

A hooded, red-cloaked man.

"You have done a very foolish thing, brigand," came the menacing voice as the horse walked closer. The red monk reached down and drew a long stone knife. "If you do not let me pass, you will not live to regret it."

The Lunumbir stood his ground. The red monk had almost reached the near rim.

"Very well." The red monk lowered the knife. "Have it your way, fool!"

But in the instant before the monk spurred his horse forward, the signal Lumana dropped a weighted net upon him from the canyon wall above. The net covered the monk in a hopeless tangle of rope, and as his horse sprang forward he tumbled backward. There was a heavy thud as he hit the ground.

"Get the horse," said the Lunumbir when his man joined him a minute later over the unconscious monk. "We'll need it to carry this bundle back to camp."

"Just as you had hoped, sir," said the cheerful signal Lumana a short while later. He handed the Lunumbir a sealed paper. "A dispatch rider."

"Very good. How's Yens coming along?"

Yens was sitting a short distance away, undergoing the necessary modifications to his appearance. He had already donned the red monk's cloak. Now, while two of the others worked to cut and tonsure his hair, another was inking his wrists with careful copies of the red monk's tattoos. The red monk himself—stripped to his stockings, gagged, and bound fast to a tree—glared at his captors.

"He's bearing up well, sir. What shall we do with the prisoner?"

"Does he still refuse to cooperate?"

"Yes, sir."

"Make him uncomfortable, but do nothing for the moment until I have a look at this. Speaking of which, I'll need the hot knife to open the seal."

"Yes, sir. Right away."

A few minutes later the man returned with the knife, and the Lunumbir sat down to his work. Taking the sealed letter in one hand and holding it still, he pressed the edge of the knife against the base of the wax. It was delicate, slow labor. If the blade touched too long against the paper, it might scorch or even ignite it. But if he cut too high or too fast, he might destroy the seal or make its breach obvious. Doing either would compromise the whole operation.

For two months the Lumanae had been moving in Aeld Gowan. They had sailed from Caeldora in a small ship of their own, and this had given them the ability to move about the great island with considerable discretion and efficiency. This was just as well, for they had soon found that they needed every bit of both.

The Lunumbir had come to Aeld Gowan in the hope of finding Morumus and Oethur, the only surviving monks from Lorudin Abbey. From them he had hoped to glean some clue as to why the Red Order had so overreached their mandate, and taken such great risks as to attack the old order of the Church. The old order was a minor faction with no patrons at court and thus no political power. The reckless malice of the Red Order made no real sense, unless—unless!—it signified something deeper.

The Lunumbir believed in a direct connection between the health of the Church and the security of the empire. A threat to the former was by necessity a threat to the latter. And that was what he must learn from those monks: was there any potential threat to the empire?

What he had found upon his arrival had surprised even him.

The Red Order was working hand in glove with the king of Mersex!

Of all the nations in the western world, only Mersex posed a potential threat to the security of the empire. Her former king, Luca Wolfbane, had spent his life forging his country into just the kind of weapon that could bring down the empire. The emperor himself had breathed easier when news had arrived last year that Luca was dead. Common opinion at court had been that Luca's son and successor, Wodic, would be a weak shadow of his father. And perhaps he would have been, too, had he been left to himself.

Why had the Red Order, which played the emperor's loyal hand on Midgaddan, taken the part of his greatest rival on

Aeld Gowan? Why did they orchestrate the unification of Mersex and Dyfann? At what game were they playing?

Taken up with pursuing the answer to this question, the Lunumbir had quite put aside his original purpose in coming to Aeld Gowan. Finding the monks could wait. The security of the empire called both him and his men to a new task: penetrate the machinations of the Red Order.

It was to this end that the Lumanae had carried off this afternoon's ambush. Their hope in intercepting the riders had not been to murder soldiers; any Lumana worth his wages could do that before breakfast. Rather, they intended to place one of their own on the inside of the Red Order, in the vital and information-rich role of a dispatch bearer. Yens, who spoke both Mersian and Vilguran, would serve them well.

Thus it was that the Lunumbir had more or less forgotten the names of Morumus and Oethur. For all practical purposes, he had dismissed last year's events in Caeldora.

Until he saw the contents of the letter in his hand.

"What is this?"

Addressed from a Brother Erworn in Grindangled to the head of the Red Order in Noppenham, the letter detailed the transfer of several high-value prisoners. The first was one Bishop Ciolbail of Dunross, a Lothairin wanted for conspiring to murder the Mersian king and queen. The second was Bishop Treowin of Grindangled, a rebel against the authority of the Archbishop of Mereclestour, who had further conspired against King Aeldred of Nornindaal. The third was Oethur son of Ulfered. He too had conspired against King Aeldred, his brother, and was wanted by the Order for aiding those who had desecrated the Muthadannach in Caeldora.

The Lunumbir had never heard of Brother Erworn. He had no idea what was meant by "the Muthadannach in Caeldora," nor had he known that Nornindaal had a new king. Yet in the letter there were three things he did recognize from his previous Caeldoran investigation: the names Ciolbail, Treowin, and Oethur.

He read on.

The Red Order at Noppenham was to divide the prisoners. The bishops were to go south to the Archbishop of Mereclestour. Oethur, however, was to be taken west into Dyfann—to somebody called "the Hand of the Mother," at a place called "Banr Cluidan."

Hand of the Mother? Banr Cluidan?

The Lunumbir frowned. He hated terms he didn't know. This letter was full of them.

It was at this point that Erworn's letter ended. Yet another hand had added its own annotations at the bottom. These were in a quick, cramped script—as though dashed off in a few brief minutes.

Reading on, the Lunumbir understood why.

The prisoners had arrived at the secret chapterhouse in Toberstan this very day. One of them—Oethur—had been beaten for churlishness. They were to be fed and watered and then forwarded south under heavy guard before sunset. Noppenham should have them in three days.

This was the end of the letter, except for one last clerical note at the bottom: *"Dispatched via Brother Gwurn."*

The Lunumbir stood up and walked over to the bound red monk. "Ungag him." When his order was followed, he stared down at the monk. "Who is this Brother Erworn?"

Despite his awkward situation—bound to a tree wearing nothing but his woolens—the red monk glared up at him with beady, imperious eyes. "If you do not release me this moment, you will die a very slow death."

"I believe you've already made me that promise. Now, answer my question."

"No."

"No?"

225

Something flickered in the monk's eyes. Clearly he recognized the dangerous edge to the Lunumbir's voice.

Good.

The Lunumbir set down the letter and took up the red monk's stone knife. He pressed the point under the man's chin. "This is your last chance. What is a Muthadannach? Who is the Hand of the Mother?"

"Pray you don't live to find out." The monk turned away his face.

"Very well. Regag him." The Lunumbir stood, watching his prisoner. "We will find the answers without your help, Gwurn."

Despite his intent to reveal nothing, the monk flinched. The Lunumbir smiled. He had been right. This was Brother Gwurn.

He turned to Yens, whose disguise was now complete, and handed him the letter. "Read it, then reseal it. Until we meet again, your name is Gwurn. You know what to do. Tell them you were attacked by brigands. We'll leave the soldiers' bodies where they fell, in case they should check your story."

"Yes, sir." Yens pulled up his red hood and moved toward the monk's horse.

"The rest of you, make ready. We are returning to the ship."

"What about this one, sir?" A Lumana pointed to the bound monk. "Should I prepare a draft?"

"A draft?"

"To erase his memory, sir."

"There is no need for that. Let him keep his memory. It will do him no good."

"Sir?"

"The draft is for fools and neutrals. This man is neither."

The Lumana's eyes widened a fraction. "Sir, are you suggesting we—"

The Lunumbir cut him off with a wave of his hand. "You all saw what his order did at Lorudin. This red monk is an uncooperative enemy, and we carry no prisoners. Yet we are more merciful than they . . ."

He stooped down to look Gwurn in the eye. "Do you wish to confess your sins to Aesus?"

Through his gag, the red monk only sneered.

The Lunumbir stood up and turned away. "Cut his throat, and leave him for the birds."

PART IV

SCARLET BISHOP

21

"**A**re you sure you want to do this *now*, my lord?" The grey-haired man arched a bushy eyebrow. "Are you not to depart within the hour?"

"I am."

"Am what, my lord? Desirous to spar, or preparing to depart?"

"Yes, Morhwen." Stonoric picked up the practice sword. "Both."

"Very well, my lord."

As Stonoric's weapons master picked up his own wooden saber, Stonoric nodded. "Shall we begin?"

"At your word, my lord."

Both men picked up their forearm-sized shields.

"Go!"

They faced one another, rotating in a wide circle around the practice chamber.

Despite the "my lord" of a moment ago, Stonoric knew that Morhwen would be ruthless now that they had joined combat. He himself insisted upon it. Training with anything less than full measure prepared nobody for real combat. Men might fight *faster* than they practiced, but they never fought *harder*.

Stonoric fought hard, whatever the situation. And at this moment, he saw Morhwen make a slight misstep. He leapt forward and scored the hit. "First blood!"

Morhwen grunted and jumped back. "Your right arm hasn't suffered, I see."

"Even my left feels stronger every day, now that I'm home."

Stonoric had been back in Hoccaster for four weeks. The king had been loathe to send him away, yet there had been little to do in Mereclestour after the assassins' capture. Meanwhile, there was much to do in his own city.

Morhwen's brow arched. "Is that so?"

Before the duke could reply, the weapons master pounced with a swift downward slash. Stonoric raised his shield, but not as fast as he ought to have done. The swing glanced off the shield—and struck the duke in his bad shoulder.

Stonoric hooted in pain.

"Still seems a bit slow," said Morhwen with a grin.

"Stronger." Stonoric grimaced. "I said it feels stronger. I never said it was healed."

They went back to circling.

"How's the shoulder?"

"Only hurts when I take a step. I suspect I will bear it to my grave."

Morhwen nodded. "The older you get, the more these things will come your way—things that just never feel right." He lunged.

Stonoric sidestepped—and agreed.

The pain in his shoulder was like the frustration he felt about the changes in his country. Stonoric would support Wodic to his grave. But he doubted he would ever grow comfortable with the merger of Mersex with Dyfann, an irreversible prospect given the latest news from court . . .

"Did I tell you that Queen Caileamach is with child?"

As the closest thing Stonoric had to a confidant, Morhwen did not blink at the sudden turn in the conversation.

"No. However did you learn that?"

"Lady Hoccaster. She returned last evening with the archbishop's retinue."

"The two shall become one," Morhwen observed. "One flesh, and one kingdom."

The duke smiled at his old friend's detached tone. He knew very well that Morhwen was no keener on the Dyfanni than he himself. Perhaps even less.

"I'm trying to see it like a pain in the shoulder." Stonoric turned his left side away and launched straight at Morhwen with a furious serious of strokes. "A man can complain about it. Or he can learn to accept it as his new limitation and compensate by favoring his remaining strengths."

"Just so." The weapons master's sword was a blur as he parried each successive blow. Then, without warning, he whirled away from Stonoric.

The duke stopped on his heel and turned—

—and found Morhwen standing on his left, with his sword at Stonoric's throat.

"By all means, play to your strengths. But never confuse a limitation for a protection. Never, my lord."

Morhwen lowered his sword, took a step back, and bowed.

At that moment, a servant in the doorway cleared his throat. "My lord, Archbishop Simnor asks me to inform my lord that the archbishop is ready to depart."

"Thank you, Burrin. Please inform His Grace that I will be along shortly."

As the servant vanished, Stonoric put down his sword and clasped his old friend on the shoulder. "You're very good, Morhwen. It is a lesson well taken."

A short time later, Stonoric and Simnor rode side by side through the outer gates of Hoccaster. Behind them stretched a long, wide line of soldiers—some mounted, but most on foot. The whole procession marched to the booming cadence of heavy drums.

Looking forward, Stonoric saw the line of the Gwyllinor Mountains stretching across the never-too-distant western horizon. They were not harsh, rearing mountains. Yet he knew that they concealed a dangerous, barbaric people.

He remembered it all too well . . .

. . . an unprovoked invasion that had nearly taken Hoccaster.

. . . a bloody but necessary campaign of reciprocity.

He would never have gone back, had it not been for the king's direct order.

"You look pensive, my Lord Duke."

Stonoric turned his head to find Simnor looking at him. Meeting the archbishop's gaping black eyes was like staring into a pit, even when he tried to show concern. "I suppose I am, Your Grace. It has been long years since I traveled west. For a long time, those mountains have been the western boundary of my world."

Simnor nodded. "It is the same for them, you know."

"Who?"

"The Dyfanni. For generations, those mountains have been the boundary of their world—only in the other direction." He smiled. "But now we have an opportunity to build a new world. With a New Faith."

"If you say so, Your Grace."

"Does it not encourage you, my Lord Duke?"

"My creed is discretion in all things, Your Grace—in faith as in food and drink. Whether the faith is Old or New is of little consequence to me. Does that make me a heretic?"

Simnor chuckled. "Far from it, my lord. The Old Faith of Dyfann has always taught that there is only one Source, only one Mother to all faiths. To this one might add the words of Aesus: 'He who is not against us is for us.' Your disdain for partisan particularities is a sign of spiritual maturity."

"That is kind of you to say, archbishop. But I daresay there are many in the Church who would speak against your liberality. Yours is not the majority view."

"Not yet, but that is part of what we are doing here, my lord."

"I beg your pardon, Your Grace, but I don't follow your point."

"The union of Dyfann and Mersex will bring many benefits to our peoples. But far more important is the merger of the Old Faith with the New. As the spring equinox brings the balance of day and night, so this year it will restore spiritual balance to our island. In two weeks' time, the Feast of the Sacred Cross-Tree will usher in a new world. A new golden age will dawn over Aeld Gowan, my Lord Duke—and from here, the light will spread to all the world!"

"Never let it be said that you are not an optimistic man, Your Grace." Stonoric did not attempt to hide the irony in his smile. "But there is little sun in the North, and methinks you will find it difficult to persuade north of the Deasmor. The Lothairins and Norns are for the old order. They will not welcome your New Faith."

"My lord is wise." The archbishop's tone chilled, and Stonoric saw the man's eyes turn to obsidian fire. "Some resist. Even in nature, no Mother gives birth without losing some blood."

Simnor went on for a few more minutes. Stonoric nodded with feigned politeness the whole time, but in truth, he had lost interest. Stonoric's moderate sensibilities—his "disdain for partisan particularities," as Simnor had expressed it—found the archbishop's enthusiasm distasteful. And then there had been the gleam in the cleric's eyes . . .

It was clear to Stonoric that, whatever Simnor said, the archbishop was just as narrow in his sentiments as the men of the North. His was a different kind of narrowness, to be sure.

But it was just as dangerous.

Stonoric returned his attention to the mountains before him. Whatever he thought of the archbishop's zeal, matters of the spirit were not his business. His business was steel.

The king's orders had been clear. Stonoric was to lead an army into Dyfann. He was to escort Archbishop Simnor to the Feast of the Sacred Cross-Tree at Banr Cluidan and to await the outcome. If all the clans submitted to the New Faith and to Wodic as their new High Chieftain, well and good. But if any resisted, Stonoric was to convince the recalcitrants by force of arms.

Almost without thinking, Stonoric touched the pommel of his sword. He cared little for the things of religion, but he cared much for his king and country. He desired no Dyfanni land—indeed, he would have preferred the king never enter upon this merger. But now that the die had been cast, he would back Wodic to the hilt.

Literally.

Besides all this, he knew a much greater storm was approaching. King Heclaid of Lothair had refused to surrender his bishop. Within months, there would be war with the North. In the meantime, his men might as well have the practice in Dyfann.

Archbishop Simnor would have his chance to persuade with spirit. Where he failed . . .

Stonoric would finish the job with steel.

22

The western passes were the highest, wildest region of the Deasmor. The ascents were steep and unremitting. What trails existed wound narrow tracks along drops that were sheer and unforgiving. Below these paths lay deep ravines, their bouldered bellies waiting to founder the flesh of an unwary traveler. And above the footways, craggy summits breached the tree line to lie exposed beneath the sky like exhumed skulls.

Above ground, all along the visible surfaces of the high country, the moisture of thick mists and the waters of many rains gathered into trickles. These trickles merged into rivulets, and the rivulets in turn ran downhill to the north. As they coalesced and collected, they formed into ever larger pools and ever swifter streams. These, in due course, grew in strength until they became the mighty Mathway River of Lothair.

Yet this high country was as significant for what it concealed as for what it did not. For while most of its water ran above ground, some of it also ran below the surface into an extensive network of caves. It was here, in these caverns connected by an elaborate labyrinth of tunnels—some natural, some not—that the Dree had constructed their stronghold.

Cuuranyth.

Morumus and Gaebroth entered the fortress at dawn. With them they carried such implements of destruction as Gaebroth had acquired or scavenged. They had staves, of course, and each carried a brace of the Dree's own knives—long, vicious stone blades that Gaebroth had obtained through personal combat in his private war. Along with the weapons, they also carried a store of provisions. These were not extensive, but they contained enough to get the two monks and the rescued girl out of the mountains to Aban-Tur—which, from this point, was much closer than Dorslaan.

A few other miscellanies had been shared between them: Gaebroth carried two coils of rope—one knotted, one not— and Morumus carried a small axe. Finally, each man carried a shielded lamp, for the ways by which they would enter Cuuranyth were deep passages unknown to the Dree.

In the fifteen years of his mountain hermitage, Gaebroth had not only learned every path of the Dree, but he had also learned the secret approaches to Cuuranyth. There were whole levels of caves and tunnels surrounding those inhabited by the enemy—secrets of which only Gaebroth was aware. None of these led to the prison cells, of course—or else he would have long ago sprung every prisoner himself. But he had found two passages that might prove most useful to today's expedition.

The first opened by a concealed nook into Cuuranyth's cavernous central gallery. From this access, they could reach the nomergenna magazine in minutes. The other tunnel branched off from the midpoint of the first. It would take them to a concealed ledge high on the wall of the Dree's torture chamber.

It was for this that Gaebroth had brought the knotted rope.

"Which way?" Morumus whispered as they stood at the juncture of the two ways.

"I think we should fire the nomergenna first. If we use a long enough fuse, we will have time to get back to this point and on to the interrogation hall before it ignites. The torture chambers are near the cells. When the flame hits the herb, most of the Dree will go to investigate. That will be our chance to get in and get the children out."

"Do you have any idea how many Dree are here?"

Gaebroth shook his head. "They never showed us their faces, so it was impossible to keep track."

The two men proceeded down the first tunnel. But they traveled at a more cautious pace. They were approaching Cuuranyth's main chamber now, and there was no telling what they might encounter. Nearer and nearer still they drew. They dropped the shield over Morumus's lamp, concealing all its light save that which escaped a single draft hole near the top. Even Gaebroth's they reduced to a mere sliver. Then, at last, they saw a glow in the darkness ahead of them.

"We're here."

As they came within a few feet of the opening, Gaebroth shielded his lamp the remainder of the way and set it down nearby. Morumus was about to follow his example when Gaebroth stopped him.

"We'll need yours when we reach the magazine. Bring it along."

Both men held their breath as they crept out into the great gallery of Cuuranyth. Although the rim of the cavern remained in shadows, parallel lines of lampstands illuminated its open central area. These lines of light, extending from one end of the gallery to the other, created an impression of two long walls. And at either end, these walls continued into yawning tunnels leading away from the hall. Yet beyond the presence of the lit candles, nowhere along the length of the chamber was there any movement or sign of life.

Gaebroth exhaled. "Empty. Thank God."

"What are those?"

239

Morumus was pointing to three massive tapestries. Hung near the center of the gallery and stretching almost from floor to ceiling, the tapestries were illuminated from the bottom by an arrangement of candelabras. Each depicted a different scene, but all three contained the same great white tree.

"That's it." Morumus turned to Gaebroth. "That's the tree they worship. You are *certain* that the tree is not here?"

"Yes. During my imprisonment, I once overheard the Dree speak of bringing the nomergenna from a great distance. And in the years since my escape, I have seen them bringing the barrels along the trails that come from the south. The tree is not here. Only its pictures."

"Still, I should have a look at those tapestries. They may give us a clue as to where the tree *is* located."

Gaebroth shook his head. "It's too risky."

"It's a risk worth taking. With the seedling in Caeldora destroyed, they only have one left. If we destroy it, we destroy their source of nomergenna forever. Besides, we don't have to stand right out in front of them. Those tapestries are huge. All we need to do is get close enough to get a clear look."

"There." The older man pointed to a spot just behind the near wall of lamps, where a natural pillar of thick stone provided some cover. "Is that close enough?"

Morumus nodded. They crept forward, and he peered at the tapestries.

In the first scene there was a lush garden. A great white tree stood at its center, resplendent amidst the brown boles and green leaves of those around it. Its form was familiar to Morumus: the same slender branches, the same scarlet leaves, as those of the tree he had seen in Caeldora. The only difference was that the tree in this image was larger and fuller than all those around it . . . and one of its branches was reaching! For fleeing from the grasp of the tree were two figures. One was a man, the other a woman. Both were unclothed.

Morumus frowned. The scene reminded him of the story of the Fall of Mankind in Holy Writ. But if so, where was the serpent? Where was the Tree of Life? Was the white tree supposed to be the Tree of Probation? If so, why was it reaching?

He looked again and saw two inscriptions embroidered at the bottom of the cloth. The first line was in a script he could not read. But the second was written in Dyfanni:

"Adinnu: Man rejects the Mother's offer of secret wisdom."

The second tapestry showed another white tree—still great, but not as large as the first. This tree was planted in a forest, and before it bowed a woman clothed in white. In the distance behind the forest was a tall mountain. Upon its heights was fixed a great ark.

Morumus frowned again.

The Flood?

The double inscription—as with the first, he could only read the second line—confirmed his suspicions:

"Llanubys: Tham's wife thwarts Yeho's flood and replants the Mother."

Morumus did not recognize the third scene, depicted in the final tapestry. Again there was a white tree—the smallest of the three. But here the tree stood alone atop a tall green hill, surrounded by a ring of standing stones. Lines of people were moving on both sides of the hill. On the right side, red-robed figures ascended, leading children dressed in white. On the left side, the red-robed figures descended alone.

Though he did not recognize the place, Morumus knew full well what it meant. But the caption glossed over the cruelty: *"Ring of Stars: The Mother welcomes her children."*

Morumus turned away from the tapestries, so angry he trembled.

"Any clues?"

He met Gaebroth's gaze. "Do you know of a place called the Ring of Stars?"

The old man shook his head.

"Neither do I. Let's go."

The two men backed away from the candlelit shrine. Staying far out of the reach of the lamplight, Gaebroth led them toward the great tunnel that exited the hall on the left. As they approached its wide opening, the old man paused and turned to look at Morumus.

"The magazine is not far, but there's no cover beyond this point. If they see us, we have to kill them before they can raise an alarm. Any hesitation could be fatal. Do you understand?"

Morumus nodded. "I'm with you, Gaebroth."

Stepping out of the safety of the shadows, the two men entered the total exposure of the wide, well-lit tunnel.

As they proceeded down the tunnel's seemingly interminable length, Morumus kept his stave at the ready. Any Dree who entered the tunnel from either direction would see them immediately, and he would have but seconds to attack. Though it seemed improbable to the point of presumption, he prayed that they might pass undetected to the magazine.

His prayer was answered.

Several tense minutes later, they reached a crossing. Here, Gaebroth led them out of the main passage and down a narrower, dark passage to their right. At its end, they came to a heavy wooden door.

A sudden thought struck Morumus, a jolt that clenched his stomach. "Do we need a key?"

Despite the tension of their situation, Gaebroth sounded almost amused. "We are in the Dree's hidden stronghold, Morumus. They don't get many intruders. There are no guards at the doors, except at the prison cells . . ." Here he reached out a hand and pushed on the door—

It swung inward without so much as a creak.

". . . and there are no locks."

Morumus had not known what to expect of a nomergenna storeroom. Though he had tasted the herb once in mead, he had never seen the substance unmixed. Gaebroth had made a remark about barrels, but that hadn't told him much.

But Morumus could not, in his wildest imaginings, have expected what they found.

The magazine looked like a wine cellar. It was long, but not very wide. The layered racks of casks lining both walls made the room seem even narrower. As Gaebroth closed the door behind them, Morumus unshielded his lamp and held it up. He could only just make out the back wall in the far distance.

One could see almost none of the cave walls for the honeycomb of small, side-lying barrels running floor to ceiling along both sides of the chamber. Morumus swallowed. "How much do they have here?"

"They've been collecting it for a long time." Gaebroth's grim smile flashed in the lamplight. "Even if you never find the other tree, destroying this will set them back by generations."

"Praise God. How do we do it?"

"Set down your lamp and get that axe out of your pack."

Morumus did so in short order. "Now what?"

"Go to the back wall and hack open a dozen or so of the lower casks. The idea is to get a sizeable heap of the herb on the floor in front of the other barrels."

As Morumus moved to comply, he saw Gaebroth withdraw three items from his pack. The first was one of the coils of rope: the unknotted one. The second was one of the spare waterskins. The third was a small wooden bowl.

A bowl? What has he got in mind?

He would find out soon enough. In the meantime, he had his own task.

He carried a bowl all this way . . .

Reaching the far end of the chamber, Morumus selected his first barrel at random and swung the axe. The lid of the cask yielded to the blow with but the slightest resistance, and as the axe came away it let loose a stream of something like dark sand.

A pungent aroma filled his nostrils.

Nomergenna.

Hefting the axe, Morumus opened a second barrel, a third, and so on. It was not difficult work, and within a quarter of an hour he had broken many of the casks. By the time he shouldered the axe, he stood ankle deep in the dusky, granular herb.

"Very good." Gaebroth came up behind him but stopped several paces away. "Now step out of that stuff, and brush it off your habit and shoes."

When Morumus was finished, the older man handed him the rope.

"Make a loop, and lay it in the middle of your heap."

"Why is the end of this rope wet?"

"It's oil. This is our wick."

Completing this, the two men began backing out of the chamber. Morumus unfolded the rope span by span. As he did so, Gaebroth dipped the section of rope into the bowl, which he refilled with oil from the waterskin as needed. It was slow labor, but they had to make certain the rope was well soaked before laying it down.

At last they reached the door.

"There," said Gaebroth. "All's ready."

"Now what?"

"We light the wick."

"How long will we have before . . . ?"

"Hard to say. But it's slow-burning oil, and with this much rope I'd guess we'll have about half an hour."

"Will that be enough?"

"Maybe."

"Maybe?"

"Oh, we won't have any difficulty locating the children in that time. But getting out—"

"I thought our plan was to use the fire as a diversion?"

"It was. But nomergenna is very explosive, and there is more here than I remembered. When this magazine ignites, it may very well bring all of Cuuranyth down with it."

"I could live with that."

"Me too. Yet if possible, I'd like to survive. And then there is the little girl."

"Right. We'll just have to move faster than we planned." Stooping down, Morumus removed the shield from his lamp and took up the end of the rope. "Ready?"

"Ready."

Morumus put the wick into the flame.

Less than a minute later, he and Gaebroth raced back toward the main gallery and their secret tunnel.

As the door swung shut behind them, the wick's flame cast a lonesome light in the darkened storeroom. But that light brightened as the determined flame spread down the length of the oil-soaked rope. The single point of light grew into a long, fiery serpent.

A serpent poised to strike at the heart of the Shadow's Nest.

23

ack in the tunnel, Morumus and Gaebroth hurried toward the torture chambers. The older man had assured Morumus that the distance was not long, yet the knowledge that they had less than half an hour before the magazine exploded made every step seem twice as long.

And every moment twice as short.

The thought propelled them down the dark passage as surely as enemy pursuit, and as they passed, their lamps cast bobbing shadows upon the rough stone walls.

A series of questions chased one another through Morumus's mind as they drew near to the interrogation hall. How many Dree would they find? Was the girl taken from Dorslaan their only prisoner, or might there be others? What would they do if the Dree were too many?

At this last silent inquiry, his hand tightened upon his stave. His thoughts strayed to the brace of Dree knives hanging at his belt. Morumus might not know the answers to his first questions, but to this last his answer was not in doubt.

There would be no turning back.

Neither he nor Gaebroth had said it aloud, but the resolution was mutual. Whether the girl was capable of escape or not, they would attack. The odds did not matter. Whether a pair of Dree or a dozen, they would not leave empty-handed so long as there was *any* hope of rescue . . .

"It's just ahead."

Gaebroth's whisper cut off Morumus's bellicose musing. The older man had stopped and was pointing up the tunnel. There, about fifty paces ahead of them, Morumus saw the rough rectangle marking its terminus. Its glow indicated that they had reached their destination. He nodded, and both men shielded their lamps.

No sooner had they shuttered the light than a most sinister, unwelcome sound reached their ears. There were noises coming from the torture chamber below them—horrible sounds that rebounded down the outer passage to lodge in their ears. Some of these were snatches of Dyfanni, cold and threatening. Others were pleas for mercy—broken, sobbing, *young* voices in Northspeech. Still others were screams—wordless, howling cries of agony. And interwoven with them all was an unmistakable, cantillating hiss . . .

The Dark Speech.

The two monks rushed forward.

The interrogation hall was an irregular, oblong cavern, and the ledge upon which the two monks emerged was one of several that jutted out along its craggy walls. Above them, the length of the drooping ceiling of the chamber hung thick with gleaming, heavy stalactites—like so many jagged, slavering teeth, waiting to snap closed upon their victims. Yet more menacing by far was the scene unfolding some distance away, below them, near the cave's center.

Within a circle of flickering lampstands, two children were bound to stone tables. Morumus recognized one of them as the girl the Dree had taken from Fheil's Delf. The other was a boy he did not recognize. Around the tables stood half a dozen black-cloaked Dree, emphasizing their cruel song with serpentine gestures. With every new hiss and writhing twist, the children cried out with fresh agony. The girl's eyes jerked from side to side, and she screamed as though surrounded by a thousand nightmares. Beside her, the boy's eyes had rolled back into his head, and he moaned as he slowly drew a knife across his own exposed chest.

"Make fast the rope—!" Morumus's growled command cut short as Gaebroth placed the line into his hand.

"Go now, I'm right behind you!"

Clutching his stave in one hand and the line in the other, Morumus dropped over the ledge. As soon as his feet hit the floor he leapt aside. A moment later, Gaebroth landed beside him.

Both of them winced as they clutched their staves. The knotted cord had burned and cut their hands as they had slid down the rope. But hotter than the pain in Morumus's palms was the wrath in his heart. "Ready?"

"Ready."

With silent prayers, the monks leapt to the attack.

There was no plan beyond a straight rush, no strategy but to smite the enemy and see him dead. It would be a hard fight—six to two—but surprise and sheer determination favored the monks. And for a time, even the Dree's evil worked against them as the girl's perpetual screams masked the attackers' sweeping footfalls.

A strange sensation overtook Morumus as he ran toward the ring of lampstands. He had experienced the same thing last year in Saint Dreunos's Cathedral in Versaden, when the Mersian bishops and a red monk had tried to dispatch him. He would have described it as waking up, only he was already awake. His awareness expanded with sudden and terrifying force. And though his heart still pounded in his chest, he felt a sort of calm enveloping him.

"For with you I will run against a troop, and with my God I will leap a wall."

Morumus and Gaebroth had closed the distance to a dozen paces before the Dree spotted them. When they did, the tenor of their dark song changed. A moment earlier it had been a threatening leer aimed at the children. Now, as they saw the impossible—two armed monks dashing toward them with weapons raised—it morphed into a hissing fear.

Morumus smashed his stave into the first Dree with the force of a forge hammer. He heard bone cracking beneath the heavy wood and did not wait to see the Dree crumple before wheeling toward the next—

Whish!

The Dree's knife sliced through the sleeve of his shoulder, grazing the flesh beneath as it passed through. Had Morumus turned but a moment later, it would have been a gouging rake across his back. Now, the unspent bulk of the blow threw the Dree off balance.

Like lightning, Morumus brought his stave around and down—right onto the back of the hooded neck. The Dree crashed to the floor, and in one fluid motion Morumus drew a knife and plunged it into his back.

Cannot afford to risk him waking up.

He spun to face the next attacker . . .

"If you do not surrender, we will kill them right now."

With face still flushed and heart still pounding, it took Morumus a moment to realize what he was seeing. A few paces away, Gaebroth too stood over a fallen Dree. That made for three down. But as the red mist cleared from Morumus's vision, he saw that the other three Dree were still standing. Two of them held drawn knives to the throats of the bound children. The third, the speaker, stood between the two tables, turning his head to take in both Morumus and Gaebroth.

The older man glowered at the monks. "You will kill them anyway. But give the children to us, and we will leave you untouched."

"*Fool!* Dozens of our brethren walk these halls, and you think you will walk out?"

"You are lying. We've just come from your great hall. Empty. If you had others with you here, you would have raised an alarm by now."

Morumus could not be sure whether Gaebroth spoke from conviction, or whether the older man's words were a wild fling. But when the lead Dree flinched, he knew they were true.

"You've already lost six. Three at Fheil's Delf, and now three more here." Morumus drew his knife and pointed it at the speaker. "Release the children now, or we will bring this whole cursed mountain down on your heads."

"You have a sharp tongue, monk. When our brothers return, I will feed it to you—"

But the Dree never finished his sentence, for in that moment the whole of Cuuranyth heaved with the rippling force of a cataclysmic explosion. The floor beneath them lurched, causing the Dree and the monks to stagger. A shower of dust fell from the cavern's roof. A moment later there was a loud explosion as a falling stalactite crashed into the floor.

The Dree let loose a low hiss. "What have you done?"

"Your precious herb, the nomergenna." Despite the gravity of the situation, Morumus gave a sardonic laugh. "Like the tree in Caeldora . . ."

The malevolent hisses of the Dree told Morumus he did not need to say anything further. They knew all about Caeldora.

"You!" growled the speaker. The other Dree's knives came away from the children, and all three began moving toward Morumus.

"Get the children out of here, Gaebroth!" Sheathing his knife, Morumus gripped his stave with both hands and backed away from the monks. But he did not move toward the knotted rope hanging from the tunnel ceiling. Instead, he moved toward the cavern's main entrance.

For their part, the Dree seemed content to let Gaebroth have the children if they could have Morumus. They spread out as they followed him, two of them moving to his flanks with their knives pointed inward. Their intent was clear: like a pack of wolves, they meant to encircle him and cut off his escape.

Morumus heard Gaebroth begin a reply, but the older man's words were lost in the echo of a tremendous groan overhead. This noise was followed by a series of sharp, splintering pops. He barely had time to register what they meant before . . .

Crash!

Another stalactite exploded into the cave floor—this time less than a dozen paces to his left. A shard of stone nicked his scalp as it whizzed over him.

Crash! Boom! Crash! Boom!

The stone spires began falling from the roof in quick succession, a hail of deadly missiles aimed at no one in particular—capable of killing without discrimination.

Without waiting to see how the Dree would respond, Morumus turned and fled toward the exit.

Please, Aesus, let the others get out safely!

But what was he going to do?

"Deeper love has no man than this, that he should lay down his life for his friends." If Morumus could not escape himself, he might at least buy time for the others.

Behind him, he heard the Dree's determined footsteps and enraged curses.

"There is no escape, monk!"

"You will die a long, slow—" But this second speaker never finished.

Crash!

Morumus felt more shards flying past him and turned his head. Though he did not stop running, he did gasp.

A massive, falling stalactite had crushed the Dree in midsentence!

With a prayer of amazed thanksgiving, Morumus returned his attention forward. He was nearly out of the torture hall now. Just a few more steps, and he would pass into the adjoining chamber. In the dim illumination provided by wall-sconced torches, he saw some kind of large pool . . .

Gaebroth's cistern!

Recognition came like the ray of a dawning sun, and Gaebroth's words came flooding back to him . . .

"In Cuuranyth there is a deep pool of water that acts as a sort of cistern for the place. We had to walk past it every day as we went between our cells and their torture chambers. . . . At the very bottom of the pool there is a small tunnel."

Morumus smiled again. Perhaps he would escape after all—

Crash!

This time the shaft of stone exploded but a footstep to his right. The blast knocked Morumus sideways with cruel force, peppering him with stone fragments as he fell. A heavy member of this hail struck him on the temple, and colors streaked across his vision like lightning. He hit the floor hard, and the impact squeezed the breath from his lungs.

"Pull him into the next chamber!"

Stunned by his fall, Morumus was powerless as two pairs of hands like crow talons fastened on his sleeves and dragged him into the cistern chamber. Here there was no floating dust to choke his gasps, nor exploding stones to crush his chest. Morumus was out of the murderous hail.

But he had not escaped the malevolent Dree.

"Lift him up and hold him fast." The grips shifted, and the Dree jerked Morumus up. One hooked his arms behind his back. The other peered at him. In the dim light, his hooded face was a void of shadow.

"Are you truly the monks who desecrated the Mother?"

"My brother? No. But me? Oh, yes." Morumus let the pleasure be evident in his affirmation, and he spat at the Dree.

Both Dree hissed with almost uncontainable fury.

"You will experience dying as few men ever have—"

"Save your speech." Morumus cut him off. "Go ahead and kill me and be done with it. It won't bring back your tree or restore your stockpile. I know all about your so-called power, and without your fairy dust you are impotent. You are defeated, and for that I gladly sell my life."

The Dree raised his fist. "You will learn how wrong you are, monk!"

"Am I?" Morumus shrugged. "Teach me, then. And take as much time as you like—though we both know that with the mountain collapsing, you haven't got much. It would be my crowning pleasure to see you die here with me."

As if to punctuate his words, Cuuranyth gave another ominous heave. Dust and small bits of stone fell from the ceiling above them, and from somewhere down the farther corridor—the one leading away from both cistern and torture chambers—there was a significant thundering echo.

An entire cave collapsing?

"No, fool." The Dree shook his head, and dark triumph laced his rasping speech. "You will not escape so easily. No hand may spill the blood of the desecrators but the Hand of the Mother himself. You are bound for sacrifice at the Ring of Stars."

"Where and how makes no difference to me." Morumus turned his head away. "I am not afraid to die."

The Dree's tone was cold. "There is death, and then there is dying."

"I put a knife into the heart of the last person who said that to me."

"Well then," boomed a voice from behind the Dree, "one must keep up the tradition."

Because he was not looking, Morumus did not see the blade point that sprouted—a moment before the voice spoke—from the Dree's middle. But he heard the gasp from the impaled man, and he heard the scream from the final Dree as he released Morumus and fled in the opposite direction.

Turning from the fleeing Dree, Morumus saw the first fall lifeless to the floor. The stump of the long stone knife protruded from his back. Over the corpse stood an old man trailed by two children.

"Gaebroth! You were supposed to flee with the children through the tunnel!"

"You're very welcome, I'm sure." The flash in the older man's blue eyes pierced Morumus with the memory of Abbot Grahem. "The tunnel collapsed before we could reach it. There's only one way left for us to go."

"The cistern?"

Gaebroth nodded. "You remembered."

The chamber about them shuddered again—with a sudden, violent intensity. Some of the water lapped up over the brink of the pool, and overhead there was a very foreboding crack.

"Can they swim?" Morumus gestured to the children.

"We can, sir." Despite their pallor of fright, both children looked determined.

"They can cling to us." Gaebroth took the girl's hand and directed the boy to Morumus. "Once we reach the bottom, it's but a short tunnel to swim to the next chamber. From there we go up and out."

"Out to where, sir?" The girl stared up at Gaebroth.

"To freedom, my dear." His blue eyes glistened. "To freedom."

24

he midnight sky above the Noppenham road was a tapestry of velvet. A brave host of stars shone like sparkling dust across the dark canvas, the only illumination on a night when the new moon had left the canopy without its pale lantern. It was thus in deep shadow that the road wound its way along the Mersian coast.

Yet the presence of the sea was never far from one's senses. Even where the surf could not be seen, the roar of its regular crash echoed in the near distance. Moreover, the presence of salt was unmistakable on the light breeze, its invigorating tang wafting into the nostrils of even the most weary traveler.

Oethur was not the weariest of the three men lying bound in the cart as it creaked and bumped along its way. Beside him on the right, Treowin had fallen into an uneasy doze. And on his other side, Ciolbail groaned in his sleep. Oethur knew how they felt. He himself felt the ache of several bruises beneath his brown habit. Yet the pain had been worth it.

They were four days out of Grindangled now, and a day south of Toberstan. Every additional league south took them farther into Mersex, farther from escape. Two more days and they would reach Noppenham, from whence there could be no realistic hope of rescue.

Acutely aware of this, the three Northmen had felt compelled to make some attempt at escape. And thus they had done.

It had seemed an opportune moment. The guard of Nornish soldiers sent by Aeldred had stopped at Toberstan, having been ordered not to cross the border. Their continuing captors—a half-dozen red monks, which was more than enough in Mersex—had called a halt that very morning. While their horses had watered, the Dree had unbound their prisoners' feet and permitted them to leave the cart for the sake of seeking similar refreshment—and for relieving themselves in less savory ways.

While all had been so engaged, an unfamiliar noise in the distance had called four of the red monks away. Taking advantage of the situation, the three prisoners had pummeled the two remaining guards—using hands bound in front as makeshift clubs. Then they had made a dash toward the sea.

The action as a whole had been doomed from its inception. The Northmen had no help waiting and no place to hide. Moreover, they were on foot while the Dree were on horseback. Consequently, the red monks had recaptured them with relative ease—and returned them to their place on the cart with the pummeling they had inflicted upon their guards repaid double.

Yet it had not all been in vain. The three Northmen had managed to reach the beach before the Dree had overtaken them. And in the moment when Oethur had been knocked, face first, into the sand, his bound hands had closed over the sharp, serrated edge of a seashell.

Lying now in the cart as it rolled along under the stars, Oethur smiled.

He still had the shell.

With the greatest care, he used two fingers to withdraw it from the place between his wrists—and beneath the covering of his bonds—where he had tucked it. Holding the shell in his hands, he felt along its edge. Not so thin as to snap, nor so thick as to lose its edge.

Will it work?

Holding the shell between his thumb and forefinger, Oethur began to cut. He scraped the shell's edge back and forth across the width of the rope binding his wrists. He could feel the vibration of each pass, feel the tension begin to slacken as the shell severed strand after strand in slow, yet steady succession . . .

Oh yes, this will certainly do!

Without the presence of the moon to give some tangible sense of time, Oethur had no way to know how long it took to free himself. It was cautious, laborious work. Once his hands were clear, he puzzled for a time as to how to unbind his feet. He could not very well sit up, as that would give him away within a moment.

Instead, he turned onto his side and curled himself into as much of a ball as he could manage. Once in this posture, it was a simple thing to reach down between his knees with the shell to his ankle bonds. A short while later, the last strand binding him snapped.

Now what?

The Dree driving the cart had not even flinched at Oethur's motions. Indeed, the entire party of the red monks—the two driving the cart, and the four riding along its flanks—traveled in stark silence through the starry night. Yet despite their lack of speech, the red monks showed no sign of slowing.

So long as the cart is moving and the Dree are watching, I can't very well cut loose the bishops . . .

Despite his normal, cheerful resilience, Oethur felt the wraith of doubt creep into his heart.

What if they don't intend to stop before daylight? I'll be discovered . . .

But he needn't have worried, for in that moment the night road erupted.

Hiss! Hiss!

The sharp sounds pierced the darkness like a serpent's kiss, setting the horse rearing and the driver screaming.

The startled horse bolted, and the cart gave a heaving lurch, sending one driver tumbling from the bench. The remaining driver called to his fellow even as he grabbed for the reins, but in the very next moment the wheel struck the fallen man.

Oethur braced himself as the pitching cart heaved, bounced . . . and overturned.

The crash flung the three prisoners from the cart with such force that for a moment it seemed they were flying. Yet before Oethur realized what was happening—and before the bishops came entirely awake—they hit the ground.

Hard.

Oethur's first sensation was pain. Not just the pain of impact, but also a sharp pain in his hand. A moment later he realized what it was. Somehow, against all odds, he had managed to hold on to the seashell. But when he had fallen, its sharp edge had cut into his palm.

As he blinked against a blackness quite independent of the moonless night, Oethur's second impression was of noise. The screams of both man and beast pierced the darkness around him. They seemed to be coming from everywhere at once, as though he were surrounded by a perishing choir.

"Sea raiders! Coming from over—"

But another telltale hiss turned the Dree's cry into mangled gurgling.

Oethur could not see the arrows raining death out of the starry night, but he recognized the sound of their flight. This close to the coast, they could only mean one thing . . .

Sea raiders!

Oethur's heart pounded. *I must get the bishops away!* He pushed himself to his feet and looked around. *Where are they?*

Though he could see almost nothing, he heard a low moan from somewhere close. Following the sound and stooping down, he reached out toward a large, dark hump . . .

His hands touched rough wool.

"Bishop Ciolbail? Bishop Treowin?" He could not tell which it was. "Your Grace, can you hear me?"

"Oethur?" Treowin's tone was dazed, and his volume far too loud. "Oethur, what—?"

"Quiet!" Oethur put a hand over his superior's mouth. "We've been attacked by sea raiders, and the cart has overturned."

"Sea raiders . . ." Comprehension dawned on the older man, and as he tried to sit up he spoke in a much quieter tone. "Help me up, Oethur. Where's Ciolbail?"

"I'm here." The low voice came from somewhere within a few paces.

"We must get away, Your Graces. Hold still while I cut you free."

Nobody argued. Oethur helped both men to their feet, and the three of them began creeping inland. Behind them, the screams were being snuffed out one by one. Meanwhile, torches had been lit near the wreckage of the cart—and voices echoed across the empty night.

"There were prisoners, all right. But they're not here."

"Spread out. Find them!"

Without a word, Oethur and both bishops quickened their pace. All three knew many stories about what happened to those who fell into the hands of sea raiders. None of them wanted to discover for themselves whether or not the stories were true.

At first it seemed they would succeed. With the darkness of new moon above and the brown of their wool habits, the Northmen were almost invisible. They hurried along, half-bent and unseen against the night, and managed to put several hundred yards' distance between them and the raiders' torches.

But then the turf in front of them erupted. A large bird, turned out of its nest without warning, took to the air with a rush of wings. As it did so, it gave a vindictive, air-piercing shriek.

It was just the sort of signal the sea raiders needed.

"Over there! Go!"

Torches began bobbing in their direction across the darkness.

"Run for it, Your Graces!" But even as he urged his superiors on, Oethur saw something that sank his heart. A few of the torches were held too high and moving too fast to belong to men on foot . . .

Horses!

Despite the futility, Oethur and the bishops flew with surprising speed. Fear of falling into the hands of sea raiders gave them an added urgency. Onward they pushed with reckless abandon, the certainty of the danger behind making them heedless of any possible danger ahead.

Yet in the end it did not matter. Heart could not outrun hoof. From the corners of his eyes, Oethur saw the flanking riders as they overtook them. And he knew without looking that there were others close behind them. Less than a minute later, they were surrounded.

The three Northmen stood back to back, facing the sea raiders.

"Don't let them take you alive, brothers," growled Treowin.

"There's no need to fight," said one of the men on horseback.

Oethur started. *He's speaking Vilguran? With a Caeldoran accent?* He straightened. "Who are you?"

The speaker handed his torch to the man beside him, then dismounted. "We are Lumanae," he answered, gesturing to his companions.

Ciolbail spat. "If you're imperial bodyguards, then I'm a—"

"A what? A *bishop?*"

Ciolbail fell silent.

Something tickled at the back of Oethur's memory. The speaker's voice ... it was somehow ... *familiar*. "Who are *you*?"

"Me?" The speaker chuckled. "I am a Lunumbir—a Lumana who works in the shadows." He lowered his hood and stepped forward. "But you know me by a different name, I think."

All three Northmen gasped.

"Nack?"

An hour later, the four of them sat in the cabin of a small ship sailing south along the Mersian coast. The lamp hanging above the table swayed back and forth as the ship swayed on the sea. The Northmen had shared their stories. Now Nack shared his.

"I have been in the service of Emperor Arechon since the days when he was but Prince of Caeldora. It was during those years that he received a letter from an unknown monk named Anathadus. My master was so impressed with the letter that he persuaded his father to make Anathadus a bishop. After being crowned emperor, Arechon gave me the supervision of Aevor and ordered me to protect Anathadus. Though he no longer agreed with Anathadus on many points, he nevertheless respected his integrity and retained a fondness for him."

Oethur leaned back. "So when the Red Order murdered Anathadus, I take it the emperor was not pleased?"

"No. Investigation of the whole matter—Anathadus's murder, the slaughter at Lorudin, and the death at Naud—fell to me. We apprehended the last survivor of Lorudin remaining in Caeldora—"

Oethur straightened. "You found Ortto?"

"Yes, but he was only able to tell me *what* had happened. He could not tell me *why* it had happened. But he did tell me who I needed to find: you, Oethur, and Morumus. It grieves me terribly to hear you say that Morumus has died."

"It grieves me, too. But I believe we will meet again, and he died well."

"Just so." Nack paused before continuing. "In the meantime, those of us who remain alive must carry on with our duties. For my part, that involves discovering what the Red Order is seeking. What you've told me, Oethur, provides some of the answer: they are seeking to establish their cult within the Church and will eradicate any who oppose them. Do you agree?"

"Wholeheartedly."

"But what has happened to all three of you—the betrayal of your brother Aeldred, Oethur, and the conspiracy to implicate Ciolbail in the assassination attempt in Mersex—means they are after more than just a foothold in the Church . . ."

"They want the whole of Aeld Gowan," said Treowin.

"And perhaps Midgaddan after that." Nack's voice was cold. "If so, then they are a clear and present threat to the Imperium."

Ciolbail studied Nack. "Does this mean you will help us stop them?"

"That involves two separate questions, Your Grace. I cannot give Lothair any direct help against Nornindaal or Mersex, for the emperor has not chosen a side in this conflict. Nor can I help you eradicate the Dree from Aeld Gowan, for this is not Arechon's land, nor his war. As soon as we have landed you three at Dunross, we are leaving Aeld Gowan. But as to stopping the Red Order in Midgaddan, you may rest most assured. Their subversive activities are a clear threat to *both* my masters."

"Both?"

Nack gave Oethur a shrewd look. "Son, do you think I spent all those years in Anathadus's service with my ears stuffed?"

At dawn the next morning, Morumus stood with Gaebroth and the two rescued children in the middle of a clearing high in the Mathway Vale. Behind them, the river took its ease by spreading out into a deep pool flanked at its head by large boulders. Before them, a small company of grassy mounds punctuated the otherwise smooth turf.

"This is where it happened," said Morumus to the others.

They had escaped Cuuranyth. Though it had soaked them through, the tunnel at the bottom of the cistern had led them to safety, just as Gaebroth had promised. Passing through a series of lightless places, they had emerged at last from the Shadow's Nest, soaking wet and without food or water—all their provisions had been carried into the mountain. They had wrung out their clothes and then kept moving. Their only hope had been to get to Aban-Tur before they froze or starved. Marching the remainder of that day and through the night, they had arrived this morning at the clearing by the pool.

Here.

They had come to the one place in all Aeld Gowan that Morumus had hoped never to see again: the vale of shadows, the place where Morumus had watched the Dree murder his father.

"Pardon me, sir, but *what* happened here?" The young boy's eyes were wide. "These mounds look like . . ."

"Graves." Had somebody come to bury Raudorn and his men, or had the land covered them itself over these last ten years? Despite the years, Morumus's memory of the slaughter and its aftermath was sharp enough for him to remember exactly where the men had fallen . . . and from the placement of the mounds, he was certain that, whatever the case, each body had been covered just where it lay.

Morumus turned toward the children. "It was here that the Shadows murdered my father and his men."

For a moment, the children said nothing. But they both nodded, and a tear formed at the corner of the girl's eye.

"Which one is your father?" asked the girl.

"Over here."

Morumus led the way to a large mound near the center of the company.

"Here is where my father lies." Tears burned in his own eyes now. "Here is where he will rise at the Resurrection Day."

From within the folds of his cloak, Morumus withdrew the only object he had carried with him out of Cuuranyth: the hilt of a broken Dree knife. Stooping, he laid it atop his father's grave.

"When he wakes, my father will find this. And when we meet, I will tell him how we broke the power of the Dark Faith on this day."

Rising, he turned north. "Come now, my friends. A brisk march will bring us to Aban-Tur before supper."

25

thin sickle moon hung low in the east as Somnadh climbed the path. Beneath his feet, the ancient track wound its way up and around the steep tor. Above him, a broad band of purple dust stretched across the sparkling canopy of the heavens. On this night in particular, the circle of standing stones toward which he climbed was well named indeed: *the Ring of Stars.*

Somnadh paused as he reached the summit, glancing up at the sky above him. *Can you see these same stars tonight, Urien?*

It was for his sister's sake that Somnadh had come tonight. It was less than a week until the Feast of the Sacred Tree in Banr Cluidan. In just a few days, he would begin the greatest endeavor of his life. And though his heart thrilled at the prospect, a dark fear gnawed at him . . .

What will become of Urien?

At present, he did not know the whereabouts of his sister, but a bird had brought word from Aeldred, his beloved brother in the north. The monk Morumus was dead, fallen into Fheil's Delf. The other desecrator of the Mother in Caeldora—Aeldred's own brother, Oethur—was bound and heading south.

Hope had surged into Somnadh when Aeldred had first told him of his plan to capture Morumus and Oethur. He had been sure that if he brought the blood of both monks, the Mother would forgive Urien her role in the desecration of Caeldora.

But will only one be enough?

Now that he stood at the brink of finding out, the wordless foreboding that had plagued him these many months surged over the barriers with which he had bound it. *Will the Mother make me sacrifice my sister?*

Gathering his courage, Somnadh stepped beneath the stones. The white runes etched in the dark monoliths seemed almost to glow as he passed under and through the towering stones. Within moments, he stood within the Ring of Stars.

Somnadh gazed upward at the Mother—and his breath caught in his throat. Despite the dark night, the great goddess tree seemed to pulse with preternatural whiteness. Her perfect form stood tall, her glory unbowed. And between her supple branches, he could see again the purple band that spanned the heavens. It seemed to him the perfect backdrop for the beauty of Genna—a royal veil to wrap the Queen of earth and heaven.

"Genna ma'guad ma'muthad ma'rophed."

There was nothing in the world for which Somnadh cared more than the Mother . . .

Except Urien?

The thought struck him like a lash, and he fell to his knees. Gazing up through streaming tears, he raised both his hands and began to pray.

"Oh Mother, must I choose? Must I sacrifice she whom you yourself once embraced as your own Heart? Must she now die, who was hounded by Aesus's dogs? Might she not yet be restored? Oh, Mother! Oh Mother, I—" But his words vanished beneath a wave of grief.

Through his wracking sobs, Somnadh heard movement in the Mother's branches. He looked up.

Could it be . . . ? Yes!

268

Though no breeze blew across the hill, though no wind whispered through the standing stones, there could be no mistake. Genna's branches were rustling . . .

"My dear child," came a whisper at his ear. At the same moment he felt a soft touch at his shoulder.

Somnadh jumped.

"Llanubys!" he gasped, his pounding heart settling back into his chest.

"Somnadh." The old woman's wispy strands of hair wrapped her skeletal face in an ethereal halo. "My dearest and most faithful son." A thin hand extended to caress his face. "What vexes you?"

Somnadh dropped his gaze. Though Llanubys was very old, her dark eyes retained a piercing fire that defied all age.

"Is it because of Urien, my son?"

Somnadh's heart caught again, and he looked up. "You know?"

"Of course I know, dear one." Llanubys's voice was soothing. "But you need not worry. Your sister can be restored."

"She can?" Hope pulsed through him.

"Yes, my son. I have received a vision from the Mother. But it will not be easy."

"I will do anything, Llanubys." Tears running from his burning eyes, Somnadh turned to gaze up at the Mother. "I will do anything, *Genna ma'guad!*" Then he looked back to Llanubys. "What must be done?"

"The desecrators of the Mother's sapling must be found. They, along with your sister, must be brought here. Though in the past she but carried the Mother's offerings, on this occasion it must be Urien's hand that sacrifices them both."

Somnadh's heart sank. *Both? But the monk Morumus was dead* . . . "Is there no other way?"

"No."

"But surely the Mother knows, Llanubys?" Somnadh heard his voice trembling.

"Knows what, dear one?"

"Knows that what she asks is only half-possible!"

"Why do you say that?"

"A bird has arrived from Aeldred. He has taken one of the two desecrators—his own brother, Oethur. Even now he sends him to us. But the other monk—the one named Morumus—is dead. He fell into Fheil's Delf while pursuing our Mordruui."

Llanubys's thin skin crinkled in a kind smile, and she patted him on the shoulder before turning to take a step toward the Mother. "I see your distress now, my son. But as before, it is unwarranted."

"I don't understand."

Llanubys's voice went cold. "This Morumus yet lives."

"He does? But Aeldred—"

Llanubys's head whipped back, and the look in her eyes froze the words on Somnadh's lips. "I have no doubt your brother's report was true, in point of bare fact. Some time ago I myself received word from Cuuranyth. Our Mordruui were pursued into the mountains, and in their flight had to cut the bridge at Fheil's Delf. In so doing, they sent a monk into the mist. All this is quite true."

"But surely if he fell, he must have perished?"

"He did not."

"I don't understand, Llanubys."

"Neither do I, my son." If the old woman's expression had been cold before, her voice was now ice—and wrath. "I do not understand how any monk could survive that fall. Nor do I understand how only two monks—only *two monks*, Somnadh—managed to overthrow Cuuranyth itself!"

"Cuuranyth has been *overthrown?*" Somnadh shook with the effort to control himself. "Surely not!"

"Not five days ago, my son. Word arrived by bird this morning."

"But our stores! Years and years of our nomergenna harvest . . ." As the realization of what he was saying struck Somnadh, he fell silent. Could it be? "Everything we harvested in Caeldora, most of what has been gathered here," he continued in a horrified whisper, "all but the barest reserves . . ."

"Lost."

The word resounded in the darkness like a dull gong. As she finished speaking, Llanubys looked frail—frailer than she had ever appeared before.

Lost.

Somnadh had come to the Ring of Stars this night in a state of sorrow over Urien. But now that sorrow gave way to rage—a great red wrath, heaving up within him. *First they desecrated the Mother's daughter. Then they stole my sister. Now they have burned our stores . . .*

His next words seethed through his teeth like smoke from a dragon's maw. "You say two monks stormed Cuuranyth?"

"Yes."

"Who was the second?"

"We do not know. The Mordruui who sent the news—the only one of a half-dozen who escaped—wrote only that one of the monks was the same man who had pursued them at Fheil's Delf."

Morumus.

"I will find him, Llanubys."

"No, my son." The ancient Heart of the Mother's expression had softened, but her voice was firm. "You will have enough to do after the Feast. Your brother Aeldred has agents in the North, does he not?"

"He does, but—"

She waved his objection away. "Then you will leave this Morumus to him. Your sister, however, is another matter. She will return to you before the end of the Feast."

"She will? How do you know? Do you have word of her whereabouts?"

"I have no word, my son." Llanubys turned back toward Genna. "But in the Mother's vision, I saw the two of you standing together once again—here, within the Ring of Stars." Her voice grew quiet. "I will be gone by then."

Somnadh flinched.

Gone?

Of all that Llanubys had said this night, this was by far the most unsettling. Though only she knew her true age, the Heart of Genna had outlived generations of men. For so long, she had waited to see the Mother's triumph. It simply was not possible that now, on the very cusp of their victory . . .

No!

Somnadh shook his head, a lump climbing into his throat. "No, Llanubys. No, you must not speak like that."

The frail face returned to him. The taut skin formed a hollow smile across her fleshless face. "Do not vex yourself for me, dear one. I have lived a long, long time. And I will live to see this first great Feast of the Sacred Tree. But I shall not live to see another."

Somnadh shook his head, wanting to object, but found he could not speak. Tears welled again at the corners of his eyes.

Llanubys returned to lay her hand on his shoulder. "There, there. You have ever been my most faithful son, Somnadh."

"And you have been like a mother to me, Llanubys . . . please don't go!"

"Only the Mother lives forever, dear one."

He dropped his gaze. "I know, but . . ."

"When I am gone, your sister Urien must take my place. Bring her to me as soon as she is ready, along with the monks. Once she has offered their blood in atonement, I will teach her the Last Secret. After that, she will be Llanubys—and I will be no more. Do you understand?"

Somnadh looked up, and in the darkness the gleam of Llanubys's white tresses seemed to blend into the Mother's own
supernal iridescence.

"I understand, Mother."

"When did this arrive?"

"Just tonight, sire."

Satticus watched his master's face. Despite the bright flames
on the hearth, Aeldred's expression was darkening.

"Did you read it?"

"No, sire. The seal used indicated it was for your eyes only."

"Here." The Crown Prince thrust the small scroll of paper
toward his private secretary. "Give me your thoughts."

Satticus took the paper and unrolled it. As he scanned
the few lines scrawled in a hasty hand, his eyes widened
and his lips pursed. "Your brother and the bishops have
escaped?"

"Several days ago, it appears." Aeldred's tone chilled. "The
question is: how?"

"You don't believe this account of sea raiders?"

"Do you?"

Satticus shook his head. "I do not. I can see why the monk
might have thought it, but his message says the prisoners
and their captors were speaking Vilguran. Our northern sea
raiders are not known to take prisoners—nor do they speak
the language of the Church."

"Exactly!" Aeldred slammed his fist onto the table in front
of him, sending a clatter through his empty dinner plates.
"But if not sea raiders, then who? And how did they know
where to find our convoy?"

"How many people knew about this secret transportation?"

"Very few." Aeldred spoke with deliberate pause. "Besides you and I—and I'm not worried about you, Satticus—there were only those handful of monks and soldiers who escorted them."

"Did you send any word ahead?"

"I sent one message by bird to Dyfann. To the south, I sent a dispatch ride—" Aeldred's voice stopped short. "Do you think it could have been him?"

"Perhaps."

"But the rider was one of our own—one of our Order!"

"Yes, sire. But betrayal isn't the only possibility. He might have been waylaid. Or one of the soldiers who remained behind at Toberstan may have lost his discretion at the bottom of a tankard."

"I will leave it to you to determine the case and to take appropriate measures. But in the meantime, there is a far more important question . . ."

"Where will the escaped prisoners go?"

"Yes."

Satticus frowned. "They will go to Dunross."

"How can you be so certain?"

"It's the only haven they have left, sire."

"I fear you are correct, but I wonder if you realize what it will mean."

"Sire?"

Aeldred turned toward the fire, and it was several minutes before he spoke. "Heclaid will cancel my engagement to Rhianwyn."

"Surely not, sire!"

"Of course he will! Oethur will make sure of it!" Aeldred turned back, and his eyes flashed with wild rage. "My brother has always wanted Rhianwyn for himself, and he will denounce me as soon as his foot hits Lothairin soil!"

"But that would be an act of war, sire."

Aeldred regained his composure before continuing. "With Heclaid's bishop returned and Treowin present to back the man's account, we will be at war regardless. But Lothair is isolated, and we have strong allies. If they had any sense, they would surrender immediately."

"They will not surrender, sire. Both King Heclaid and your brother will fight to the last man."

"I'm counting on it, my friend."

"Just so, sire. But if your brother should marry Rhianwyn, his claim against you might be strong enough to draw away some of our—"

"I have no intention of allowing Oethur to marry Rhianwyn, Satticus."

"But how will you stop it?"

"You remember my agent in Urras?"

"Yes, sire. But—"

"I have an agent in Dunross, too."

Satticus drew a sharp breath. "Will you kidnap the princess?"

Aeldred shook his head. "No. There is too much risk of failure."

"But then what will you do?"

"If I cannot have Rhianwyn, I will ensure that no man does."

26

"I used to think you were nothing but a false grabber," said an accusing voice from somewhere quite close. "But I see now I underestimated you. You are also an accomplished false *die*-er!"

Morumus had been standing quite lost in thought by the windows of the palace library in Dunross Castle. Now he had just enough time to turn before Oethur's arms engulfed him.

"My brother!" cried the Norn. "I cannot tell you how good it is to see you! I thought you had died!"

"And you, Oethur!" Morumus gasped for air against Oethur's bearish embrace. "But if you don't unhand me soon, I may yet fulfill your fears!"

A moment later they separated, standing at arms' length and looking at each other with the delight of reunited family. For a full minute, neither man spoke.

Morumus found his voice first. "The king told me you had arrived, along with Ciolbail and Treowin. He did not tell me how or why, but he hinted that you had found trouble in Grindangled."

"More than you know, brother." The rays of the dying sun through the library windows cast long shadows behind

Oethur. The Norn looked grave indeed. "More than you can imagine."

"Oh, I don't know about that. After these past weeks, you may find my capacity for imagination somewhat enlarged."

"So I've heard—or at least heard hints. And since you seem to have imagined a means of cheating death, I look forward to tonight's council. I fear we may both have need of such a means again—much sooner than we'd like!"

Before Morumus could reply, a heavy bell struck the hour, its booming timbre reverberating through Dunross Castle to reach them as a dull echo.

"Speaking of the council," said Oethur when the noise faded, "I believe there is to be a dinner beforehand—for which that is the bell." He turned and began moving toward the door. "Are you coming?"

Morumus spared one last glance for the sunset over Dunross before forsaking the view to follow his friend.

About two hours later, dinner was a contented memory as King Heclaid sat down to council. As he sat, so the others summoned to join him followed his example. Immediately flanking him were the four thane-wardens of Lothair— Morumus's brother Haedorn among them, at the king's right hand. Beyond the two thanes on the king's left were the two bishops, Ciolbail and Treowin. Opposite them sat Gaebroth and Morumus. Opposite the king himself, at the far end of the table, sat Oethur.

"Friends," said Heclaid as they took their seats. "This is a grave occasion, and one for which I want us to have the greatest possible freedom of deliberation." He looked around the table, meeting each gaze in turn. "Let us therefore set aside any reticence with respect to speaking our minds. This is a privy council, and the rules by which we are honor-bound in public do not apply. Our purpose here is to share information and forge strategy, not to stand on etiquette or fuss about ceremonies. Is that clear?"

"Yes, sire," said the council members in rippling succession.

"Good. Now that's settled, I want to begin with Bishop Ciolbail. Your Grace, our enemies have seized upon your prolonged absence from our court as an occasion to accuse you and us of conspiracy against the Mersian crown. Be pleased to explain to this council how you came to be so long missing."

As Ciolbail unfolded his account, buttressed by Treowin, Morumus's eyes widened. But as the bishops and Oethur came to the decisive interview with Aeldred in the dungeon, he felt his blood rising.

Aeldred was behind his father's murder!

Glancing to his left, Morumus saw Haedorn looking back at him. They both nodded. Whatever else was revealed, Aeldred of Nornindaal was now their enemy.

Yet when Oethur and the bishops recounted their rescue, Morumus was so surprised that he nearly forgot about Aeldred. "Nack? You were rescued by Nack? Nack is a *Lumana*?"

"He sounds like a very capable man," said the king. "I wish I had met him."

"He would not even come ashore, sire." Ciolbail shook his head. "But he assured us that he will pursue the Red Order on Midgaddan. Hearing us convinced him that the Red Order is not simply trying to establish a foothold within the Church. Their machinations in Mersex, Dyfann, and Nornindaal show they are out to seize total power in Acld Gowan—and, as Nack himself said, 'perhaps Midgaddan after that.'"

"Shrewd as well as capable." Heclaid nodded. "I agree with this Nack's assessment."

"Is it simple lust for power, sire?" Morumus had been turning matters over in his mind while listening, and things had begun to connect.

All eyes, including the king's, turned to him. "What do you mean, Morumus?"

Morumus took a deep breath. "If the Red Order is nothing but a group vying for power and treasure, then how do we explain the risks they have taken to perform their secret rituals? If their goal was only to gain control, why did they risk detection on Midgaddan and Nornindaal by kidnapping children?"

At this, a couple of the thane-wardens began murmuring. "Sire, what was this kidnapping of which this monk speaks?"

The king looked pensive. "I see your point, Morumus, but since my lords have not heard your full story, you'd best explain it to the council."

Morumus did so. Without giving away Urien, he explained to those gathered what had happened in Caeldora: how they had tracked murdered children to a Mordruui sanctuary, and how in escaping they had learned that the Mordruui were the Red Order. When he reached the part of his tale where he fought Ulwilf in Naud, he paused to explain.

"Right before he died, the red monk Ulwilf said something very interesting. When I accused him of lying about his conversion, he denied it, saying that he *had* embraced the Church. I remember his very words: 'Where she corrected the Old Faith, I heeded. But to embrace the refinements of the New Faith does not mean discarding the truth of the Old.' He went on to insist that the white tree worshiped by the Mordruui is the Mother or Source of all faiths. I remember how he said it: 'It is she whom my people worshipped as our goddess, and it is her Son whom the Church calls Aesus. They are the same.'"

"My brother Aeldred said something very similar," interjected Oethur. "When I accused him of betraying our God by embracing the Mordruui, he scoffed and claimed that 'the true Aesus' had been a servant of the Mordruui's goddess."

"That wasn't all he said," added Ciolbail. "He denied the resurrection, saying it was unnecessary. 'There is no need!' he insisted. 'Sons and daughters may die. . . . Yet it matters not, for all return to the same Source. Death brings return to the Mother.'"

"'It is only she who lives forever.' That's how the murderer ended his self-righteous reverie." Treowin growled at the memory.

"You see, sire," concluded Morumus, "I think the Mordruui are after more than just power. It seems to me that they intend to merge their Dark Faith into the True Faith of Holy Writ. Their goal in infiltrating the Church and in murdering children is the same: to perpetuate the Dark Faith."

"So they pour out the blood of their victims to the white tree?" asked one of Heclaid's thane-wardens.

Morumus met the man's outraged gaze. "Yes, and from this tree they harvest an herb called nomergenna. It is the source of their power."

"Their power?" The king's frown deepened. "What do you mean?"

Morumus turned to Gaebroth. "Brother, why don't you explain what happens when one ingests nomergenna."

He listened as Gaebroth detailed how nomergenna rendered a person obedient to the Dark Speech, and how the Mordruui leveraged this effect to make their victims do and see horrible things. When Gaebroth finished, Morumus then related two confirmations: the first being his own experience on the night the Mordruui had murdered his father, and the second being Colba's report from the Mordruui's raid on Dorslaan.

"And that was just before you fell into Fheil's Delf, was it not?" The king's tone was somber.

"Yes, sire."

"Explain to the council how you survived—and what followed."

Morumus obeyed. His account of the battle at Fheil's Delf evoked several approving nods from the thane-wardens, and he saw Oethur smile as he told them of waking up on the mist-enveloped lower bridge. But what really evoked the council's approval—and made Oethur's eyebrows climb his scalp—was the account of Morumus and Gaebroth's storming of Cuuranyth.

"The two of you have dealt the Mordruui a devastating blow," said the king. "Well done!"

Several voices rose, accompanied by resounding thumps on the table.

"Hear, hear!"

When the cheering subsided, King Heclaid straightened in his chair. Even before he spoke, the council could sense that the period of informality had concluded.

"My lords"—he turned his head toward his thane-wardens— "you have all now heard the accounts of these men. You have heard the many crimes of Aeldred of Nornindaal. Not only did he murder our beloved Raudorn Red-Fist, but he has confessed to the murder of his own father and brother. He imprisoned our dear Bishop Ciolbail and used his token to provoke war between Mersex and ourselves. As though this were too small an evil, he has sold his soul to Belneol and joined forces with the Mordruui, who intend to destroy the True Faith of Holy Writ. Is it not so, my lords?"

The four thane-wardens spoke in unison: "It is so."

Haedorn's agreement sounded particularly vehement.

The king inclined his head. "For these several reasons, it is our sovereign will to dissolve the engagement of our royal daughter Rhianwyn to Aeldred of Nornindaal. My lords, do you consent?"

"We do."

"Furthermore"—the king still used his official tone and the royal plural—"it has been testified to us by these bishops that the ascension of Aeldred to the throne of Nornindaal was never the will of his sire, and it seems evident that such an ascension would undermine both the spiritual and temporal peace of the North. Is this not so, my lords?"

Again, unanimous consent.

"For these reasons, it is our sovereign will to exhort our brother, Oethur of Nornindaal, to denounce Aeldred as a heathen and a murderer, and to make his own claim to the throne of his nation. We exhort him to do so with the seal of these bishops and within a fortnight's time—before the seven lords of his land confer the crown upon his brother. In harmony with this exhortation we pledge to our brother the full support of Lothair, and do hereby recognize him as the true king of Nornindaal. My lords, do you concur?"

At this point, the thane-wardens of Lothair paused.

And no wonder!

The enormity of what was transpiring before him stunned Morumus. King Heclaid was offering to help put Oethur on the throne of Nornindaal.

King Oethur.

King Oethur!

It was no wonder that the thanes of the realm paused. If they passed this resolution, they committed themselves to war with Nornindaal—in addition to the war that already loomed with Mersex.

Do we have any hope of winning such a war?

"We do."

King Heclaid looked down the table at Oethur. "My lord, what say you? Will you accept the exhortation and support of Lothair?"

Morumus had never seen Oethur look more grave. But instead of speaking, the Norn bowed his head. For a long moment he remained thus. Morumus had no doubt that his brother was praying . . .

Oh Lord, give light! Sweet Aesus, give Oethur wisdom!

At last the Norn raised his head and faced the council. He took a deep breath. "I will. God help me, I accept."

No sooner had the words left his lips than King Heclaid's four thanes were on their feet, beating upon their end of the council table and shouting acclaim.

"Long live the king of Nornindaal! Long live the king!"

Though stunned by the outburst, the rest of the table—the bishops, Gaebroth, and Morumus—joined them forthwith.

"The king! The king! Long live King Oethur!"

When the cheering subsided, Oethur looked graver than ever. "You're very good, all of you. May our Lord give us joy of victory."

"Indeed, my brother." King Heclaid was beaming. "And we have much work ahead of us to see you on your throne. But for now, there is but one thing further to settle." He looked again at his four thanes, then raised his voice to the servant by the door. "Ask the Princess Rhianwyn to enter!"

As the council chamber's door opened to admit the princess, all the men at the table—already on their feet—turned.

"Lest any man, abroad or at home, doubt the sincerity of our commitment," said King Heclaid in his most formal tone, "and in pursuit of the harmonious union and mutual support of our two peoples, it is our sovereign will to decree that, within a week, our own daughter, Rhianwyn, Crown Princess of Lothair, should be given in marriage to King Oethur. My lords, do you consent?"

"We do!" came the booming affirmation.

The king looked to his daughter. "My dearest Rhianwyn, do you consent?"

Rhianwyn looked at Oethur. "The last time we spoke, Lord Oethur—or rather I should say, sire—I asked you a question. Do you remember what it was?"

Oethur nodded, and his voice trembled as he spoke. "You asked whether we would ever know a happy tale between us."

Rhianwyn's clear blue eyes filled with tears. "I am willing to try if you are."

King Heclaid's final question was for Oethur. "My brother, will you consent to receive my very dearest treasure, the fairest jewel in all my realm?"

Morumus could hear the joy in Oethur's reply.

"With all my heart."

27

even days later, all of Dunross blazed with color as Princess Rhianwyn's wedding day arrived. Despite the haste in arrangements, the city had turned out its very best face. Orange pennants hung in every window, and nearly every creature abroad in the streets—man, woman, and beast—wore a ribbon of red, green, or black. The streets themselves had been swept clean to an exceptional degree, and many a shopkeeper could be seen standing outside his premises keeping close watch over a spotless patch of walkway.

Six days ago, the palace had issued two proclamations. The first was Oethur's denunciation of his brother, which gave a detailed account of Aeldred's crimes, a statement of Oethur's own claim to the throne, and a consequent call to all loyal Norns to rise against the usurper. This proclamation, certified and sealed by both bishops, was heralded in Dunross and then sent by royal messenger to the seven lords of Nornindaal. The second was King Heclaid's announcement that Lothair recognized Oethur as true king of Nornindaal and would cement the alliance by a royal marriage at the week's end.

Overall, the mood in the city was buoyant. Both proclamations had set every tongue in the city wagging, of course.

On one hand, the prospect of war with Nornindaal had lain dormant for so many generations that most found it difficult to fathom. On the other hand, the promise of royal nuptials captured the popular imagination. Almost everybody knew something of weddings, and more than a few elders remembered the pageantry of King Heclaid's own wedding some thirty years prior. Thus it was that the talk of the town turned more and more upon the pleasant and familiar. By the time the great day arrived, the looming conflict seemed all but forgotten to most.

But not to all.

In Dunross Castle high atop its mound, the two kings, four thanes, and four clerics held close council for several hours each day. The fact was well known about the palace, yet none looked on it askance. After all, they were only doing their duty. And besides, everybody knew that apart from giving the initial orders to set preparations in motion, even kings and bishops were well advised to leave the details of wedding preparation to the ladies and chamberlains.

But amidst all this general benevolence, there was one other in Dunross for whom the approaching wedding could not erase the shadow of war.

Muthadis.

The Mother's Maiden.

None in Dunross knew her by this name, of course. Aeldred's agent had spent several years in deep cover, a servant girl well placed in the palace service. It was she who had uncovered the secret correspondence between Rhianwyn and the traitor Oethur. And it was she who had received a secret correspondence of her own just a few days past . . . a message from her lord himself:

The robin must not nest with the rook. Take all necessary measures, but spare the rook for the fowler.

Muthadis understood its coded meaning perfectly well. *Robin* was the name used for Rhianwyn, *rook* stood for Oethur, and the *fowler* was Aeldred himself. So Oethur must live—at least until Aeldred overtook him. As for Rhianwyn . . .

The princess must die.

The only question was: how?

Muthadis had turned over the possibilities in her mind. Which method of dispatch would inflict maximum damage upon the enemies of the Mother? Gruesome murder had its place and bore a certain attraction. And yet a private massacre, however macabre, could be concealed in its details. A public death could be concealed from nobody . . . and if done right, could be made to drive a most effective wedge between King Heclaid and his would-be son-in-law.

Poison.

Yes, poison it must be. And poison of such a painful sort that it would cause horrid convulsions and screams as it did its work. A potent dose, but not too fast-acting. The guests at the wedding feast must see the treacherous Rhianwyn writhe in agony before she gasped her last.

And they must see Oethur tip her the glass!

This would be the masterstroke. According to protocol, the first toast of the wedding feast would involve 'King' Oethur praising his bride—and then offering her the first taste from his own glass. It was this glass that Muthadis intended to lace with a most lethal poison.

It was a perfect plan. And as one of those servants chosen to wait upon the high table at tonight's feast, she would be in a position to see it done.

The High Princess murdered . . . by the hand of her husband.

Walking down the corridor of Dunross Castle in her finest livery, Muthadis licked her lips. She could almost taste her triumph.

It had been a long time since Morumus had felt such joy.

At present, he stood on a balcony just outside the feasting hall of Dunross Castle. In the great chamber behind him, the assembled guests awaited the arrival of the wedding party. Meanwhile, away before him, the sun had sunk half its girth behind the horizon. But the half that remained aloft sent jubilant orange rays shimmering across the Mathway estuary . . .

Orange, like the banner of Lothair!

It was a whimsical thought, but one that suited the festive occasion.

The wedding ceremony itself had been magnificent. It had begun at noon, with Oethur riding in martial splendor from the harbor up through the streets of Dunross to the cathedral. After this, King Heclaid had escorted the princess down from the castle's high mound in a grand show of royal finery. Both entourages had passed through wide avenues lined with cheering throngs. The whole city had turned out for the occasion—awash in vicarious cheerfulness.

From his post high in the cathedral tower, Morumus had been well placed to observe both processions. Though a close friend of Oethur and brother to a thane-warden of the realm, he was not of sufficient rank to ride alongside either. Nor did he qualify for a place of honor at either the ceremony or the feast. Oethur had apologized with sincere profusion. Such places had to be distributed with great delicacy among the thanes and minor nobles.

For his part, Morumus had been relieved. He possessed no great love of high tables, nor of the speechmaking that such positions required. He was much more comfortable with empty balconies and quiet sunsets.

Bishop Ciolbail had officiated the ceremony himself. Morumus had found the homily to be very fine, and he had beamed from ear to ear when the bishop had pronounced Oethur and Rhianwyn man and wife. It wasn't just the fact that he esteemed the estate of marriage—though that was true enough. Morumus's joy stemmed in no small part from the fact that his friend was so obviously happy.

"I have long admired her, Morumus," Oethur had confessed to him on the evening after the king's council had pledged them to be wed. *"But for as long as she remained engaged to Aeldred, I could never permit myself to see her as more than a sister."*

But now the positions of both had changed. Oethur was no longer a monk, but a king. And Rhianwyn was no longer his future sister, but his present queen.

"Give them joy," Morumus whispered as he watched the sun sink lower, "and may God grant us the victory to secure it!"

"Indeed," said a voice behind him.

Morumus spun. "King Heclaid!" He made a hasty bow. "Your Majesty!"

"Please, stand." The king came up beside him to stand near the rail. "I am glad to have found you alone, son."

"Why is that, sire?"

"Though this is a day for merriment, I cannot but muse upon the dark days that lie ahead."

Morumus nodded.

"What do you think of our prospects, Morumus?"

"It is not for me to say, sire. I am no captain, and I have little—"

"Don't evade my question, son. If your king asks for your candid opinion, it is most certainly for you to say."

"My apologies, sire. I meant no offense."

"I know it, son." The king smiled, his face benevolent despite his firm tone. "But I want you to answer the question. Honestly."

"Well, sire . . . to be honest, I think we will need a miracle. I do not doubt the courage of my countrymen, nor the justice of our cause—"

"—but the combined forces of Mersex and Nornindaal outnumber us greatly. To speak nothing of Dyfanni conscripts."

"Yes, sire."

"I am of your opinion, Morumus." The king looked out over the bay beneath them, his gaze distant. "However righteous, our situation is grim."

"But I do believe in miracles, sire. And I am sure our Lord favors us against the denizens of the Dark Faith."

"I am sure he does." Heclaid turned to look at him. "But what would you say, Morumus, if I told you that you might be able to help work the miracle we need?"

At the king's words, a sudden sense of apprehension struck Morumus. "I would welcome such news, sire, but I confess I would have little confidence."

"It's not your confidence that I require, son. Only your tongue."

"I do not understand, sire."

"You were friends with Donnach mac Toercanth. And you speak Grendannathi. Do you remember what I said some time ago, that I would require your aid in explaining Donnach's death to his people?"

"I do, sire."

"Very good. That time will soon be upon us. I have sent messengers north to arrange an embassy with the heads of their clans. You will accompany me. You will explain Donnach's death, laying special emphasis upon the identity of his murderers—and the fact that their allies now control the better part of our island. If the Grendannathi agree to join with us, we may just stand a chance of victory."

Morumus took a deep breath. *An alliance with the northern barbarians?*

"Sire . . . the Grendannathi are pagans. Surely it is among them that the Dree and the Dark Faith have found the most shelter?"

"For generations it has been so. And even a decade ago, few could have disputed your words. But much has changed since you left Lothair, Morumus. Our missionaries have been active among the Grendannathi. Donnach may have been the most prominent convert, but he was by no means the only one to renounce the old gods. Clan by clan, the Grendannathi are coming to Aesus. But it is a touchy thing. That is why Donnach's death was so disastrous. But I am hopeful—and I am praying—that with your assistance we may turn their just wrath toward its proper objects. What do you say to that?"

For a moment Morumus said nothing. He looked out over the bay, remembering his last conversation with Donnach:

"You must finish the work." The light in the Grendannathi's eyes was beginning to fade. "You were born of a noble house—a prince— and you are rooted in the two things needed: languages and Holy Writ." He smiled. "Do you see it, brother?"

"Yes." Morumus's voice broke as he wept. "Yes, Donnach, I see it."

"Finish the translation, Morumus. Bring the good news to my people, Prince of Roots. I will wait for you in Everlight."

When Morumus turned back to the king, he felt the sting of a tear at the corner of his eye. But his resolution was firm. He bowed. "I am your servant, sire."

"Very good. I knew you could be relied upon, son. Both you and your brother are true sons of your father, and Raudorn Red-Fist was never a man to shun his duty—however difficult it might prove."

"Thank you, sire."

"Not at all. And now, we should get indoors. It wouldn't do at all for them to begin without—"

Heclaid's words were lost as a sudden scream shattered the evening air.

"What was *that?*" Morumus stared at the king. But both he and Heclaid knew full well what they heard.

It was a woman's scream . . .

It was coming from the feasting hall . . .

. . . and it would not stop.

EPILOGUE

Banr Cluidan had changed.

Urien had finally reached her childhood home—only to find that it was lost forever.

The village itself, lying round the hill, remained much the same as she remembered. As in Cyrdol almost two weeks prior, so here she observed the traditional sights and sounds of Dyfanni life. Most of the homes were still the small, traditional crofts. Most of the narrow streets between still found space for chickens and children. And in most cases, the latter still outdid the former for volume of noise.

Yet alongside these familiar sights appeared bleak indicators of transformation. Several large stone buildings now stood amidst the modest lanes of wood and thatch. They loomed over their neighbors like great lumpish ogres. And then there were the Mersian officers. These rode through the village as though they owned Banr Cluidan, each with a heavy infantry trailing in his wake. The soldiers on foot regarded their surroundings with malicious suspicion: hard set faces and pikes held ready.

From what Urien could observe, the suspicion was mutual. Villagers averted their gazes and stepped lively when the patrols approached. Parents herded oblivious children out of their path lest they be trampled—or worse. At present, all sides were on their best behavior for the Feast. Yet despite the tranquility of the moment, it was clear that neither side was comfortable with the other.

How long had it been like this? How long would it remain thus?

A long shadow fell over Urien's soul as she walked the once-familiar streets.

The Red Order had not brought freedom to Dyfanni.

It had brought occupation.

The New Faith was no salvation to the Dyfanni.

It was slavery.

But the greatest sign of change did not lie in the village. The most significant token of things to come stood above it. The ancient hill fort was gone . . .

In its place stood the Cathedral of the Sacred Tree.

The cathedral was a monument to the Red Order's religious alchemy. In its rough shape, it looked much like an Aesusian cathedral. Yet the closer one looked, the fewer resemblances remained. White stone might not have been entirely foreign to church construction, but red glass for the windows certainly was. But worse than this subtle innovation was the overt symbolism: above the cathedral's main entrance the builders had carved the same image Urien had seen in the chapel at Cyrdol.

It was a great likeness of the Mother, cradling a baby in two of its lower boughs while two others made the sign of the cross over the crèche.

From the moment she first had laid eyes upon it, Urien had loathed the cathedral. Nothing would have pleased her more than to watch it burn. Nothing would please her less than to enter beneath that abominable idol inscribed above its doors.

And yet today, the day of the spring equinox, she was doing the latter. Disguised in her red robe with the hood pulled up, she had joined a great procession of red monks as they canted and chanted up the wide path to the cathedral.

For the Red Order, this was a day of celebration!

Today was the Feast of the Sacred Tree!

Today the Archbishop of Mereclestour would consecrate the first cathedral in Dyfann—the first sanctuary of the New Faith in the land of the Old!

But Urien cared little for the archbishop or his feast. *Today, I will find Somnadh.*

Today, she would confront her brother with the evil he had embraced.

How will it end?

As the procession drew nearer to the cathedral, Urien's thoughts drifted back to the last time she had ascended this hill as a little girl, on her way to do the work of the Mother.

Urien shuddered. And yet for all the horror of that day, there had been one bright spot.

She had been with her father and brother.

They had welcomed her into the inner circle of those gathered to honor and worship the Mother.

For many years, Urien had looked back on this memory with fondness.

But no longer. Now the memory held no innocence. Now Urien knew that the Old Faith of her childhood was a lie, and that lying just below its ancestral surface was something far more sinister.

The Dark Faith.

Even in those distant days, her brother had followed a path bathed in blood.

Urien took a deep breath as she entered the cathedral. *Is there any hope for you, Somnadh?*

"On this historic day, we celebrate more than just the balance of day and night," intoned the red-hooded Archbishop of Mereclestour from before the altar at the front of the nave. "Today, we applaud the spiritual balance brought by the union of two peoples and two faiths. A new dawn has come to the ancient land of Aeld Gowan!"

As the archbishop raised his arms in benediction, a choir of red monks began singing. As the music filled the cathedral, Urien noticed that the current of the cantilation had a most peculiar double quality. On the surface it was ethereal and haunting. Yet below this . . . there was a rougher strand— punctuated by what sounded almost like rasping hisses.

"Come forward, my children, and lift up your hearts! Take the Sign of the Son, and behold the Miracle of the Mother!"

At these words, the assembly stirred to life. Beginning with those in the front, the congregation formed a long procession moving toward the altar. Before she could avoid it, Urien found herself nudged into the queue by the surge.

From her place near the back, Urien scanned the host of moving faces. *Where are you, Somnadh?*

Somehow, she could sense her brother's presence.

But where?

As the first congregants partook of the sacrament and peeled off toward the sides of the nave, gasps and exclamations filled the cathedral.

"I see it! Oh, I see it!"

"The Miracle!"

Urien paid little heed to the growing commotion. Whatever the archbishop was up to with his ritual, her only concern was to find her brother—

There!

As the first of the red monks reached the altar rail and knelt, he threw back his hood and looked up at the archbishop.

Could it be?

Yet as the monk stood and turned, Urien saw that she had been mistaken.

Never mind! Look to the next!

The next red monk was not her brother, nor the one after him. Yet Urien saw to her delight that it would not be difficult to identify Somnadh when he did appear, for as each monk knelt he was required to lower his—

—his cowl!

The realization of her danger struck Urien too late. *I will be discovered!*

But by now she was far too close to the front. She could not step out of line. There was no way to go but forward . . .

She was only three places from the altar rail.

"Go in peace, my son."

Another monk rose and turned, his face revealed to all.

Not Somnadh.

She was two places from the hand of the archbishop.

"Go in peace, my son."

The final monk before Urien knelt . . .

And now, at long last, she saw her brother.

"Go in peace, my son."

Kneeling before the rail, Urien looked up at the archbishop. There could be no mistaking those all-black eyes . . .

Her cowl fell, and his black eyes widened.

"Hello, Somnadh."

GLOSSARY

New Terms First Occuring in *The Scarlet Bishop*

Aberun: one of the seven lords of Nornindaal

According to Iowan: Holy Writ's fourth account of the earthly ministry of Aesus

According to Maerc: Holy Writ's second account of the earthly ministry of Aesus

Adinnu: Dyfanni for the First Garden—mankind's original home

Caileamach: the High Princess of the Dyfanni and Queen of Mersex

Calum: first missionary to Lothair and founder of Urras Monastery

Calum's Hall: main hall of Urras Monastery, named for Saint Calum

Corised: one of the seven lords of Nornindaal

Cuuranyth: the mountain stronghold of the Dree

Cynnig: a board game popular in courts and monasteries

Cyrdol: a village in Dyfann

Dorslaan: a village in southern Nornindaal, near the Deasmor

Droelum: an apothecary's potion used to erase memory

Eolas: name in the Dyfanni Old Faith for the first Mother tree, known to Aesusians as the Tree of Probation

Erworn: personal chaplain to Aeldred

Fersk: a river in Nornindaal

Fheil's Delf: a great chasm in the high Deasmor; its name means "Shadow's Digging" in Old Nornish

Geraan: one of the seven lords of Nornindaal

Gwyllinor Mountains: mountains forming the border between Dyfann and Mersex

Halbir: one of the seven lords of Nornindaal

Jugeim: one of the seven lords of Nornindaal

Lothair the Wise: the ancestral founder of the Lothairin people

Lucky Jug: a dingy public house in Dericus

Lunumbir: Vilguran for "Shadow of the Moon"; a high-ranking, deep-cover operative of the Lumanae

Malduorn: king who led the Norns to Aeld Gowan; grandson of Nuorn

Malduorn's Keep: the inner keep of Grindangled Castle

Meporu: one of the seven lords of Nornindaal

Muthadis: an agent of Aeldred, masquerading as a servant girl

Nornshaam: the ancestral homeland of the Nornish people

Nuorn the Valiant: the ancestral founder of the Nornish people

Rhianwyn: daughter of King Heclaid, Crown Princess of Lothair

Satticus: private secretary and advisor to Aeldred

Stonoric: the Mersian Duke of Hoccaster, cousin to Wodic

Toercanth: a Grendannathi chieftain, friendly to the Lothairins

Tham: in the Dyfanni Old Faith, the husband of the woman who saved the Mother by carrying Eolas' seed into the Great Ark

Threefold Cord: a potent symbol in Lothairin heraldry and legend

Tree of Probation: in Holy Writ, the tree whereby God tested man

Urras Abbey/Monastery: island monastic community off the western coast of Lothair

Wodic: the King of Mersex, son of the late Luca Wolfbane

Wyris: village matron from southern Nornindaal; mother of Colba

Yeho: Dyfanni name for the God of Holy Writ, regarded in the Old Faith of Dyfann as a jealous son of Eolas who flooded the world in an attempt to kill his Mother

Yorth: one of the seven lords of Nornindaal

Jeremiah W. Montgomery is the pastor of Resurrection Presbyterian Church (OPC) in State College, Pennsylvania. He has been a blogger, essayist, and pipemaker. He and his wife have four sons who love to read and a little girl who cannot wait to begin.